The Protégé

The Protégé

BRIANNA HALE

THE PROTÉGÉ by BRIANNA HALE

Copyright © 2018 Brianna Hale

| All Rights Reserved |

Cover design by Maria @ Steamy Designs

No part of this book may be used or reproduced in any manner whatsoever without written permission from the publisher, except brief quotations for reviews. Thank you for respecting the author's work.

This book is a work of fiction. All characters, places, incidents and dialogue are drawn from the author's imagination and are not to be construed as real. Any similarities between persons living or dead are purely coincidental.

Where words fail, music speaks
HANS CHRISTIAN ANDERSEN

THE PROTÉGÉ

Chapter One

Isabeau

Now

I came to say sorry, but it didn't work out that way.

"A cellist?" says the woman with the clipboard, looking between me and my instrument case as if we've ruined her day. "I've only got one cellist on my list and his name is Roger Somers. Who are you? Is Mr. Valmary expecting you?"

My heart bangs like a timpani drum against my ribs hearing his name. Laszlo Valmary, conductor and musical director of the Royal London Symphony Orchestra and my former guardian and mentor. I've come straight from the train, luggage and all, to face the man I haven't spoken to in three years. Now that I'm in London again I feel him on every street I walk down, in every strain of music I hear, in the very air I breathe. But he's not expecting me and I wasn't expecting this, whatever this is that's happening today.

The woman cuts across what I was going to say. "Never mind. The flautist hasn't turned up so the schedule's a mess anyway. Go through and wait." She gives her clipboard a pained look and marches away, and I'm left in the alcove by the stalls as musicians file past me. I draw back into the shadows letting my thick red hair fall forward, not wanting to be recognized.

The Mayhew Concert Hall in the West End is a huge, stately venue of plush velvet and gold scrollwork. An enormous crystal chandelier hangs overhead and the auditorium is lit by dozens of sconces lining the balconies. The seating goes up and up to the dizzying nosebleed sections where people crowd together for five pounds a head for a glimpse of the orchestra on stage. For those paying upwards of three hundred pounds a ticket for a stalls seat every string of the violins is visible, the notes on the sheet music, the precise movements of Laszlo's large, skilled hands as he conducts. It's a more intimate experience down in the stalls but up in the gods the music is just the same. The music soars.

I breathe in the memory of remembered notes. I've missed this place.

At this time of day on a Thursday I expected to find Laszlo in his office but rehearsals seem to have gone on longer than usual. No, not rehearsals. Auditions by the looks of things. If Laszlo's lost orchestra members then he'll be impatient, distracted. This isn't the time for me to untangle my feelings for him or ask for his help. I should go, but curiosity holds me in place. What has happened? Has a swathe of the ensemble walked out again? He's not the "callow youth" that he was accused of being thirteen years ago when he took over the orchestra. He's a man of thirty-eight and the darling of the British classical music scene. The best musicians in the country clamor to be part of his ensemble.

I listen to threads of conversations going on around me and try to discover what has happened to the orchestra. Then I tell myself to focus and plan what I'm going to say to Laszlo; how I'm going to have to tell him that after all his training and effort I've ruined my musical career before it's even begun.

"Isabeau."

My hand convulsively grips my cello case. I turn and see him standing by the rows of red velvet seats, the man who took me from my home when I was eight years old. Who taught me almost everything I know about music. About life. The man I've spent the last three years in turmoil over. Missing him like crazy. Being angry with him. Wanting him.

I don't need to get close to know that he'll smell like sweet peppercorns and smoky Arabian nights. He looks good, but then he always looks good, tall and lean and smartly dressed in a dark shirt and suit. A sultry mouth and hawkish nose, and not quite enough facial hair to call it a beard but just enough to scratch your nails through and feel the lovely rasping of the bristles. Hazel eyes that always seem to be moments away from warm pleasure or flashing emotion, and fine, sandy brown hair that's too long as usual, growing down to his collar. I used to tease him about that, telling him that he has conductor's hair, the careless mane that *maestros* grow so they can toss it about in passion to the music and look romantic in journalists' black and white photographs. I was the only one who could tease him. One of the few who could make him smile.

Laszlo steps forward, and my heart leaps because I think he's going to fold me in his arms and hold me close like he used to do. But when he reaches for me his hand closes around my upper arm, cold and hard, and he leads me out of the auditorium and along a corridor without a word. Hopeless tears prickle in my eyes. He's still ashamed of me. I look up at the ceiling and breathe in sharply, a trick that a makeup artist once taught me before a solo student performance, the first one of my career that Laszlo wouldn't be watching. *Suck those tears right back in, pet. Don't go ruining your face.*

THE PROTÉGÉ

He takes us into to his office, closes the door behind us and then just stands there with his back to me, one hand braced against the door. A clock ticks on the wall and I count the seconds in three-four time, a minuet clashing with the pounding of my heart.

I should speak first but I don't know how to unravel the apology that's become snarled on my tongue. The last three years without him have been hell and losing him was like cutting off a limb. No, worse, like taking a sledgehammer to my cello. My world shattered the night of my eighteenth birthday and I can see that he still hasn't forgiven me for what I did. I hid the broken pieces of my heart deep down where no one would ever find them and I don't know what he'll do with them if I show them to him now.

His hand slides down the wood and he turns to me. "Isabeau—"

The door opens and a man puts his head in. I recognize him. Marcus Sabol, Laszlo's first violin and concertmaster. "Laszlo, that oboist... Oh. Hello." Marcus comes to a halt when he sees me. He's a stringy man in his late fifties with a shock of white hair and the energy and bubbliness of a much younger man. We never met as he joined the orchestra after I went to university in Durham, but I've seen him play. He and Laszlo are perfect together, working in tandem to get the most out of the ensemble.

Marcus' eyes travel from my face to my cello case and back again. "You're Isabeau Laurent. I saw you play in Cambridge last year. Absolutely phenomenal. Are you coming with us?"

He sees my blank face and smiles. "Laszlo didn't even tell you why you're here, did he, he just called his protégé back from university. Former protégé? Anyway, we're trying to put this last-minute fiasco together with half a damn orchestra. Thank god you're here."

Laszlo's expression doesn't change but I see how his jaw clenches. Marcus has just put him in a difficult position. The first violin is the most important person in the orchestra after the conductor and he gets a say in the principal players. I should correct Marcus and come back another time. It's not just the graceful thing to do, it's the only thing to do if I want to put our past behind us and ask for Laszlo's help.

The atmosphere is as tight as a bow string and Marcus' smile dims. "You are here to audition, aren't you?"

There are so many things I want to say to Laszlo. Most importantly that I'm sorry, but also that the happiest time of my life was when I was his protégé. That my musical career has stalled and I don't know what to do about it. That when I play the music doesn't even sound like me anymore.

That I need him in ways he doesn't understand and I'm only just beginning to.

THE PROTÉGÉ

I've never been good at saying what I feel but Laszlo always knew how I felt when I played my cello. It's not everything I want to say but it's a start, and if he's leaving for a tour then I need to say it now.

I lift my chin and look Laszlo in the eye. "Yes. I'm here to audition."

Chapter Two

Laszlo

Now

She's even more beautiful than I remember. Cheekbones finer, features more delicate. The years apart haven't changed how I feel about her, but nothing could change that. Not my regret, my pain, my guilt. My anger. Even when I've been mad as hell I've still wanted her, the one woman in the world I can't have.

I watch her smiling at Marcus as he takes her coat and suitcase so she can unpack her cello, her curtain of red hair falling in front of her face. She used to wear it up at home and while she was practicing, but she always, always wore it down while she was performing, the thick tresses spilling over her shoulders. I want to step forward and put a stop this but the thought of seeing her like that again, sitting at her cello and playing for me, holds me rooted to the spot. She and Marcus move past me out of the office, deep in conversation about the best audition piece for her. I listen to their voices as they fade away down the corridor.

What would I have said to her if Marcus hadn't come in? I don't even know where to start with all the things I want to say to her. I've never forgotten how things ended between us and I regret how I lost her. She left a hole in my world and my heart that I've never been able to fill. I don't even know if she wants these truths from me. In three years she never tried to contact me.

And now she's here.

The keening notes of her cello reach my ears. They've started without me. What is she playing, Bach?

No. It's our piece. She's playing our piece.

I picture her sitting with her mother's cello between her knees as she draws the slender bow across the strings. The long column of her neck bent just so, her eyes drifting closed as she plays. Before I know it my feet are leading me out to the auditorium toward her. I need to see her for myself.

She's seated at the front of the empty stage. The sleeves of her lightweight sweater are pushed back past her elbows and she's wearing calf-length boots with a green plaid skirt. She definitely didn't come here to audition. Isabeau would never dream of auditioning in anything but black. She's playing *Vocalise* by Rachmaninoff arranged for cello and piano, though the piano to the right is standing silent and she's playing alone. There are dozens of pieces for those two instruments together but this one was ours. The last year she lived with me we played it often, on our quiet Monday nights or tired Sunday afternoons, after the work was done, the practice finished and the rehearsals over. The steady and questing piano phrases. The insistent, plaintive cello, asking and leading before drawing back again. Not for an audience or applause. Something just for the two of us.

And she's playing it by herself.

She opens her eyes and fixes her gaze on mine. Unbidden, the fingers of my right hand are tapping out the piano part against my leg and before I can stop myself she sees, and her playing falters. Just for a split second, but I hear it. I hear other things as well. The cello is like a human voice and the music she's making is filled with sorrow and regret, as clear as if she's speaking the words aloud to me.

I'm sorry, Laszlo.

I don't want her apologies. There's nothing for her to be sorry for because I'm the one who let her down. For ten years she looked to me for protection and safety and when she needed me most I betrayed her.

Isabeau reaches the end of the piece and instead of tapering slowly into silence she stops abruptly and leans back from her cello as if she can't bear it anymore. Her eyes are full of hurt. I know how much it hurts because I feel it too.

Marcus turns to me with an appraising look. He's smiling, waiting for me to tell Isabeau that she's perfect, that she's hired. He doesn't understand what was said between us through the music. He only heard one of the most proficient cellists in the country.

"Well, Laszlo?" he asks.

Well, nothing. The point wasn't for her to audition, the point was for her to show me how she feels. I wish Marcus and the Mayhew and everything else would just disappear so I could tell Isabeau that she has nothing to be sorry for.

I move forward and put my hand on the stage at her feet and look up into her eyes. "Thank you, Miss Laurent."

I'm not being cold, addressing her like that. It's part of the etiquette of the concert hall. Later when we're alone I can call her Isabeau, and we can talk. I still have her number and I'll text her when I get back to my office and ask her to wait and give me a chance to explain.

I turn to go but she calls out, stopping me. "Mr. Valmary."

She's standing, one hand wrapped around the neck of her cello. There's a new look in her eyes, something bright and determined.

"Do I get the place?"

I stare at her, not understanding. Marcus is looking at me with an expectant smile. I know what he's thinking. I'd be crazy to refuse a cellist like Isabeau, especially when we need her so badly.

Isabeau, part of my orchestra again. Turning toward the string section and seeing her just a few feet away, looking back at me. Feeling that exquisite happiness that only comes from knowing she's close to me.

But Isabeau can't come on tour with us. Spending every day and night together for the next five weeks is out of the question with the way things ended between us. This tour is meant to be an escape for me, a way to get out of the funk and uncertainty that has invaded my life so I can consider what I want next. Is the answer Europe? Is it New York? Somewhere further afield? Where is up, what is onwards when you have achieved your lofty goals by the age of thirty-eight? That's the whole reason I said yes to this "fiasco", as Marcus called it, with parts of the orchestra on leave. To stretch myself and help clarify things. But I won't be able to think straight with Isabeau close to me.

They're both still looking at me, expectant, so I reach for the first phrase to hand. "My assistant will call you."

Marcus starts to say something but I go back to my office, close the door behind me and rest my back against it. I picture the way Isabeau's hair fell across her shoulders as she played just now, thick and soft and beautiful. I remember how it felt running through my fingers that night. The memory comes back as clear as a single note from a Stradivarius violin. How she felt in my arms at last. My perfect, untouchable girl, finally mine.

A knock on my door startles me out of my reverie. *Fuck. Isabeau.*

But when I open my door I see, not Isabeau, but a smiling man in his forties holding a cello case. He beams at me. "Sorry I'm late. Roger Somers, here to audition."

Somers. I remember now, he was suggested by our third violin as a very good cellist. I saw him play in Oxford two years ago. The sensible choice. The right choice for the tour.

But when I imagine standing at the front of the orchestra and turning to the string section I don't see this man looking back at me. I see Isabeau.

I want Isabeau.

"The place has been filled. Thank you for coming." I shut my office door in Somers' startled face, take out my phone and call my PA. "In thirty minutes' time call Isabeau Laurent. Tell her I want to see her tomorrow. At my house. No, she has the address. I'll forward you her number."

I end the call, send the contact information and close my eyes, certain that I've just made a huge mistake. Isabeau in my orchestra. Isabeau in my life again. Marcus' confusion about what she is to me, my protégé, my former protégé, something else entirely, is my confusion.

When she was a child it was so easy. I was her mentor, her guardian, her safety and her home. But then she grew older and things changed, so slowly that I didn't even realize what was happening.

I look at my phone and watch the minutes tick by. Half an hour later the email comes through from my assistant confirming my meeting with Isabeau at the house tomorrow morning. It's done. I'll be alone with her, just Isabeau, and all the things that have been left unsaid since the night she turned eighteen. I rest my head against the door and close my eyes, my mind turning back to that wintry day thirteen years ago. The first time I ever saw her.

Chapter Three

Laszlo
Then

The sound of the cello makes me stop dead in the street. A single, bright note strung out on the air with a purity that belies the smoggy London day. I look around for the busker. The sound is too clean for an amateur; the musician will be a professional who's come out on the street to play and pass an hour in the fresh, cold air. Perhaps they need work and I can persuade them to join my ensemble. I'm in need of a cellist for my new orchestra. I smile to myself, thinking of the newsprint tucked into my music case: LASZLO VALMARY, 25, YOUNGEST EVER CONDUCTOR APPOINTED TO THE ROYAL LONDON SYMPHONY. The piece is riddled with clichés about new blood stirring things up and the ruffled feathers of the old guard. *"I'll not call that upstart maestro," says Rickard Andersson, former cellist who quit the orchestra in protest yesterday after a forty-one year tenure.*

Let them be ruffled. I've arrived.

The cello plays on and I recognize the piece. *Reverie* by Sibelius, played with simplicity and skill. But where is the musician? I turn on the spot, trying to find them. And then I do, outside a coffee shop. Or rather I find the sound and my eyes have to drop three feet to find the cellist because she's a child. Her small fingers ply the strings, carving the bow across an instrument that's so tall she has to play it standing up like a double bass. I'm mesmerized by the sound she's making and I want to grab passers-by and make them listen until they understand what they're witnessing. Raw, natural talent. A child's simplistic style, yes, and she seems to have developed a few bad habits in the way she holds her bow, but these things are easily corrected. As she grows she could get much, much better. She could be world class.

I have places I need to be but I can't leave her. Beyond all musical considerations, why is a girl of seven or eight standing on a busy London street playing for money? It's not safe. She's so small that anyone could snatch her up and disappear with her, and that instrument looks like it could be tempting to a thief with a knowledgeable eye.

I go over and kneel down in front of her so that my face is on a level with hers. "Hello." She raises her eyes and they're a beautiful shade of jewel green, thickly outlined with dark auburn lashes. "What's your name?"

The bow twists in her fingers. "Mrs. Davis says we're not supposed to talk to strangers."

"Who's Mrs. Davis?"

"My teacher."

Cello teacher? No, more likely a school teacher. Where are her parents? Why aren't *they* impressing on her that she shouldn't talk to strangers? She's so small and slight that she could be picked up like so much fluff and spirited away. Whoever has her in their charge is neglecting their duty of care and I find myself growing angry with this unknown person.

Swallowing that down, I hold out my hand to her, and after switching her bow into her left she puts her small one into mine. Her fingers are freezing. I wonder how she can she possibly play with fingers so cold. "My name is Laszlo Valmary. Pleased to meet you."

Solemnly, she shakes my hand. "Isabeau Laurent. Pleased to meet you, Mr. Valmary."

I smile. Isabeau. A beautiful name for a beautiful girl, and her manners are as lovely as her playing. "That's a nice cello."

"It was my mother's."

Ah. That explains why it's too big for her. "Where is she?"

"She's dead."

My lips compress with sympathy. "And your father?"

Isabeau chews the corner her lip. She doesn't want to answer. I examine her shabby coat with a button missing; the twenty coins or so of change that have accumulated in her cello case. She's probably not getting the lessons she needs to develop her talent. She doesn't even seem to be getting the basic care she needs. "Do you like playing the cello, Isabeau?"

She holds the instrument closer to her body as if I'm going to take it away from her and stares at the ground, defiant. "Yes. I like it a lot."

Sweet girl, you needn't be defensive about your love of that beautiful instrument to me. I understand perfectly.

I tilt my head down a few inches and catch her eye. "Is your father at home? Will you take me to meet him?"

"Why?"

I open my leather music case and pull out the newspaper article. She reads the headline and looks at the picture that accompanies the story. "That's me, Isabeau. I have an orchestra filled with musicians like you. Only the very best people, and I think one day you might be one of those people."

Isabeau takes the newsprint from my hands and studies the picture and then my face, comparing my features carefully. She passes the page back and packs her instrument away, scooping the few coins from her cello case into her pocket. Then she looks up at me, her face a serious oval. "Yes please, Laszlo."

I know then that Isabeau Laurent is going to be very, very important to me. She's going to be my protégé.

She lugs her cello case two-handed down the street, her feet moving in an awkward one-two, one-two fashion. I hold out my hand for it. "Let me carry that for you."

Isabeau lets go with reluctance, and as we walk she keeps her eyes fixed on the instrument as if she daren't let it out of her sight. Her house is two streets away and as we walk I feel my apprehension grow. This is one of the more unpleasant areas of London but I try not to allow my North London privilege make assumptions about Isabeau's home life.

When we get to what I assume is her front door Isabeau lets herself in with a key. It's a two-story Victorian terrace with grubby windows and a front door that looks like it's had one lock broken and another badly fitted. I follow her inside and she takes her cello from me and disappears upstairs with it, taking pains not to let the instrument bang on the steps as she goes.

The rooms on the ground floor smell sour and there's a man with a thin face lying in the front room on a mattress, asleep. He seems to be using the lounge as a bedroom as there are discarded t-shirts and jeans lying across an armchair.

"Mr. Laurent?"

The man opens his eyes and fixes me with a look of blurry surprise. "Huh? Who are you?"

I don't answer right away, letting my eyes travel around the room and then back up the stairs. "I found your daughter playing her cello on the high street."

The man grunts and hauls himself to his feet, using the back of the sofa for support. This takes effort, as if he's in pain. So that's why he's sleeping down here. When he pushes past me on the way to the kitchen he notices the way I'm looking at his uneven gait.

"Broken back," he grunts.

Mr. Laurent finds what he was looking for, his cigarettes, and sits down heavily at the kitchen table. There are the remains of someone's breakfast. Isabeau's presumably. Toast crusts and marmite. There's a chair in front of the toaster, so that a child might reach up onto the high counter.

THE PROTÉGÉ

I examine Mr. Laurent in the light from the window. He's not much older than I am but his face has been lined with pain. Or at least I think it's pain. He starts to cough, and what begins harmlessly enough turns into his thin frame being wracked with wheezing and spluttering.

Going to the cupboard I find a clean mug and fill it with water. As I do my eyes fall on a half-open drawer and I see a battered spoon with scorch marks on the underside. A couple of hypodermics. A tourniquet made from a leather handbag strap. A small plastic bag partly filled with a white substance. It takes me a moment to understand what I'm looking at.

Heroin. In the same house as a child. As Isabeau.

Mr. Laurent has stopped coughing and has noticed what I'm staring at. He looks at me with pathetic neediness in his eyes. "I'm in pain. They stopped my meds."

My empathy is at war with my revulsion. The chronic pain of spinal damage must be a terrible thing. He was probably prescribed painkillers at first but then they were taken away, leaving him with an addiction.

"Don't call the cops. I'll go to jail."

Anger rises in my chest. Not *I'll lose Isabeau* but *I'll go to jail*. He'll be cut off from his supply. He should be thinking how this is affecting her, not himself.

I've never been a patient man. I've never liked waiting for what I want, or for what I think is right. I start speaking in a low voice without even knowing what I intend to say. "I'm not interested in you or what you do. I'm here about Isabeau. She displays a talent for playing the cello that is rare for one so young. Rare for anyone. She needs proper training." I look around at the squalor, remember her averted eyes when she asked about her father. I meant to offer to pay for her tutelage but that's not going to be enough. If she stays here I'll never forgive myself if something happens to her.

"She needs to get out of this place. I'm leaving, and I'm taking Isabeau with me."

I have no right to do any such thing. Removing her from her father's care is not only immoral, it's illegal, but when I think of the care she's not getting and the way she held her cello tightly as if someone might take it from her I know I can't leave her here. She's so slight, so defenseless. I feel a surge of protectiveness for the girl. How long until she gets hurt by someone? How long until he sells her cello for drug money? When you love music more than anything else in the world losing your instrument is not the same as losing a possession. It's like having part of your soul ripped away.

Mr. Laurent is so blindsided by my words that his cigarette is burning away to ash, unsmoked. "No you're fucking not."

"Yes, I am. I can give her what she needs."

"You're a fucking pervert."

"If I was a pervert I wouldn't have brought her back here. I would have just taken her. She was out there alone, unprotected, and I brought her home." I look at the needles in the drawer and my lip curls. "To this. But I'm not going to leave her here. She's coming to live with me and I'm going to give her the training she needs to become one of the best cellists in the world."

Mr. Laurent is still looking at me as if he doesn't understand what I'm doing here or what I'm saying, but *cellist* seems to stir something in him. "Her mum was good. Said Isabeau was good and all."

"She's more than good. She's a natural, and perhaps she'll even be famous one day. But more important than being famous, she's going to be happy and safe, two things she isn't while she lives here."

We watch each other in silence, my gaze angry and his filled with guilt and suspicion. I pull out a chair and sit down.

"This is how it's going to work, Mr. Laurent. I think you'll find you want to agree to my terms."

Chapter Four

Isabeau
Then

I half-listen to Laszlo talking to Dad downstairs. I can't hear the words, only the rise and fall of their voices. Mostly it's Laszlo talking.

He wants to teach me to play the cello. No one's taught me since Mum died a year ago in the car accident. Since then no one's even wanted to listen to me play. Dad doesn't like music in the house so I don't play inside very often. When I do I make sure it's after he's taken the medicine for his back. It makes him so sleepy that he doesn't hear the notes.

Laszlo is coming up the stairs and sit up expectantly. He's smiling, but there's a funny look on his face like he's not certain about something.

"There's been a change of plan, sweetheart."

Hope flickers out. So it was too good to be true, that this strange man who appeared like a fairy king out of a hillside would help me to learn to play. He's as handsome as a fairy king, too, with the loveliest greeny-brown eyes and too-long hair; the sort of fairy king who would ride a stag or some fantastical golden creature. I turn away to my cello, running my fingers over the instrument case. He's going back to those people who've asked him to help them with their music. An orchestra, he called it. I had hoped I'd get to meet them but I guess I won't.

"How would you like to come and live with me?"

He keeps talking, something about a house on the other side of London and a room to play music in but relief and happiness is singing too loudly in my ears. It's not just lessons he's going to give me, but a whole world of music, like those people in the orchestra have.

"Will you still teach me how to play? Properly play?"

He looks at me for a long time, as if he's trying to decide something. I try and look like a person who really, *really* wants to learn how to play the cello.

"Of course."

He helps me pack up a few of my things into my school bag and a holdall and we take them downstairs. Dad's at the kitchen table, smoking a cigarette. I hesitate, looking into the kitchen. Then I go through and stand in front of him. I don't know him very well lately. He sleeps a lot, and is sick and in pain a lot. I wonder if Mum would have known how to make him better. I wish I knew.

"Dad, I'm going to learn how to play the cello, like Mum could."

He seems to sort of nod but he doesn't look at me, and so I turn and go to Laszlo, who's standing by the front door with his hand on the top of my cello case and my holdall and his music bag in his other hand.

I leave the front door key on the hall table, and I close the door behind me.

I've never ridden in a black cab before and it's so big in the back that there's room for a cello case. There's room for three, even. Laszlo's on his phone, changing the times of meetings I think, and I watch London slip by with my nose pressed against the glass until he taps me on the shoulder and tells me to put my seatbelt on. The cab goes over the river and past the palace where the Queen lives and I see the gleam of the big golden statue out front. We keep driving past a park and onto streets lined with redbrick houses. There's another park, a big one, with people walking spotty dogs and skinny dogs and hairy dogs. *Hampstead Heath*, reads a sign. The road goes up and down and winds about and everything's so pretty and green. A few minutes later the cab slides to a halt in front of a red brick house. It has a shiny black front door. Laszlo pays the cab driver and takes me inside.

His home is a very beautiful house with shiny surfaces and music things everywhere. There are photographs of musicians on the walls, sheet music in neat stacks, funny old instruments displayed on side tables and in glass cases. I don't even recognize some of the things but I know they've got something to do with music. He shows me all over the house, ending in a music room that he calls a rehearsal studio, a large airy space with a great big shiny black piano on one side.

"Do you feel like playing your cello?" he asks me.

I always feel like playing my cello. I get it out and launch into a piece and he listens, hands clasped behind his back, head bent. It's funny to be listened to for minutes and minutes at a time. I try a few new things out and some of them don't work and sound horribly squeaky, but his face doesn't change. When I finish he asks me if I want to play some more, but holding my bow and my cello a slightly different way. I do, and the things I tried before don't get squeaky.

After, he goes through his shelves and gathers an armload of books and we go down to the sofas. He gives me the books to look at while he cooks dinner. Some are about reading music and I'm astonished that you're supposed to *read* these black squiggles like words, and I start learning how. Other books are stories about famous cello players, and I look at pictures of them with their instruments. Every one of them loves their cello. I can see it in their hands.

Laszlo puts the stereo on while he's cooking and hums to the music. Not the melody, the other harmonies that I barely even notice are there at first. Occasionally he stops to think or take a phone call and I see his long fingers moving on the counter, sometimes not even to the notes. Sometimes to the spaces between the notes as if he hears those, too. He does even the most ordinary things while moving through the music, though not like a dancer moves to a song, using it to make something else. A *conductor*, that newspaper piece called him. I wonder if this is what a conductor is, someone who stands at the very center of all these sounds and silences and hears every one of them.

After we eat and I tell Laszlo about what I've read, I read for a bit longer and then go to bed in a large, plain room. It's the guest room, he says, but it's going to be my room if I want and I can change how it looks. My cello is beside my bed and he says I can play it whenever I like, even in the middle of the night, so I don't know what else I could need.

Except when I close my eyes in the darkness I can't sleep.

Sometime later I get out of bed and go downstairs. Laszlo's reading on the sofa and he looks up in surprise when he hears me come in. Something's wrong. I look around the room, trying to figure out what it is, but it's not the room.

Laszlo watches me, a finger in the closed pages of his book. "Is everything all right, Isabeau? Do you miss your father?"

I go to the window and peer through the glass, looking into the dark garden. I open the casement and lean out into the chilly night air, listening as hard as I can.

Laszlo has come up behind me. "If you're ever unhappy here I want you to tell me. You can go home whenever you want."

I turn to him, finally figuring out what's wrong. In my part of London there are always noises. The neighbors arguing. Pounding electronic music. Cars going past at all hours. "It's too quiet here."

Laszlo looks out the darkened window, and then goes and switches on the stereo. After perusing the CDs for a moment he selects one and presses play. Music expands throughout the room in a soft cloud and I immediately feel better. I go and sit on the sofa and Laszlo sits beside me, and we just listen.

"This piece is called *Dream 13*," he says finally, and sketches his finger back and forth in the air like a bow. "That's the cello. Do you hear it?"

I do hear it, and put my head down on the cushion and close my eyes, letting the music cocoon me. There's a cello, and a piano too. The piano sounds like watching rain fall on leaves through shiny clean glass. The cello is a sigh first thing in the morning after a long sleep. "It's so pretty," I whisper.

"If you want, I can start to teach you how to play some of this piece tomorrow."

Just like that, as if it's nothing to take a piece of music and make it your own for a while. To have a thousand such pieces sitting waiting in CD cases and written out on sheet music that you carry can around. A whole room for making music in. I never knew that people like Laszlo existed.

I open my eyes and look at him. "Who will play the other part?"

"The piano? I will."

"Are you good at playing the piano?"

He smiles. "I get by."

"Yes, please, Laszlo. I want play this." Sitting here with him in this magical house of music I feel brave enough to tell him a secret that I've never told anyone before. "I want to play everything."

THE PROTÉGÉ

He doesn't tell me it's silly to want to play *everything*. Everything including the whistling of the kettle? The bins being collected? Every song on the radio and every sound from the stereo? Maybe I do mean everything. And why not? I've heard all sorts of things in my cello and I want to know how to find them again.

Laszlo nods. "Then you shall."

I listen to the music, feeling sleepy but with lots of thoughts and questions buzzing around in my head. I wonder if Laszlo just *gets by* on the piano, or if he's actually very good. I wonder if Laszlo is married. I wonder if one day he might marry me. I would like that, and then we could play music together, always.

I wake early in the morning and look out onto the street. There are only houses on Laszlo's street, no shops, but there are people walking past in coats and hats, the women in high heeled shoes. They're not the sort of people I'm used to seeing but they might like music, too. Everyone likes music, don't they?

Laszlo's big house is hushed as I carry my cello carefully downstairs and prop the front door open with an umbrella so that I can get back in again. I'll have to ask him for a key so that I can always get back in.

Down on the corner I set up my instrument and start to play. I don't know any of the names of the pieces. My mother taught me these songs and I think of them as *the one with the nah-na-nah part* or *the one that gets really fast at the end*. Every now and then I mix all the pieces I know together and come up with a new song, and sometimes it works and sometimes it doesn't.

There aren't as many people walking by here as there are on the main street near home and most of them frown at me. A few give me coins. I'm lost in playing the *nah-na-nah* piece when I hear a sharp voice behind me.

"Isabeau. What are you doing out here?"

When I open my eyes I see Laszlo towering over me, and he's frowning like the other people. Maybe I was wrong and people in this part of London don't like music. Maybe I've upset everyone. I rub the back of the bow against my jeans, uncertain.

He kneels down before me, his frown disappearing. "It's all right. I was just worried because I didn't know where you were. Why are you busking? You can play in the house. I like hearing you play."

I believe him, and I didn't come outside because I thought my cello would bother him. But I don't know how to tell him why I did come outside, not when there are only three coins in my cello case.

"You can tell me. I won't be angry."

"For the money. In case there isn't enough. So you don't sell my cello."

He looks pained. "Oh, sweetheart. I would never, ever do that. No one's going to take your cello away from you. Not me, and not anyone else. I won't let them."

I look at the three pathetic silver coins and I know that they're nowhere near enough to pay for music lessons or a place to live or even the dinner we ate last night. "I don't understand why you would do that for me."

"Because you love music like I love music. One day people will be very moved when they hear you play and knowing that I helped with that will make me very happy."

"Is this what a conductor does?"

He thinks for a moment. "Yes, in a way. Like in a piece of music, I'm here to see that everything unfolds as it's supposed to. That's my job. You play the very best you can, in a way that makes you happy. That's your job. You're not to worry about anything. The worrying is my job, too."

"Doesn't worrying keep you awake at night?"

He smiles. I like his face so much when he smiles. His canines are pointed and he should look strange with teeth like that but he just looks interesting.

"No, I like it. It's not worry to me." He looks at me holding my instrument and frowns. "But I do think you need a second cello, for now. One that you can play sitting down, like a real cellist, and get your arm around properly. Would you like that?"

I stare at him. *Two* cellos. Who could possibly ever possess two whole cellos all to themselves? Even Laszlo who lives in music only has one piano. But the idea of a cello that's my size sounds exciting.

"I would still keep this one?"

"Of course. This is a beautiful cello for a grown up young lady to play on and it will be waiting for you when you're ready to play it."

We go back inside and I try to give him the money I got from playing. It's only thirty-five pence but I want him to have it.

He shakes his head. "You keep it. I conducted a symphony two nights ago and they gave me some money."

"How much did you get?"

He smiles his pointed smile. "Thirty pence."

"Don't be silly, Laszlo! How much really?"

"All right, you got me. It was only twenty pence."

Later after breakfast he takes me into town to a music shop and Laszlo and the salesperson discuss half-size versus three-quarter cellos and something called *playability*. I try a few of the cellos and settle on one that's not quite as tall as I am and makes sounds that I like when I play it.

Laszlo finally stops talking and stands with his arms folded and just listens to me.

I finish *the one that gets loud at the end* and smile because it was so much fun to play on this cello. I didn't need stretch my arm so much to get the longest notes.

"Is that the one, Isabeau?" Laszlo asks me, and I nod. I like this one.

The salesperson looks at me with her eyebrows raised as she rings up the purchase on the till. "Quite something, isn't she?"

"Oh, yes. She's quite something."

The pride in Laszlo's voice makes me smile again. He sounds even better than a cello.

As we're walking home I remember the umbrella I stuck in the front door. "Laszlo, can I please have a key to the house?"

"Why would you need a key?"

I look at him in astonishment. "So I can get back in, of course. If I go out."

"What would you go out for?"

"School. Milk. I don't know. I've had a key for the last year."

"I noticed that. Sweetheart, it's not safe for you to come and go like that. I'll be here to take you to school and collect you, and if I'm not then I'll make sure someone I trust is.

And if we need milk, I'll get it." He thinks for a moment. "And you'll have to come with me for that because it's not safe for you to be alone at home, either."

"Why?"

"Because you're eight."

"Oh, Laszlo. You're so strict."

He laughs. "Am I? Well, maybe I've had some practice. There are a lot of people in my orchestra."

"How many?"

"Nearly a hundred."

A *hundred*. That's so many people, and so much music.

He looks at me thoughtfully. "Do you mind going to a new school? You'll have to transfer to the local one."

I shrug. "They probably won't care much about my cello there, either."

"No, probably not. But there are a few good high schools in London that care very much about all sorts of instruments. That's a thought. There are probably waiting lists as long as my arm. I'll have to call around my contacts, get recommendations. You'll need a cello tutor…"

He trails off, abstracted, and I watch his face, wondering if he minds all this thinking about high schools and waiting lists and having me with him every time he gets milk, but he doesn't seem irritated. In fact as we stand at a set of lights I can hear him humming under his breath.

Back at home he helps me unpack the new instrument, and I find myself looking at Mum's, hoping it doesn't feel left out.

Laszlo notices. "If you ever want to play this one, just because, I want you to feel like you can, all right?"

I nod, but I know I'm not going to play it until I'm older. *A beautiful cello for a grown up young lady to play on*, Laszlo called it. I'll play it again soon. I'll grow into it, and it will be here, waiting for me.

Chapter Five

Isabeau
Then

Laszlo puts a plate of pancakes and bacon in front of me. "Happy birthday, sweetheart."

"Thank you, Laszlo," I say, before attacking my breakfast. At my elbow are a dozen cards from tutors and youth orchestra people and Laszlo's musician friends who come to the house, some of them proclaiming *Fourteen today!*

Laszlo flicks through a score while we're eating, his fingers absent-mindedly tapping the pages to a melody only he can hear. I sneak looks around the kitchen, trying to find my birthday present. He always gives me my present at breakfast but there's nothing next to my plate or on the kitchen bench.

When we're finished eating I help him clean up, and then I can't bear it any longer. "Please can I have my birthday present now?"

He raises his eyebrows in surprise. "Your birthday present? But you've had it already."

"I have not! Don't fib!"

Laszlo seems puzzled as he looks around the kitchen but I can see the ghost of a smile on his lips. "That's very strange. I could have sworn… Why don't you go and look in your room? Maybe it's there."

I race upstairs and see my cello propped up against the wall with a pink ribbon tied around the neck. My first cello. My mother's cello. I hear Laszlo come up the stairs behind me and turn breathlessly to him.

"Do you really think I'm tall enough—big enough—good enough—" I break off, running my fingers down the glossy wood, in an agony of excitement and doubt.

"If you want to, Isabeau. It's always been your cello to play whenever you like."

Yes, I want to play it now. I touch the strings which have been silent for six years but my hands feel shaky and clammy. "Will you tune it for me? I feel all funny."

He sits on my bed with the cello between his knees and I watch as he twists the tuning pegs at the top of the neck and plays scales until the notes are just right. I've seen him do this with dozens of different instruments over the years though he only ever plays music on the piano. He hands the cello back to me and I take his place. What to play first?

I know. *The Swan.*

I didn't know what it was called when Laszlo put on a recording of *The Carnival of the Animals* when I first came to live with him. I listened to all the unfamiliar tracks, liking *Royal March of the Lion* and *Fossils* the best, but then *The Swan* started and I sat bolt upright, exclaiming, "My mother used to play this. My mother was going to teach me this but then…" And I broke off before I could say it, but Laszlo knew. She was going to teach me this but then she died. He's since taught me to play the piece, accompanying me on the piano and now I know it by heart. We play it together sometimes just because.

I put the bow to the strings and begin, the notes plaintive and slow like the composer asks for on the sheet music. Normally when I play this piece I imagine a beautiful white swan gliding on a lake, but this time I see someone with a cello.

Halfway through a huge well of emotion opens up inside me and I burst into tears, my bow arm dropping to my side.

Laszlo kneels down before me. "Isabeau, what's wrong?"

"I can see my mother," I manage in a thick whisper, tears dropping into my lap.

THE PROTÉGÉ

Laszlo gets up and sits beside me on the bed, hugging me to him, not saying anything. I close my eyes and lean into him, holding onto the memory of my mother playing this piece on this cello. There are so many feelings in music and I'm starting to notice them more and more. A piece isn't just *pretty* or *interesting* or a challenge anymore. I can feel anger in the music, or happiness, or love. *The Swan* has so much love in it, but so much loss, too. It feels like my mother but she's very far away where I can't reach her.

When the tears stop I wipe my face and reach for my bow, determined to play the whole thing, but Laszlo touches my arm.

"Do you want to see your father?"

I twist the bow in my hands, not looking at him. He asks me this about twice every year, usually around my birthday and then again at Christmas. I feel so conflicted because when I remember my father I remember two men. How he was before my mother died and he had the accident, and how he was after. The man he was after frightened me and I don't think I want to see that man. Last year Laszlo explained to me why he was different. That he was in a lot of pain that would never go away and he was using very strong medicine to help with it. When I asked him why dad's medicine would be brought round to the house by people that scared me he looked furious for a moment and then took a deep breath and told me that sometimes people prescribe themselves medicine when they feel like they can't cope.

"Not yet, Laszlo. Thank you."

"All right, sweetheart. Happy birthday."

He listens to me play for a minute and then heads for the stairs, but before he disappears he stops in the doorway and says, "Oh, I forgot—your real birthday present is in the music room."

My real present? I follow him out of the room and see that there's a large box sitting on the piano done up in ribbon the same color as the ribbon that was tied around my cello. When he gets it down and passes it to me I see the name Lou Lou on the box in gold embossing. Lou Lou is a boutique in town that sells very fancy dresses. We walk past it on the way to the Mayhew and I always look and see what's in the front window. I open the box and hunt through the tissue paper to find a pale pink satin dress. The neckline and straps have ruffles and the skirt is very long and very full. I hold it up against myself, marveling at how pretty it is.

Laszlo watches me thoughtfully. "The shop assistant said that the dusky pink color would go with your hair. I wasn't sure at first, a redhead in a pink dress. But I think she was right. It's a lovely color for you."

I stroke the heavy pink satin, loving how it spills like water over my hands but feeling perplexed at the same time. "It's so *beautiful*, thank you. But…"

He raises his eyebrows. "But what?"

"But where am I going to wear it? I only go to school and cello lessons."

Laszlo strokes a thumb and forefinger over his chin. "Hmm. That is a good question. It's such a lovely dress that a lot of people should see you in it, and on a special occasion. A very special occasion. Maybe…your professional debut?"

I stare at him. I've already performed in lots of shows and competitions and with several youth orchestras but they've never been called debuts or required satin dresses. "Where? What debut? How?"

He smiles, showing his pointed canines. "With my orchestra. At the Mayhew."

His orchestra. Perform with *his* orchestra. He's never even let me come to one of their rehearsals as he says they're kept strictly professional. I've seen his orchestra perform several times while he conducts and they're formidable. Laszlo always wears black tie and tails and he's terribly formidable as well. The orchestra is huge and the audience is enormous. I suddenly feel very small and quiet, like a mouse squeaking in a church.

"You think I'm good enough to perform at the Mayhew with your orchestra?"

"I do. On your mother's cello, if you like. A solo with the orchestra behind you."

A solo. Sit at the front of the orchestra and have my name in the program. Be announced and walk onto the stage with Laszlo. That's why he chose a dress in such a lovely vivid color, so that I would be seen. Soloists always stand out and the women especially because they wear beautiful evening gowns. I imagine myself sitting at the front of Laszlo's orchestra, close to him, playing my mother's cello, and feel breathless with excitement.

"What would I play?"

"What would you like to play?" He explains that a short piece would be best, something orchestral but that has a prominent cello solo throughout. Most importantly it should be something that I love to play.

I barely need to think about it. "I'd like to play *The Swan*, please."

Laszlo takes my hand and squeezes it. "Good girl. I thought you might."

We do what Laszlo calls some sectional rehearsals in his music room. When I first came to live with him he told me it was called the rehearsal studio, but to me it will always be the music room. I've said *music room* to him so many times that he's started calling it that, too. I hear him correcting himself on the telephone sometimes. *We'll use my music room—I mean, my rehearsal studio.* He leaves the door open when he's rehearsing with his musicians and the sounds permeate every room. When the entire violin section comes around the house is filled with drama and heartbreak. I keep out of the way because I know how seriously Laszlo takes rehearsals, but I also want to listen so I sit just out of sight on the landing above, hearing them play and Laszlo giving directions. *Less bow on the string. Make your diminuendo later.* Always polite, but firm, and they do exactly as he asks.

Just the harpist and one of the violinists come to the house to help me practice before the proper rehearsal. I've played the piece many times with Laszlo while he accompanies me on the piano and I love the piece that way, but it's beautiful with the harp and violin, too.

On the day of the rehearsal we take the Tube from Belsize Park down to Leicester Square and walk from there to the Mayhew. Laszlo's dressed in a suit jacket and shirt, but no tie, which is what I usually see him head off to rehearsals wearing, and I've put on a black pinafore dress with a white t-shirt underneath. It's what I wear for performances. At rehearsals I usually wear jeans but Laszlo expects musicians to be smartly dressed at the Mayhew at all times. I know this because at my last lesson my cello tutor, Mr. Goldstein, finished our session with a list of rules that Laszlo has for his orchestra. As he enumerated them my eyes got bigger and bigger.

No eating or drinking anything except water from bottles. No phones. No conspicuous yawning. No talking back to the conductor. No arguing with the conductor or questioning his intention or directions. No playing in between sections or when he's called for a stop. No playing anyone else's part just to see if you can. Don't tune too loudly. Don't tap your feet or whistle or hum. Don't wear a lot of perfume or cologne. No chatting between movements and never, *ever* talk while he's talking, even if he's not talking to you.

"And don't be late. He hates that. But you'll be going with him so that's not something you need to worry about."

I had no idea Laszlo had so many rules. It's more strict than school. Thank god I know because I might have embarrassed him horribly otherwise. I'm sure I've yawned at rehearsals with my other orchestras and we chat all the time and pass around snacks. Some people even swap instruments for fun when the conductor is helping someone else with their part. "Why didn't he tell me all this himself?"

"I expect he didn't want to make you nervous, and in any case you've got lovely manners. I doubt for a second he believes you would do anything to embarrass him or yourself."

Mr. Goldstein apparently does or he wouldn't have told me all these rules. Or perhaps he just thought it was best I know. "When did he tell you all this?"

"He didn't. Some is just orchestra etiquette and with Mr. Valmary you work things out, and quite quickly if you know what's good for you."

"What does he do if you break the rules?"

He just raises his eyebrows in a *don't ask* expression.

"But Laszlo's so *nice*."

Mr. Goldstein gives a choking sort of laugh. "Nice. Oh. Well. He'll never shout or bully or do anything cruel but people have been known to leave his rehearsals in tears. Or fired."

There must be an alarmed look on my face as my tutor adds, "Don't worry, he won't fire you. You're a guest soloist, not one of his orchestra. Besides, he's very indulgent with you. If any of the ensemble knew he played Saint-Saëns with you while you were both in your pajamas they'd drop down dead."

I don't want him to be indulgent with me, I want to feel very grown up and professional so I think carefully over the rules as the Northern Line train plunges through the tunnels. When we pull into Euston I say to Laszlo, "People in the orchestra call you *maestro*, don't they? Do I call you *maestro*?" *Maestro* means "master" in Italian and it's a term of respect musicians use when addressing the very best conductors.

"No, as you're a guest soloist you can call me Mr. Valmary, and I'll call you Miss Laurent."

Laszlo call me Miss Laurent? How funny. "Why do you have so many rules for your orchestra? Mr. Goldstein told me about them."

"Lots of conductors have rules. Or rather, etiquette."

"But why do you?"

He stands aside for someone who wants to get out at the next station. "How we behave while we play shows how much respect we have for the music and the people who composed it. Not all orchestras are so structured but we are because we play the most respected pieces by the best composers, in one of the most beautiful concert halls in the world."

"And then the audience feels safe coming to hear you because they see how much you respect the music?"

Laszlo thinks about this for a moment. "Yes, that's a very good way to put it."

"Why were people so upset when you took over as conductor?"

He looks at me in surprise. "You remember that?"

"Of course. It was the very first thing I learned about you."

I see the ghost of a smile. "Some people in the music community thought I was going to challenge the established order of things. That I was too young to know what I was doing and that I wouldn't show the music respect. It's true I like to try new things and interpret things my way. A conductor always has their own vision they want to impart. But I always, always respect the composers, and the music. That to me is the most important thing."

"Not what people in the music community think?"

The ghost of a smile again. "You can't control what people think, only what you do. Do what you set out to do, and do it well, and nothing else matters."

I brought some schoolwork at Laszlo's suggestion as the rehearsal will go on all morning and I won't be needed until the end. I sit to one side and take out my history textbook but it lays unopened on my lap. I'm too interested in the orchestra and the things Laszlo says to them as they rehearse. They're playing *Scheherazade* by Rimsky-Korsakov and he keeps stopping during the movements to ask some sections to be louder, some faster, some musicians to play slightly differently. He doesn't do rude things like shout or click his fingers at someone or moan, "No, no, no, not like *that*," as some of my conductors do. Laszlo's very calm and thorough, and soon the music coming off the orchestra is exactly what he wants it to be.

Before I know it he's looking over at me. "Miss Laurent, we're ready for you now."

My heart starts to pound in my ears and I collect my bow and cello, which I tuned at the beginning with everyone else. Some of the musicians smile at me as I take my place, particularly the harpist and the violinist I practiced with. There are so many of them, nearly a hundred, and they're mostly strangers.

But Laszlo's not a stranger. Laszlo is Laszlo, and once I'm sitting down in front of the other cellists I'm very close to him. There's a warm look in his eyes and I recall what Mr. Goldstein said, that Laszlo's very indulgent with me. But I don't feel spoiled. In fact quite the opposite. It's like my tutor said, Laszlo never told me a list of rules, he just behaves or talks in a certain way and I find myself responding. And I like that about him. I like that very much.

Sitting here surrounded by the order that he's put in place and upholds I feel very safe. He won't let anyone tell me I'm too silly or young to be here, or talk over my playing or call me names. If I make a mistake no one will laugh at me, because he's there. I smile up at him and he gives me the ghost of a wink.

When I'm settled and my bow is poised I look at his hands. He brings them to resting position, forearms parallel to the floor, palms raised and fingers bent, and the baton is held lightly in his fingers. The baton is because it's such a big orchestra and it helps the people at the back see what he's doing. He raises his arms slowly and brings them down just as slowly, showing the orchestra what tempo he wants. The harp starts to play and the rest of the string section joins in, measured and gentle. All around us the rest of the orchestra is hushed. I wait for my cue, keeping Laszlo's hands in my peripheral vision, and then I start to play.

For a few bars I'm too nervous to become lost in the music, but then there's just the poignant strains of my cello and the swell of the strings all around me, and Laszlo. He's told me that the gestures he makes while he's conducting reinforce what the composer has written on the sheet music and remind the ensemble of what he's asked for during rehearsals.

When we get to the end and the sound of my cello fades away he smiles at me, and I like that because he hasn't smiled at anyone else the whole rehearsal. I've been watching.

All right, maybe I'm a little bit indulged.

I wonder if he's going to adjust my playing but there are only directions for the orchestra. "Beautiful, Miss Laurent. Once more? Violas, a little softer from twenty-eight to thirty-four, please."

When we've finished the piece a second time the rehearsal ends. I wait to one side with my cello as the rest of the orchestra put their instruments away or stand about talking. A few of the musicians are talking to Laszlo.

Finally we leave, and Laszlo suggests we go to Covent Garden for a late lunch. As we're walking over the cobbles I say, "Are you sure my playing was all right? You didn't have any corrections for me."

He looks down at me in surprise. "Solo pieces are a collaboration between the soloist and the conductor. You bring your own vision for the piece and I interpret it for the rest of the orchestra so that your playing sounds its very best."

"How do you know my vision? I never said anything."

"Sweetheart, I've heard you play *The Swan* so many times. You don't need to tell me because I know what it means to you."

My vision for the piece. He's arranged his whole orchestra—well, the strings anyway—around my vision for the piece. It's such a lovely thing for him to have done and I don't know what to say.

"Did you enjoy yourself?" he asks.

Trying to convey just how wonderful I found the whole experience I say emphatically, "It was *so* nice. I've never felt like that during any rehearsals or even practice, that I was within something so beautiful and that everything around me was flowing like water. Your orchestra is wonderful."

"Thank you, Isabeau. I think so, too."

I take a deep breath. "You're a really wonderful conductor, Laszlo. It was a bit scary at first, but I felt very safe with you there."

He looks down at me, and then puts an arm around my shoulders and squeezes me briefly. His voice is husky when he says, "Thank you, sweetheart. That means a lot to me."

The night I'm to perform comes around quickly. There are two soloists visiting the Mayhew and playing with Laszlo's orchestra, a violinist and a pianist, and I'm to come on at the end.

I watch the orchestra from the wings wearing my pink dress. Mostly I watch Laszlo, who looks very handsome and dramatic in his tuxedo. I love seeing him wind up to a crescendo, the movements of his arms getting bigger and his hair flying about. The pianist plays with the orchestra first, and then there's a break, and then the violinist. And then there's me.

The applause goes on for a long time when the violinist finishes and there's a lot of shouting and cheering. Laszlo takes his bow with the violinist and then comes off stage and approaches me. "Are you ready?" he asks in whisper.

I nod, gripping my cello tightly. He watches the audience for a moment, waiting for them to settle, and then we walk out together. The applause erupts immediately and it's so loud. The lights are so bright that I can barely see the audience sitting in the dark, but I think that might be a good thing. I stand beside Laszlo with butterflies rioting in my belly.

He smiles at me and turns to the audience. "Ladies and gentlemen, over the years it's been my pleasure to introduce for you many world-class soloists at the Mayhew, and tonight is no exception. But this is the first time I've had the honor of presenting a soloist's debut. Miss Isabeau Laurent is an award-winning cellist with the North London Youth Orchestra, a soloist of great talent, and my protégé."

The applause erupts again and so do my nerves as we take our places, but when I look up and see Laszlo just a few feet away I feel better. Nothing bad can happen as long as he's there.

Laszlo never speaks to musicians except his concertmaster while he's on stage but he looks at me expectantly and I nod when I'm ready. Once the strings start and I play the first note everything falls away. I don't see my mother again, but I feel her, and I'm playing for her.

When the piece ends and the last long note from my cello fades I find I have to open my eyes because at some point I've closed them, and the world comes rushing back in a storm of applause. All around me a sea of bows are tapping in unison, the string section's version of clapping, and Laszlo has his hand out to help me up. We take bows, and then the two other soloists are there as well and there's so much applause that I feel bewildered by it all. Laszlo's looking closely at the first few rows, a smile on his face. Finally we're able to get off stage and the soloists and the ensemble are congratulating me and telling me how well I played and I'm trying to say *you too* and *thank you* to everyone.

Finally it's just Laszlo, looking pleased, his hair rumpled from pushing his fingers through it. "Isabeau, that was so beautiful you made some people cry."

So that's what he was looking at during the bows. "Did I make you cry?" I tease, because I'm elated now it's over. I know I didn't make him cry because I saw his face at the end and he was only smiling.

Laszlo puts his hand over his heart. "You made me cry in here. I'm so proud of you, sweetheart."

He hugs me, and his familiar sweet peppercorn scent envelops me. *How long,* I wonder, hugging him back fiercely, *until he falls in love with me and asks me to marry him? It's taking so long to grow up. I love him so much already.*

Chapter Six

Isabeau

Now

I'm on Laszlo's street ten minutes before the appointed time but I don't go to the front door and knock. Not yet. Instead I stand by a garden wall a few doors down, stomping my feet in the cold.

This was my neighborhood for ten years and it's more familiar to me than any other part of London. I was happy all the time here. Frustrated some days, yes, by school or by my fingers if they wouldn't coax the sound I wanted from my cello. Some days I was sick, and some days I missed Laszlo if he had to go to away to perform. But those were only minor blips, and the thread of my days was always one of happiness.

Every day except that last one.

When I was younger it was so simple. I loved Laszlo, and once I'd grown up he'd fall in love with me, too. I never considered that he might not feel the same way about me. That he couldn't feel the same. Other people seemed to assume that I thought of him as a father but to me he was my protector, teacher and friend, and the most important person in the world. We never told each other we loved each other but if I had I would have meant it in the romantic sense. That I was *in* love with him.

I don't know if I still love him. I don't know what he thinks about that night or what he thinks about me now. I do know why he wants to see me at the house: so he can ask me why I came to the Mayhew out of the blue and why I auditioned when I wasn't there to audition. Why I asked for a place in the orchestra when I know nothing about the tour. I've lain awake most of the night thinking about how I will answer these questions. We may quarrel again like the night of my eighteenth birthday only this time the rift will be permanent. I'm frightened that I'll lose Laszlo forever.

Yesterday I wanted to play for him so he'd understand how I feel. When I opened my eyes and saw that his fingers were moving to the piano part of *Vocalise* I felt a longing for him so great that it was almost unbearable. A longing to make music with him again. I could see from his normally so shuttered face that he missed that, too, and it was like a lance had impaled me through the chest. I miss his clever hands. The sound of his voice. Opening my eyes from a solo to see the warmth in his eyes.

But this is not about what I miss. This is about what I need, and I need his help. I want to be a soloist but for that I need vision. Authenticity. Inspiration. My sense of who I am as a cellist has been devastated and I need Laszlo as my mentor again. To feel the peace and happiness that comes from his strong and subtle presence. His strictness and high expectations of me.

I've played in many ensembles over the last few years but no conductor makes me feel like Laszlo makes me feel. Safe. Happy. Protected. And other things, things that I barely understood before I left his house. Things that I was just starting to discover about myself.

During the three years away from Laszlo I learned about music, exploring unfamiliar styles of performing and playing. I discovered that there's peace to be found in walking alone through the beautiful university grounds at Durham and hearing music float out of open windows and choral singing echoing from within the cathedral. I learned that going to bed with someone when your heart's not in it is one of the loneliest experiences you can ever have.

I discovered that it's unwise to look to anyone else for your happiness. I tried to find my own happiness, in all the ways, but the memory of Laszlo was everywhere. His voice, his direction unexpectedly filled my fantasies. Playing well and imagining that he was listening to me would make me slick and restless. Recalling the sound of his voice as he'd corrected something in my playing or told me I'd done well would, with the help of my fingers, bring me to orgasm. I knew some of this while I was living with him. That I was attracted to his authority, his confidence, and that pleasing him made me feel so very good in unexpected ways. But I didn't know how much I craved that all the time until I lost him. I didn't know then how important it was to my music.

I glance at my watch: three minutes to eleven. I'm not asking him to love me, touch me, take me to bed. What I want goes deeper than that. I have to speak it aloud for him because this is one thing that music won't be able to tell him.

I want what only Laszlo can give me. I want to be his protégé again.

I check my watch again: one minute to eleven. I peel myself away from the wall and head toward his door. It's time.

Chapter Seven

Laszlo
Now

I see Isabeau at the end of my street ten minutes before our appointed time, huddled close to a wall, the lower part of her face swathed in a thick knitted scarf. One gloved hand is holding her cello case and the other is wrapped around a shoulder bag that will be filled with sheet music. She's shaking despite her heavy winter coat because her legs are clad only in tights and there are black court shoes on her feet. She's dressed for the stage, not a freezing London street. Every now and then she glances at her wristwatch. At one minute to eleven she straightens and walks up the street. The bell rings at exactly eleven.

When I open the door I see from her pale, tight face that she's nervous. No. Terrified. Of me? It was the same when I said her name yesterday and she turned toward me, and I hate it because she's never been afraid of me. I want to reach out to her, reassure her, but there's too much distance between us even though she's only two feet away.

Her chin lifts and she says in a clear voice, "Hello, Laszlo."

I take her up to the studio where she gets out her cello and begins to tune it. We should talk, but it's wonderful seeing her in this space again, sitting behind her cello. Her bloodless fingers slip on the strings and I step forward automatically and take her small hand between mine, as I've done in the past. Warming her fingers. She looks up at me with those clear green eyes that have haunted me since that night.

Tell her you're sorry. For everything. Even the things she doesn't know about.

I clear my throat and release her. "Bach's Sixth. Do you have the sheet music?" She doesn't so I find the cello part for her and place it on the music stand.

She plays excellently. Her technique, her pace. This is one of the symphonies I want the ensemble to perform on tour and there's not much time to rehearse so it's important everyone can play it. "The second movement—"

Isabeau cuts across me without raising her voice. "Aren't you going to tell me how that was?"

I feel a lurch and the room goes out of focus.

"You never say good girl anymore." The feel of her body close to mine. The deep pools of her green eyes as she looks up at me.

"Don't I?"

"No, you don't. Daddy."

The miniscule hesitation right before she says it. Daddy. "What? Don't call me that."

"Why not?"

"Because I'm not your father."

"I know. I didn't mean it that way."

I was always Laszlo to Isabeau. She didn't call me daddy until the night of her eighteenth birthday. I said "good girl" a lot when she was younger, when correcting her and praising her had been easy. Before it started taking on new and unexpected dimensions. Before I started thinking about her in ways I knew I shouldn't.

Isabeau slips like a fish into my lap, making my breath catch. My desire for her paralyzes me as I'm caught between acting on my fantasies and pushing her away. I should push her away. Her fingers stroke my short beard, her nails scratching through the bristles. Her soft, pink mouth is very close to mine. "Do you like that, daddy?"

Yes. Yes I like that. Her touch, her weight in my lap. That word. Daddy. It sounds decadent and more than little slutty from her grown up but still very young mouth. And when she presses her lips against mine I let her. My hands slide around her hips and I pull her tightly against my thickening cock, letting her feel my length through her underwear. What she does to me. What she's been doing to me for months even though I've hated myself for it.

Her sharp intake of breath. The way she looks wonderingly down at the evidence of my arousal and then slides back and forward against me, tentative, holding onto the lapels of my suit jacket. Her soft cry of pleasure as rubbing her clit against my cock seems to send sparks through her. Raising her eyes to mine, eloquent with arousal.

"Good girl," I murmur, encouraging the back and forth of her sex against me, holding her lightly, guiding her. Just a little longer and she'll be coming in my lap. Fuck, I've wanted this. This, and so much more. She moves faster, breathing hard, her eyes filled with need for me. Isabeau's perfect green eyes.

Isabeau, and the green eyes that have looked to me for ten years with trust and love. Since she was a child. And now, what? I'm going to fuck her on her eighteenth birthday? Is this all she means to me? Shock and guilt sluices me like an icy waterfall and I shove her off my lap and onto the empty sofa seat.

"No. Isabeau. We can't."

She's barely a woman and she's naïve about men. If I hadn't known that already from spending just about every day with her since she was eight years old I would have felt it in the tentative way she moved against me, the surprise on her face that rubbing her clit against me had felt so good.

"Laszlo?"

Her voice pulls me back to the present. She has a neutral, expectant expression on her face that I've seen a thousand times on the faces of my orchestra, but when I look closer I'm certain she knows exactly where my mind went.

"From forty-four," I say, naming a measure at random.

I turn toward the window as she plays, closing my eyes to the painful memory that's waiting in the wings. I try desperately to keep it at bay but it crashes over me.

Isabeau looks up at me in surprise, her mussed hair falling into her eyes. "What's wrong, daddy?"

All the ways I've thought about her since she turned seventeen flood my head, swiftly followed by self-loathing and the horror that she's somehow discovered that I've thought about how good it would be to take her to bed and teach her about things other than music. Discover what she wants. Show her what I want. Hear her say Yes, sir *when I ask her if she likes the way I touch her, if she wants more. No, what she said.* Yes, daddy. *Fuck, that's much better. That's perfect.*

My protégé, who is not only a virgin and in my care but half my age. I need to explain to her why it would be wrong for us to have a sexual relationship but I can't think straight. I'm torn between my desire for her and my instincts to keep her safe, keep her happy, and never, ever touch her like that. All the pent-up need and self-recrimination wells up, and when she reaches for me again I grab her wrist and growl, "Isabeau, what the fuck are you doing?"

The second the words were out of my mouth I regretted them, not just because I was lying about how much I liked what she'd done, but also because how much it hurt her that I talked to her that way. Her nearly bringing herself to orgasm in my lap was the sweetest moment of my life, but I was so used to berating myself over my feelings for her by then that the guilt erupted at a ten on the Richter scale and I lashed out at her. Ever since then the sweetest moment also became the most shameful, because I hurt her. And I've never said sorry.

She stops playing and the silence in the room stretches. This room was never meant to stand silently. It was meant to be filled with music. Anger. Joy. Danger. Heartbreak. I need to speak but I don't know what I want to say more, that I'm sorry or that I want her. That I did then and I still do now.

"All right, next—"

"Laszlo. I didn't even finish the last piece." The seconds tick past and we just look at each other.

She speaks first. "I didn't come to the Mayhew to audition yesterday."

I sit down on the piano stool and fold my arms. She's holding her bow like it's a weapon, gripped tightly in her hand. "I know. You wanted to talk, and when we were interrupted you wanted to play. What I don't understand is why you then asked if you had the place in the ensemble."

"Because I do want the place, on certain conditions."

I wait, watching her closely. Isabeau has conditions for me. It's not just her features that are finer and her hair that's longer. She's got a firmness about her that I've never seen before. She's scared but there's something she wants.

Isabeau takes a deep breath. "This isn't easy for me to say. I've only ever made you angry with me once in my life, but I've never forgotten that and I know I'm risking your anger again."

I want to interrupt, to say that I was never angry with her, only myself, but she keeps talking.

"For ten years you made me feel nothing but safe and happy, even during the scary parts of my life. Performing at the Mayhew. Before exams. And just…every day. I always knew you were there if I needed you. You gave my life structure and meaning and made me do my best."

I frown, because while I'm glad she always felt safe and happy living with me I don't like the idea that I pushed her to do anything. "Isabeau, I didn't do that. You did it. You were always the most dedicated student, at school and in your lessons. You never gave me a moment's worry. I barely did a thing."

It wasn't just in school. Day to day she was polite, well-behaved, sweet. Not one tantrum or transgression that I can remember. I never caught her smoking or had to wait up because she was out past curfew. Isabeau was an angel.

She shakes her head. "You made me *want* to be like that. You showed me kindness and respect and told me what you expected of me, and I wanted to make you pleased with me. I *loved* that. And you did correct me, all the time, the way you correct your orchestra. *Good, but softer this time. Pianissimo.* Except with me it would be, *You've done so well in Chemistry this semester. Why don't you see if you can do as well in French? I know you can.* Or, *If you eat at this time of night don't you think it will keep you awake?*" The corner of her mouth turns up. "*You practiced that piece so beautifully, sweetheart. Why don't you try it slightly slower next time. Good girl.* Don't you remember, Laszlo?"

I rub the back of my neck, thinking. "Yes, I guess I do. It just felt natural to talk to you that way. I didn't notice I was doing it."

She moistens her lips. "I liked the way you talked to me. The expectations you had of me. That's sort of what I wanted to talk to you about. I've never been good at putting into words what I want. You always seemed to just know. It's the conductor in you, I suppose. You can feel what music needs instinctively. You could tell what I needed. But we haven't been able to hear each other for some time now so I'm going to have to tell you in words exactly what I want. I don't want there to be a misunderstanding like…" She falters, and takes a breath. "Like last time."

I don't quite know what Isabeau's asking for but something tells me it's not cello lessons.

"I want what we had when you were my mentor. I want how it was between us just before we last saw each other. Because of the way it made me feel. To be good for you."

My heart starts pounding. Isabeau was always such a good girl and I thought that was just the way she is. I didn't know she was doing that for me, because she liked that it made me happy and that that in turn made her happy. That it became something more for her. I think that's what she's telling me but I'm not sure. I have to know for sure. "You don't need me to be your mentor any more. Your playing is superb. There's nothing else you need from me."

She takes a deep breath. "You don't know this, but in those last months I started feeling differently about some of the things you would say and do. The way you would correct me. The way you would praise me. The feelings you gave me made me a better player, a happy person. I want to feel that way again."

What way, Isabeau? I still don't know what you mean. The old self-loathing rises up, that I shouldn't be hoping for what I think she's asking for, but I let it fall away. She's twenty-one now. She can ask me for whatever she likes.

She turns her green eyes up to mine and they're filled with pain. "I've been so unhappy without you, Laszlo. I rarely enjoy playing anymore and I can't face auditions and performances because I'm sure that everyone will hear my unhappiness in the music. I'd rather you just know what I want and risk you getting angry with me again than long for something and never—"

"What sort of feelings?" I ask quickly. My chest feels tight. I have to know what she means. I can see how much it's costing her to talk like this but I need her to brave for me, just a little longer. Her hands gripping her bow are white-knuckled.

"It's sexual, Laszlo. Your voice, your words, the way you talk to me. Especially the way you are with me when you're conducting or we're playing together. It does something to me. I understand why you reacted the way you did that night I turned eighteen. I was... I was pushy. I sprang my feelings on you and shouldn't have."

I hate hearing her apologize for something that wasn't her fault. She needn't feel ashamed for kissing me. "Isabeau—"

She puts up a hand to stop me. "Let me just finish. I'm not asking for—for that. What I called you. What I did."

Do you like that, daddy?

My hands clench on my biceps. If I'd known half of this three years ago things would have been very different. I still wouldn't have touched her, but I would have known how to tell Isabeau that we needed to take things very, very slowly. That if she wanted me to keep praising and being strict with her even though she didn't need it anymore, just because she liked it, because it was good for her playing, for her happiness, that I could do that for her. That I *wanted* to do that for her. That it was very easy for me to start doing those sorts of things consciously for her, to give her pleasure. Because making Isabeau happy is my keenest joy.

"I've been away for three years. I'm twenty-one and I've thought about things. Realized things. I'm asking you to make me feel safe, give me instruction, but this time knowing how it makes me feel. If the idea is horrible to you and you can't do it I understand and I'll leave. But if I come with you on the tour I want you to be my mentor again, I want you to be strict with me, and I want you to know why I need it."

She takes a short breath and drops her eyes. It seems her measure of bravery has run out, but she's said enough. I more than understand. She's asking me to be her dom, though she doesn't seem to know that's what she's asking for. Not with sex, not with physical discipline, but with words. Instructions. There's a great deal of power in words, in expressions, in body language. She's asking to give up a measure of power to me because it makes her feel free. Despite everything that's happened between us, she trusts me.

Relief and gratitude pour through me. Isabeau still trusts me.

I might not remember how much I corrected her but I do remember how good it felt to praise her, to tell her she'd done well, to see her smile and turn a little pink with pleasure at my words. I remember how toward the end seeing that happen made me want to put my hands on her, touch her, taste her, and the horror that I wanted to do that to a seventeen year old girl, to *Isabeau*, made me never question why she reacted that way.

I gravitate toward the dominant. I enjoy it very much, not with humiliation and a lot of pain, but with control and severity. I prefer the women I take to bed to be on the submissive side and enjoy certain things, react a certain way when I say things.

The way Isabeau reacts to me.

I know exactly how to be Isabeau's dom. I really fucking want to be Isabeau's dom.

She shifts uncomfortably in her seat. "You're not saying anything. I've made you angry again."

"Isabeau." Sunk in uncertainty, she doesn't look up. More firmly, I say, "Isabeau, look at me." She raises her eyes to mine. "Good girl. Play Beethoven's Fifth. The opening eight measures. Then stop."

Eyes glowing, she does, and I hear that sweet sound again after all these years. Isabeau. Isabeau happy. It's tentative, she's still not sure if I'll do what she's asking, but she's hopeful and I hear it and it's the most wonderful sound in the world. When she finishes I step forward and cup her chin lightly with my hand.

"Beautiful," I murmur. She melts before my eyes, all the tension going out of her body and she angles her face into the warmth of my hand. Sweet girl. I didn't see before how submissive she was. It would have been wrong to see it. But I see it now.

Do you like that, daddy?
Yes. Yes I like that.

I step away, pretending to be considering what she's asked for but really trying to gather my thoughts. I put a hand on the glossy black piano top, knowing I have to be serious, to be stern, but aching to tell her how happy I am that she's come here today and said all this.

I turn back to her. "All right. You've told me what you want. Now I'm going to tell you my conditions."

She looks at me expectantly, so different from the look of fear that's been in her eyes until now.

"You will remember that I'm a thorough man. If you are to take this part in my orchestra and become my protégé again then I'm going to be strict with you. More strict than before, because this is more serious than before. This is my work. You'll be one of my musicians answering to me. Are you prepared for that?"

She nods, and I wait pointedly.

"Yes, Laszlo."

"The things I tell you to do won't be a negotiation. I'm not asking for your opinion, I'm demanding your obedience."

Almost under her breath, she says, "No one talks back to the conductor."

"I beg your pardon?"

She shakes her head quickly. "Nothing."

Little tease. She always did have an impish streak and I have to fight to keep a straight face even though my heart is bursting. She's smiling, her color's back. My sweet girl is happy.

With a calmness I don't feel I take out my notebook, turn it to a fresh page and hand it to her with a pen. "Three years away at university you will have picked up bad habits. Write down for me your schedule. When you practice. When you sleep. When you eat. Everything."

She accepts the book and pen from me and starts to write. I go and stand on the other side of the room, leaning against the window ledge, arms folded. I never used to be so obviously controlling with her but the point is that she feels someone cares what she's doing with her time. Questions race through my mind. What *has* she been doing with her time? What else would be good for her? How do I keep a level head right now when all I want to do is scoop her into my arms and kiss her? Isabeau wants my control, my dominant side, the part of myself that I keep tightly leashed almost all of the time. I see Isabeau sitting naked at my feet, her expression radiant with submission, and arousal surges through me. How perfect that would be. How I want that, more than anything I've ever wanted in my life.

But Isabeau hasn't asked for that and this isn't about what I want. I take a deep breath and push the seductive image away.

When she's finished I give the outline she's written out a cursory glance and then close the notebook. "All right. Leave that with me."

"No lectures? It's terrible. I can see that from your face."

"I said leave that with me, Isabeau." I wait for a beat, watching her closely. Then I sit down on the piano stool again and say, in a gentler tone of voice, "I'm going to send you an email about the tour and I want you to think about it, and about being my protégé again, and if you want both. If you want just one, or neither, that's fine. I'll still want us to be close, if you do." I smile, my eyes running over her face. I've missed her so much, my beautiful girl, and now she's here. "And I want you to know I'm so happy to see you, sweetheart."

Her eyes get very bright and she reaches down and fumbles with her cello case, letting her hair fall in front of her face. I want to reach out to her, hold her, but it's still so tentative between us. It's important that she doesn't make a quick decision or feel like it's the only way we can have a relationship again. I need her in my life and I'm afraid that if we reach for too much too soon we'll lose everything again.

"You too, Laszlo," she says in a soft voice. "What are you going to do in the meantime?"

"Me?"

"With um, that." She nods at the notebook in my hands.

"I'm going to do what I always did, seeing as you asked so nicely. You'll be hearing from me soon." I won't be demanding of her until she agrees to what we've discussed, but I want her to feel like I'm expecting her to be good in all the ways she used to be for me. Her tentative smile lets me know it's the right thing to do.

I take her downstairs to where her coat is hanging in the hall, and when it's clasped in her hands she turns back to me.

"Does this make you feel strange? Because of who we used to be to each other?"

Nothing about this feels strange to me and I want to do this for her for so many reasons. For the happiness it brings her most importantly, but the pleasure it brings me as well. Taking on roles that require me to lead and support at the same time is at the very core of who I am, the same as it is for her to feel safe and cherished and watched over so she can flourish. Being able to do this for Isabeau on so intimate a level is all the reward I need. The intense sexual satisfaction that comes from knowing that my words, my instructions make her feel good is something I'll keep to myself. "Not strange at all. You're very special to me and knowing that you're happy is important. I'll always enjoy looking after you, however you want me to do it."

The smile she gives me and the faint flush in her cheeks is like the dawn breaking after a long, dark night. If she'd asked for more... I watch her wind her scarf around her neck, wondering what she'd taste like if I took her in my arms and kissed her. What I'd find if I backed her slowly up against the wall and slipped my hand between her thighs. If she'd be wet if I got my fingers inside her underwear. If she'd come apart in my arms as I rubbed the nub of her clit in firm circles, whispering *good girl, Isabeau, come for daddy* while she looked up at me with those deep green eyes filled with need. It would be the perfect end to the meeting. Giving her a reward for being so brave and telling me what she needs.

But she didn't ask for more. She was very specific about what she wanted from me and so that's what I'll give her. I've got Isabeau back, and that's the most important thing in the world.

Chapter Eight

Isabeau
Now

There's a knock at the door at eight-thirty and I know without a doubt before I've answered it that it's going to have something to do with Laszlo. He always was an early riser even when he'd been up late conducting. If his habits are still the same, by this hour of the morning he'll have finished his run around the heath, drunk his coffee and perused the Arts section of the newspaper. I don't expect it to *be* Laszlo, and when I open the door, wild-haired, berobed and yawning, I see that my assumption is correct. It's a delivery person from one of those impossibly gentrified supermarkets in Belsize Park. They pass me a box of groceries and a note, and I read it.

Good morning, Isabeau
Something better than the breakfast you had planned
Laszlo

I remember what I put on the schedule he asked me to write out for him yesterday. *Saturday dinner: pizza. Sunday breakfast: cold pizza.* Hayley and I did have pizza for dinner last night, at nearly midnight. She'd been performing and then having drinks with the string section of her orchestra. I got distracted practicing pieces that I know are in the orchestra's repertoire. Or used to be, at least. When I got back to Hayley's flat after meeting Laszlo I was gripped with the terrible fear that I could arrive at my first rehearsal and find that all they've been playing for the last three years are obscure Bruckner symphonies.

If I say yes. I don't know anything about the tour and what expectations he'll have for me.

We didn't get to sleep until late because Hayley opened a bottle of red wine and we talked until nearly three in the morning. It wasn't good wine but it was a very good talk. Hayley and I were in Laszlo's youth orchestra together and when I fled Laszlo's house on my eighteenth birthday it was to this flat I came, unannounced and in tears. She knows everything about what happened between me and Laszlo that night.

Do you like that, daddy?

Almost everything.

It was difficult telling her what I've asked Laszlo to do for me, with his words, with his manner, but it didn't seem to surprise her. Grinning over the top of her wine glass she said, "You always did enjoy being the conductor's pet. He loved it, too. None of the other girls could get him to smile at them. He never smiled at me and I played that bloody first violin *Scheherazade* part for him."

I thank the delivery person and take the groceries through to the kitchen, remembering what Hayley asked me last night. "How was it seeing him again? Was it really awkward after, you know, kissing him? Do you still want to kiss him?" She let me talk and plied me with the terrible red wine, which I drank because I've been so jangled lately and the wine soothed my nerves. I told her that even though it was embarrassing and painful at first I'm happy I went to the Mayhew and then to Laszlo's house because I value our friendship so much and I want to rebuild it. "And I don't want to kiss him again. I know he doesn't want to kiss me."

"But you must have thought he was interested in you back then? Otherwise why did you kiss him in the first place?"

Hayley and I have known each other since I was fourteen and she was fifteen. She saw Laszlo and I together several times a week for three years and knows how I came to be living with Laszlo at the age of eight. If she thinks I was weird or gross for being attracted to my guardian she's kept that to herself.

I gave Hayley a pained look over the top of my wine glass. "Thinking? When I was eighteen? Of course I wasn't thinking, and he was totally disgusted with me."

But I remember too the way he kissed me back. The way his hands gripped my hips as I rubbed against what I was sure was his…his hard-on. His gentle words of encouragement.

Then his furious rejection.

I woke up this morning with a dry tongue from the bad wine and an uneasy feeling in my belly. Yesterday I told him that the way I want him to talk to me makes me react sexually, and what if that makes him angry with me again?

But look what he's sent me. Groceries. Groceries mean not angry, right?

In the kitchen I unpack the box, smiling to myself because it's so very Laszlo what he's chosen but he's remembered all my favorites, too. Fresh orange and mango juice. Creamy yoghurt from Devon. Bircher muesli. Apples and nut butters. Raspberries and blueberries. A packet of ground coffee that smells heavenly when I open it and hold it up to my nose; I haven't been able to afford coffee like this in forever. Wholegrain bagels, herb cream cheese and smoked salmon.

I slice off a piece of apple, stick it straight into the jar of almond and cinnamon butter and immediately hear Laszlo's disapproving voice in my head. *Three years away at university you will have picked up bad habits.* I smile and dip the apple into the jar again, because I can't unlearn every bad habit at once. Besides, I'm hungry.

This is so sweet of him. I haven't had anyone do nice things for me since I went to university. Cake on my birthday from friends of course, but no one had the money for posh breakfasts when we had to buy rosin and strings and sheet music, get instruments repaired and buy smart clothes for performances. Music is expensive.

When I've set out the fruit and yoghurt and Bircher, made coffee and toasted the bagels, I call out the door to Hayley that breakfast is ready. She comes sleepily into the kitchen a few minutes later, a fluffy robe on over her pajamas and rubbing last night's mascara beneath her eyes. "Where did all this come from?"

"Laszlo."

Hayley raises her eyebrows and sits down. "Mr. Valmary sending around breakfast. If I told my orchestra about this they wouldn't believe me. Not the musicians who've actually worked with him, anyway."

I hide my smirk behind my coffee cup, remembering what my tutor once told me, that Laszlo was very indulgent with me. It's not a bad sort of feeling, to be indulged by a man whom everyone sees as so formidable. Maybe all that talk of him being strict with me was bluster and he's really just going to be sweet. I like when he's sweet. Maybe he'll spoil me like his little pet while I play perfect, joyful notes. I could be very happy with that. I take a bite of Bircher and berries and think of the warm look in his eyes when he'd cupped my chin yesterday and said, *Beautiful*. Oh god, yes, very happy.

Hayley is watching me, suspicious and amused at the same time. "You're so transparent. Stop thinking about him."

I sit up straighter, plastering an innocent look on my face. "I'm thinking about the tour."

"Uh-huh. I'm not going to judge you for what you're doing and if you sleep with him then godspeed and orgasms to all. But be careful, won't you? He was your guardian. It's all kinds of messed up. People might be judgy and cruel or think that he touched you while you were underage. And Mr. Valmary…"

"Mr. Valmary what?"

She shrugs, uncomfortable. "He seems decent enough but people can be kind to their friends and family and not so kind to the people they take to bed. You don't know what he's really like. You know, as a man."

To date. To sleep with. He could be cruel. He could be a womanizer. He could be callous. He could be, but I know he's not. You don't live with someone for ten years without getting a good idea of the sort of person they are.

But none of that is relevant as I don't plan on sleeping with Laszlo. I've set out exactly what I want from him and I'm deciding in my own time whether to accept this arrangement. Nothing can go wrong. "I told you last night that I don't plan on kissing him again and I meant it. There's nothing of that sort between us."

Hayley mutters into her bagel, "Just some mild to moderate dominance and submission, what could be more ordinary or mentorly than that."

"*Hayley.*"

She smiles brightly. "Yes, Isabeau?"

I can't even be mad at her because she's right. It's not strictly mentorly what I've asked Laszlo to do for me but I don't care. I have Laszlo close to me again, the only man I've ever wanted and the only man I ever will. Laszlo and music. That's what I want my life to be.

I get out my phone and text him. *Thank you for breakfast*

His reply comes through almost straight away. *You're welcome. Is the pizza in the bin?*

Yes, Laszlo

Good girl

The lower part of my belly clenches. *Good girl.* Such a simple, innocuous phrase, but so much more than that. I can hear Laszlo voice as if he's murmuring the words in my ear, like a caress. *Good girl.* He feels so close to me even though he's on the other side of London. How different it is from just two days ago when I arrived back from Durham and the memory of him all around me made me want to cry because I missed him so much.

I take a shower after breakfast and then Hayley and I play the Brahms Double Concerto for violin and cello together. I watch her, envious of the fact that she performed this piece as a soloist in Philadelphia last year. She's got more dates lined up in this country and in Europe and nearly twenty thousand followers on Instagram. How has she done this? Where did the last three years even go for me?

A few hours later my phone buzzes and I see I have an email from Laszlo.

Isabeau,

I promised you more information about the tour. Normally these are arranged at least six months in advance but this time I've had to pull everything together at the last minute. Ten days ago I was contacted by a booking agent looking for an orchestra to fill a series of dates. There was a problem with another orchestra's insurance and they couldn't travel, and despite several key members of the ensemble being on leave I agreed. Several, not "half" the orchestra as Marcus Sabal stated yesterday.

I'm in need of an excellent second cellist. The itinerary is attached. It's an opportunity that was impossible for me to refuse.

There isn't much time for preparation as we leave in two days. It will be a demanding schedule and we will rehearse as we go. I've been given a free hand in what we perform due to the orchestra's excellent reputation and the pieces we play will vary from city to city. Everyone on the tour needs to be one hundred per cent committed to performing at their best. We can't merely trade on our reputation, we have to deliver world-class performances every night, and that means hard travel, focused rehearsals and devotion to perfection. I need people who can function together, under pressure. This isn't a holiday.

I would like you to join the orchestra for the tour and I'll need your response tonight. Rehearsals begin 12pm at the Mayhew tomorrow.

Thank you for coming to the house yesterday. It was timely, in more ways than one.

Laszlo

After I finish reading Laszlo's email I read it again. I've never heard him sound like this before. Not rude exactly, but abrupt. No, that's a lie. I've heard him be brusque plenty of times, just not with me. It's clear that if I come along on the tour he's going to treat me like any other member of his ensemble.

The last line of Laszlo's email makes me snort with laughter and indignation. It was *timely* for me to try and repair our relationship. What does he mean "in more ways than one"? Is that his way of saying he missed me, too?

I open the attachment and look down the list of city names and my eyes widen.

Singapore
Kuala Lumpur
Hong Kong
Hanoi
Taipei
Phnom Penh
Manila
Jakarta
Bangkok

The furthest afield the RLSO has been while he's been conductor is Moscow. I suppose that's what he meant by this tour being impossible for him to refuse, because of the locations. I can see how he would jump at the chance.

Going on tour with the RLSO. Butterflies start to beat in my belly, so I do what I always do when I feel nervous: I practice. I spend the afternoon and well into the evening playing my cello, all the pieces that I know Laszlo is fond of or has performed in the past. Before I know it it's dark outside and very late.

I eat a few bites of bagel for supper, brush my teeth and get into bed, and then I reach for my phone, trying to decide.

Laszlo.

The tour.

The butterflies are back, stronger than ever, and I don't know which part is making me more nervous: the thought of going on a long, professional tour or working for Laszlo. I've never performed professionally and I'm terrified of screwing up while playing with his prestigious orchestra.

I'm going to be strict with you. More strict than before, because this is more serious than before. This is my work. You'll be one of my musicians answering to me. Are you prepared for that?

Am I? I don't know, but I went to Laszlo to ask him to push me to develop my career. I open the messaging app on my phone and with shaking fingers I type, *It's yes*

Nothing comes through for several minutes, and then I see, *To what?*

To both parts, please. I want to be your protégé, and I want to come on the tour

He takes his time replying again, leaving me on read for several minutes. I wait, staring at the screen, anxiety churning through my belly. Then my phone buzzes.

Can you please explain to me why you're up so late? Your schedule states that you should be asleep by now

My mouth falls open. That's why he left me on read, to go and check his notebook? No *Thank you*? No *welcome to the orchestra*? The ungrateful... I think of all number of indignant replies, that I was thinking carefully about what he was offering me, like he told me to do in the first place. That if he's going to be so ungracious then he can just shove the tour up his ass. But he did warn me he'd be strict. I take a deep breath and reply, *I was practicing Dvořák's Ninth, Mr. Valmary*

Laszlo hasn't told me to call him Mr. Valmary in private conversations but I like the formality of it and I suspect he will, too. He takes his time yet again, and then replies, *Please add the Seventh and Eighth to your practice as well*

Yes, Mr. Valmary

Now, go to sleep, we have rehearsals tomorrow and I need you to be rested

Yes, Mr. Valmary

Isabeau?

Yes?

It's good to have you on board

I'm not letting him get away with just that. This wasn't just about the tour. *On board with what exactly? The tour or being your protégé?*

Both. Very much both, sweetheart

My toes curl with pleasure. Sweetheart. How I love it when he calls me that, his endearment only for me since I was eight years old. I put my phone on my bedside table and turn out the light, smiling to myself. Tomorrow I'll be playing as part of Laszlo's orchestra again, his proper orchestra, and I feel happier than I have in three years.

Almost as happy as I was before I turned eighteen.

I'll never be that happy again because back then I was whole-heartedly, uncomplicatedly in love with Laszlo, and nothing makes me as happy as loving Laszlo. He understood me as no one ever has, my thoughtful, handsome and clever guardian. I loved him while he was in control of a vast, musical throng, but I loved him most when it was just the two of us, playing together, living together. Being together.

In the loneliness of the last three years I fell out of love with him. He won't ever be able to return my feelings. To him I'll always be that eight-year-old girl he calls sweetheart.

I think of the rehearsal tomorrow and seeing him in his element, strong and commanding and in charge. A warm sensation fizzes through me, and my hand smooths down my belly and into my underwear. Music and Laszlo. Laszlo and music. One almost can't exist without the other for me. I haven't touched myself thinking about him since my second year at university, when I made myself stop because the loneliness was unbearable. I find that I'm slick and swollen merely from my text message exchange with him. I wonder if he's in bed now, thinking about me. If he's naked between the sheets. I close my eyes and rub my clit, remembering the way he cupped my cheek and murmured, *Beautiful*. My hand slides down and I slip a finger inside myself, imagining that it's his finger, exploring gently, enjoying the tight, slick grip of my flesh. I wonder if he'd like touching me there.

I told Hayley that I don't want a physical relationship with Laszlo. I'm such a liar. I want him so much it aches, and I drive another finger into myself, curling my fingers over and over, trying to ease the burning desire for him. I need something thicker than my fingers. I need him.

Isabeau, what the fuck are you doing?

Laszlo's voice, cold and angry. My eyes fly open and I yank my hand out of my pants. He'd be furious if he knew I was doing this. He can't possibly know but that's not the point. I need the security of him more than I need to get off and that means not cheating the little things. I trust him and he should be able to trust me.

I turn over in bed, wrapping the blankets tightly around myself. I won't masturbate over Laszlo. I'm keeping to our arrangement. I'm a good protégé. A horny, unsatisfied, but good protégé.

Now all I have to do is keep this up for the whole five-week tour.

Chapter Nine

Laszlo
Then

Warm air indolent with the scent of late-summer roses is drifting into the lounge and Isabeau and I are sprawled at either ends of the sofa. I keep one eye on the score spread out in my lap and one eye on her, waiting for her to look up from the copy of *Fahrenheit 451* she's reading for English class.

I liked having her in my orchestra for her debut last week and it's given me an idea. Finally she places a bookmark between the pages and I say to her, "Isabeau. How do you like your youth orchestra?"

She looks up in surprise at my question. "It's fine. I mean, good," she amends quickly, as if anxious not to seem disloyal. So, she's not overly attached to it.

"How do you like your conductor?"

Isabeau hesitates, and then says with a wrinkle of her nose, "He's all right. Not as good as you. Not as patient as you, either."

No loyalty for him? I have to hide a pleased smile. Even better. "How would you like me to be your conductor?"

She sits up, excited. "But you've already got eight cellists and I'm only fourteen. Or do you mean you're going to take over the youth orchestra? Please say yes."

"No. I want to start my own, from scratch, and I'd like you to be the very first member." The thought came to me yesterday as I looked around the empty Mayhew stage at three in the afternoon, around the time that schools were getting out. Why should the space go to waste so many afternoons a week when there are promising young musicians who could be playing there? I have the time. What's more I have Isabeau, and why should she be playing for some second-rate conductor when she could be with me? I want more of her music in my life. She does so much of her playing without me and I feel like I'm missing out on something precious.

Her eyes grow wide. "Really? You mean that? Yes *please*, Laszlo. Will we play at the Mayhew? Will it be a proper big orchestra that performs symphonies? Can we do *Scheherazade*? I love *Scheherazade*."

I feel my heart glow golden at the excited expression on her face. "Yes, at the Mayhew. And we can play *Scheherazade* and all sorts of other pieces."

Isabeau squeals and comes over to hug me, knocking the score out of my lap and onto the floor. "I'm so happy you're going to be my conductor!"

I hug her back fiercely, feeling very happy about that, too.

Auditions for the new Royal London Symphony Youth Orchestra begin the very next week but it takes nearly a month to put a full ensemble together. The amount of young talent that I hear is heartening. Every now and then there are rumblings in the classical music world that young people are all learning the guitar rather than the flute and violin, but my worries are put to rest by the dozens of talented musicians I hear.

I want to make Isabeau first cello because she's the most talented, but she's also the youngest and I worry that the sixteen- and seventeen-year-old cellists will make things hard for her or tell her that she's only first because she's my favorite. It wouldn't be a stretch because she damn well is my favorite but there are orchestra politics to be mindful of. In a year or two I'll move her up to first or second, but for now she's fourth, and delighted with her place.

For our very first concert, just before Christmas, we perform *The Carnival of the Animals* and *Peter and the Wolf* back-to-back, and it's a massive hit. All the parents and friends of the orchestra give them a riotous standing ovation, but most important of all is that my orchestra is incandescently happy. I don't think I've ever seen Isabeau smile as much as she does when she takes her bows with the rest of the orchestra. The next morning there's a small, amused piece about the performance in the Arts section of the newspaper and I find the journalist's tone both irritating and pleasing: my *little* orchestra that did so well.

When she's fifteen I move Isabeau up to second cello and the orchestra learns and performs *Scheherazade*. The piece has a difficult first violin solo throughout but a sixteen-year-old called Hayley Chiswell is more than up to performing it. I notice that she and Isabeau have become good friends and I'm glad of this because I want Isabeau to have more music friends her own age. That was one of the reasons I set the orchestra up. But not the main reason. The main reason is looking toward the string section and seeing Isabeau looking back at me, smiling. That year she wins all the cello competitions she enters and I'm there for every single performance.

I find that working with the youth orchestra is as rewarding as working with my main orchestra, and sometimes more so. I don't have to be so formal as they're good kids who are happy to be there. I like leaving the suit and tie at home and rehearsing in my shirtsleeves, without a baton, and when we perform I tell them they can wear whatever they like as long as it's black and doesn't clutter up the stage. One season a trumpet player arrives at three performances dressed as Neo from *The Matrix*. It's the Mayhew, but they're kids. They've got the rest of their lives to be serious about classical music. Isabeau wears black jeans and sneakers or long black dresses, whichever she's in the mood for. Sometimes the sneakers go with the dresses and she wears winged eyeliner as well. She's finding herself and I love watching it happen. I have Isabeau close to me and I get to hear her play and watch her pretty, studious face. Conducting and orchestras are my life and it's wonderful to share it with her. She cares as deeply about the orchestra as I do. I think about having her in my symphony orchestra in a few years' time. I want that very much. But then, she won't have time if she's a soloist and I want that for her as well. I think it's what she wants most of all, too.

That's a long way in the future, though. For now she's here, and I couldn't ask for more.

But one day, when she's sixteen, I don't have such a wonderful time at rehearsal.

When Isabeau and I arrive it's the same as any other day at the Mayhew. The ensemble is making excellent progress with Holst's *The Planets* which they'll be performing at the Winter Concert. Isabeau is happy because she's just received top marks in her Grade Eight cello exams and I'm always in a good humor when Isabeau is smiling.

As the rehearsal progresses my mood takes a nosedive. I don't know what's got into everyone tonight but the ensemble is restless, talking in between pieces, getting up and down, slumping in their chairs. I don't expect them to be as respectful and professional as my orchestra because they're not professionals, they're a bunch of teenagers and this is supposed to be fun, not work, but tonight they're really testing my patience.

Something's off in the woodwind section. I keep listening for a badly tuned instrument or sloppy playing but everything sounds as it should. One of the clarinet players is talking a lot, and in the middle of a discussion I'm having with the section about their part in the third movement he yawns conspicuously without covering his mouth, and I've had enough.

"Mr. Reese. If I'm keeping you up you're welcome to leave."

His mouth closes with a snap and he sits up straight. "Yes, Mr. Valmary."

A ripple goes through the orchestra as everyone adjusts the way they're sitting. I look around slowly, driving the point home that I'm not feeling as tolerant as I usually am and they shouldn't press their luck. Everyone is silent and still. Good. Perhaps that's the end of it.

I finish what I was saying and we keep playing, and twenty minutes later the rehearsal is over. I start packing up and out of habit glance at Isabeau, just to check on her, and notice that a flautist called Ryan Taylor has left the woodwind section and is standing next to her while she puts away her cello. Thinking back I realize that he was looking at her throughout the whole rehearsal. It wasn't Kieran Reese getting to me all this time. It was Ryan.

He's standing by her chair while he takes apart and cleans his flute. I try to follow their conversation by their body language. He seems to be asking her a question and she's hesitating, not wanting to answer. Finally, she glances at me and then gets up and comes over, her fingers running through the end of her ponytail.

She purses her lips and looks up at me with hesitant eyes. "Laszlo…"

I smile at her, wanting to put her at her ease. However I'm feeling tonight it's not her I'm irritated with. "What is it, sweetheart?"

"Laszlo, Ryan has asked if I can go with him to a concert on Monday night."

My hands still on my sheet music. As she's sixteen I suppose I should have expected this. Over the years she's grown taller, more slender in places, filled out in others. There's still a coltish uncertainty about her limbs and the way she holds herself sometimes but even that will disappear in a year or so. Her childhood prettiness has turned into loveliness. My ward is beautiful, and I know I'm not the only one who sees it.

I'm going to have to starting dealing with Isabeau dating. My irritation expands. I don't want dozens of spotted youths calling at the house to take Isabeau out and worrying every minute that she's gone. I swallow down the outright refusal that's clamoring to get out of my mouth, and think, *What concert?* Mentally running through next week's performances and soirees I can't come up with a single event that would be worth Isabeau's time. Besides, Monday nights have always been our night. Usually neither of us have to perform. I cook. She does her homework at the kitchen bench and after we've eaten we play something together. I like it. I look forward to it.

"There aren't any concerts on Monday night."

Isabeau smiles and tugs on her ponytail. "Not that sort of concert, silly. A band. Electro pop or something."

She's expecting me to tweak her nose and tell her not to be cheeky as I usually do when she teases me, but I'm not in the mood. A band. A dark venue. Dancing. Ryan's arms around her to protect her from the press of sweaty bodies, but really so he can feel her up. A thick, ugly sensation spreads through my chest. She's too young for that. She's too...*mine.*

She's too young for that, I correct myself quickly. I'm just being protective. It's what I do. But I feel the same angry, resentful sensation that I get when I catch men looking at her in the street. That they're coveting what's mine. If anyone's going to put his arms around Isabeau to protect her it's going to be me. Knowing that I can't and shouldn't want to doesn't seem to change that. If I was actually her father it wouldn't be so complicated. I wouldn't feel like men were encroaching on my territory and I could just let her go.

But I don't want to let her go, and certainly not to a dark, sweaty pop concert with fucking Ryan or anyone else.

I clear my throat, sorting through the sheet music as if I'm looking for something. "I see. Do you think you have time for dates, what with orchestra rehearsals, practice and schoolwork?"

"No."

I look up at her in surprise. I was expecting an argument, pleading, but she's regarding me with perfect calmness.

"You're right, Laszlo. I'll tell him that I'm too busy."

She turns away but I reach out and grasp her hand, tugging her back. I smile at her, puzzled and pleased at the same time. "You don't want to go?"

She squeezes my hand and leans close to whisper, "Not really, Laszlo. I've already told Ryan no three times saying that you wouldn't agree, but he insisted I ask you. Now I can just tell him you don't want me to go and he won't dare ask me again. Please keep being so strict and scary. Then I won't have to date anyone at all."

Her cool fingers slip from mine and I watch her go back to Ryan and tell him that her strict, scary guardian has told her she can't go. The boy's face flushes with annoyance and I make sure I'm busy with my music case when he glances in my direction. It's petty and it's beneath me but I'm fiercely pleased by the whole exchange. Isabeau doesn't want to go on a date with Ryan. Isabeau doesn't want to date anyone at all.

She picks up her cello case and comes toward me, leaving a disappointed Ryan in her wake. I take her instrument from her, feeling in a better mood than I have all night. As we walk through Leicester Square on our way to the Tube I watch the faces of the men we pass, seeing how their covetous eyes roam over Isabeau. When their gaze falls on me and the hostile expression in my eyes they look quickly away. She has no idea, talking to me of the evening's practice. I smile down at her, liking her where she is. Liking her close to me, being able to keep her safe even as I feel a creeping sense of guilt that I shouldn't like it quite so much.

But Isabeau's only sixteen. She's asked me to be strict and scary so men with leave her alone and I'm more than happy to do that for her. More than happy.

Chapter Ten

Laszlo
Now

I wake in the morning with a sense of completeness like I haven't felt in three years. The orchestra is whole again and everything is just about in place for the tour. But it's not that making me feel so full up with happiness. It's Isabeau. I always wanted her in my orchestra and now I have her.

I let my mind wander over the memory of her the day before yesterday in her black skirt with her slender legs in tights, asking nervously but determinedly to be my protégé again. Last night she called me *Mr. Valmary* without any prompting, and soon I'll tell her to call me *sir* in private. I imagine her saying it. *Yes, sir.* It will sound so good from her pretty pink mouth as she looks up at me with supplication in her eyes. I feel my cock twitch and realize I have a raging hard-on. I'm thinking about Isabeau and I'm hard.

This tour and various other commitments have kept me busy and I haven't had sex in weeks. I reach for my phone to text a singer I know to set something up for later tonight, but my desire for her or any of the other women I enjoy taking to bed has evaporated, and I put my phone down. I just want to lay here in the dim morning light thinking about Isabeau with an expectant expression on her heart-shaped face. How I loved seeing her looking at me just that like while she was in the youth orchestra. She was always so well-behaved and attentive, not like the other unruly teenagers in the ensemble. Always my sweet Isabeau. In a few short hours she'll be sitting just a few feet from me in the string section of my professional orchestra with just that look on her face. Playing exquisitely, her very best, for me. Watching my hands, watching my face, listening to my voice, the only things on her mind me and the music.

It's sexual, Laszlo. Your voice, your words, the way you talk to me. Especially the way you are with me when you're conducting or we're playing together.

The way I am with her makes her happy. *Probably makes her wet, too. Jesus Christ. Do I make her wet?* I groan and roll over, trying to put such delicious thoughts out of my head.

THE PROTÉGÉ

Being a conductor imparts a great deal of control. A hundred people look to me day after day, night after night for instruction and employment, people who have to do as I say or else. Unlike some conductors I'm careful not to abuse this power but I feel a thrum of dark satisfaction that Isabeau finds the way I am when I'm working and guiding her arousing. *Yes, sir* in private. *Yes, Mr. Valmary* in front of the rest of the ensemble. *Yes, maestro* during rehearsals and on stage.

Yes, daddy when I unbutton her blouse and pull down the lacy cups of her bra to stroke my thumb over her nipples.

I realize my hand has strayed to my cock and I stroke myself, imagining licking the dusky pink tips of her breasts. Making her kneel before me and pushing two fingers into her mouth. Feeling her suck them while she plays with her clit, her hand inside her underwear, white cotton briefs of the sort I used to pull out of the dryer and try not to look at. Or has she moved on to little lacy things and G-strings now? I hope not. I like the school-girlish white cotton, wedged tight into her ass for a spanking or pulled temptingly aside so I can lick her, and then ease her tight pussy down onto my cock. Powerful arousal surges through me. *Fuck, I'm going to come in a minute.*

I let go of myself with a groan. This isn't very mentorly. In fact it's exactly what I shouldn't be doing. If I give myself free rein to think about Isabeau sexually it will be too tempting to act on those desires and she's told me she doesn't want that. Besides, I've never thought about Isabeau while jacking off and I'm not about to start now.

Almost never thought about her while jacking off.

I throw back the blankets and stalk to the shower. While I wait for the water to heat up I wonder how long I'll be able to keep this up. The whole tour? While I'm close to her every day, being strict with her, seeing her be obedient and respectful to me and oh so sweet and good? Christ. I'll go mad.

Whatever I have to deal with it's my problem, not Isabeau's. I'll just have to be as disciplined with myself as I've promised to be for her. As she wants me to be with her, because she responds sexually to my control.

Fuck.

My hard-on surges anew and I switch the taps to cold and thrust my body under the freezing deluge. The icy needles of water do nothing to drive thoughts of Isabeau out of my mind.

Two hours later I'm showered and suited at the Mayhew. When I come onto the stage I shake Marcus' hand and talk to him for a moment while the last of the orchestra takes their places. I'm focused squarely on my concertmaster but

I can see Isabeau in my peripheral vision, tuning her mother's cello and straightening her sheet music. Neat and pretty in black with a black velvet bow holding up her half-ponytail.

She's here. In my orchestra. Mine.

But why she is here? Or, specifically, why is she free to join me on this tour? A cellist like her should be in great demand and yet she was able to accept the place just like that, as if she had no prior engagements. It doesn't seem right.

As soon as everyone's settled I walk to the lectern and address the ensemble, thanking them for being on board with the tour at such short notice. "I want to run through five symphonies today. Not every note as there isn't time, but the most complex and important sections. When we reach Singapore, our first destination, we'll start practicing the pieces for later in the tour. Southeast Asia has diverse musical tastes so we need a diverse repertoire. As I've already said, this isn't going to be a holiday." I look slowly around the ensemble, driving my point home. "I know you're all up to this. You've never let me down and I'm proud of you."

My eyes graze over Isabeau. She sitting very still and looking up at me, her bow laid across her lap. I feel warmth spread through my chest at the sight of her, more beautiful than ever, a glow in her cheeks that wasn't there yesterday.

"To the new faces in the ensemble, welcome, and thank you. Listen to your section leaders. Listen to me. Play your best. We're happy to have you, and we couldn't do this without you."

There's a smattering of applause and the string sections tap their bows against their music stands, but I cut it short by announcing the first piece we're practicing. I raise my baton while relaying the starting measure, and the music begins.

As the strings swell I look to where Isabeau is sitting. She's second cellist, not necessarily because she's the second-best cellist—she's the best—but because it's my second cellist who's on leave. That's how orchestras work, the whole section doesn't move up because one member is absent. The person filling in simply takes their place. It can make for interesting orchestra politics when the person filling in is much less experienced than the people sitting below them. Or much younger. Or both. I'll have to keep an eye on the others because even though my orchestra are professionals that doesn't mean they're above cattiness and putdowns if their noses get out of joint. I glance over the other cellists, wondering if anyone is getting their nose out of joint over Isabeau. Orchestra tenure is long and most of the musicians have been around long enough to remember ten-year-old Isabeau coming backstage to see me after performances. Fourteen-year-old Isabeau performing her first solo with us. The fact that she's inordinately talented won't endear her to the cellists sitting below her and above her. The fact that she was—is, secretly—my protégé won't either. Ensembles can catch even the slightest whiff of favoritism so I'll have to be careful. Even so, if anyone upsets her they'll answer to me and I will be merciless.

She's not really only my protégé, though, is she? She's my sub. We just haven't used that word. My eyes follow the curve of her cheek. Isabeau Laurent is my sub. How I love the way that sounds.

We get though every section of the five symphonies I wanted us to cover and I'm clear about how I want the pieces played. Everyone has dutifully penciled in my instructions on their sheet music. One cello sounded in my ear over the other instruments in the orchestra, every note perfect.

The rehearsal over I glance at Isabeau, and she's packing up her cello and talking to her stand mate, Domenica, the section leader for the cellos. I've got more work to do and Isabeau will be going home. To Hayley's flat, not my home.

Our home.

I want it to be ours again. While we're on tour I'm going to ask her to move back in. I need her close to me, always. I was so happy living with her and I think she was, too.

I want to see her alone right now but I don't have a good excuse. She's got all the information she needs about the tour and the rehearsal went beautifully.

But I don't care about need. I *want* to see her alone and the beautiful thing about it is there's no reason why I shouldn't. I've always been hungry for more of Isabeau and now I can have as much of her as I want.

Feeling like Tchaikovsky's wolf coming out of the dark forest, I put my baton away in its case and call, "Miss Laurent, can I see you in my office, please?"

Chapter Eleven

Isabeau
Now

My stomach clenches at the sound of Laszlo's voice and I wonder if I've made a mistake. I try to read his expression but it's closed and inscrutable. As I pack up my cello I notice one of the viola players looking at me while talking to her stand mate. She's a woman in her mid-forties and I can't work out what she's saying but I don't like the unfriendly look in her eyes. Then she turns away, still talking, so maybe it was just coincidence she was looking at me.

I carry my cello and handbag over to where Laszlo's standing, intending to follow him to his office, but he takes the instrument from me as he always used to do after rehearsals. I look at the case in his strong grip, happy memories surging through me. There's a soft expression in his eyes and I know he's remembering, too.

In his office he closes the door and sets the cello carefully down. I've always liked this room. I don't know why as it's an unlovely, windowless mess of sheet music, violin and cello strings, rosin and discarded bowties, but it feels like Laszlo, and it smells like Laszlo.

"How did you find the rehearsal?" he asks.

I stand with my back to the closed door, hands clasped in front of me. It felt good sitting in the second cello chair and Domenica was welcoming and explained patiently how and when she wanted me to turn the sheet music. We're sharing a stand and as I'm sitting below her that job falls to me. Some musicians can be fussy about how and when it's done. Her bowing was easy to follow, too, as she sets the left and right patterns for the whole section so we're moving in unison. After Laszlo, Domenica is the second most important person in the orchestra for me.

"Very good, thank you, Mr. Valmary."

His expression flickers darkly. "I want you to call me *sir* when we're alone."

Heat flashes low in my belly. Sir. I've never heard anyone call him sir before. Is this something just for me? "Yes, sir."

THE PROTÉGÉ

Something glints in his hazel eyes. I see it in the split second before he turns away and reaches for his notebook. It's like a flash of victory.

He likes it when I call him sir.

"I have something that I want to talk to you about. We discussed your career before you went to university and you said you wanted to become a soloist. You're too good to be wasting your time in an orchestra." He taps a long forefinger over his knuckle. "And yet, here you are. Now, if in your heart you don't want to be a soloist anymore I understand. There's nothing wrong with playing as part of an orchestra. But being my protégé means helping you with your career, and for that you have to tell me your goals. What do you want, Isabeau?"

I wasn't expecting this and I try and collect my thoughts. What *do* I want?

I've hated every performance I've given these last three years. Every note I've played hasn't sounded right to my ears. I've tried to ignore it because I haven't known what else to do, but that's not how you win the hearts of audiences. They can tell when you're faking it.

He comes and stands right in front of me, his eyes scouring my face for answers.

"I don't know," I say, pulling at a button on my shirt. I look at what Hayley is doing and I'm envious, but at the same time that doesn't seem quite right, either.

"It's all right, sweetheart. You're my protégé. I'm going to help you to figure what you want."

I gaze up at him, relief and gratitude pouring through me. *Just you. I'm happiest when I'm with you.*

But there were things that I wanted before. Playing as a soloist was one of my keenest pleasures and I want that back. If Laszlo helps me find that pleasure again maybe my happiness will be complete.

I look at the foot of empty space separating us. Almost.

"Yes, sir."

For the merest fraction of a second I think his eyes drop to my mouth but then he's looking at his notebook again. "Good girl. All right." He frowns down at the pages and then clears his throat. "Is there anything you need to know about the tour? Do you have what you need?"

His hand strokes down the creamy paper and I watch the path of his fingers, remembering my fantasy last night. Hayley said the dynamic between us is one of dominance and submission. What would Laszlo do if I submitted just a little bit more?

I let my gratitude and deference fill my voice, to see what effect it has on him. "Yes, sir. Thank you."

His lips part, just for a second. Then his face clears. "Are you all right at Miss Chiswell's? Are you sleeping well? It's not uncomfortable or noisy, is it?"

I'm still reveling in the effect I have on him—*I have an effect on him, and it's not like anything I've ever seen from him before*—and it takes me a second to catch up with what he's saying. "Oh, yes, it's fine thanks."

Could I make him look at me like that again? What does he like about being called sir, exactly?

He closes the notebook and folds it in his arms across his chest. "Your room at our home is still your room, Isabeau. Always."

Our home. Longing for that house fills me. The large, airy rooms. The sound of music cascading down the stairs. The feel of Laszlo all around me. I want to ask if I can go with him now, but this foot of space between us is not only a good idea because of our working relationship, but because of everything that happened before. We haven't talked about that night and I don't think I'm strong enough to be in those rooms with all those painful memories.

Fumbling for the door I say goodbye, and he watches me go.

That night I pack my meager belongings, which are eighty per cent black performance clothes, set my alarm for five am and get into bed. Our flight to Singapore is at eight twenty-five. It takes me a long time to fall asleep and then my alarm is going off what feels like two minutes later.

I make a cup of tea and drink it in the shower, brush my hair and teeth and swipe some mascara over my lashes. The flight time is thirteen hours and airplanes are cold so I wear a pair of tight, stretchy trousers, lace-up knee boots and an oversize sweater, and throw a scarf into my hand luggage. I left my cello at the Mayhew with all the other instruments to be shipped so I feel oddly empty-handed when I get into a cab downstairs with only a small suitcase and a cabin bag.

I see Laszlo at the gate, dressed in jeans and a dark sweater, looking comfortable and warm. I always liked him in winter best. I love the soft wool sweaters he wears and heavy dark coats, his long hair brushing his collar. His hard body beneath all that warm fabric. He nods at me across the sea of orchestra people and gives me the tiniest of smiles. I feel wistful, wondering how we're going to be able to spend any time alone together with this busy schedule of travel, rehearsals and performances.

I sit with my fellow string sections as we wait for our flight to be called and listen to them chat. I can't see anyone from the brass or percussion sections so I guess they must be on a different flight.

One of the viola players strikes up a conversation with me. "Is this your first time playing with an orchestra of this level?"

I recognize her from rehearsal, the woman who was looking at me with an unpleasant expression on her face. She seems friendly enough now, though. "Yes, professionally. Though funnily enough I played with this orchestra when I was fourteen at the—"

"Oh, I remember. Little Isabeau, the conductor's ward. Landed on your feet, haven't you? Second cello." She's still smiling, but suddenly it's not a very nice smile.

"Uh, yes, I suppose so?" I feel my face flush and I wish she'd go away. The cello section has been so welcoming to me and I didn't think I was going to have to deal with any comments about my age and inexperience. I know this is a big step up for someone as young as I am but it's also temporary.

And I'm a good cello player. Confused; uninspired, perhaps; but technically good at least. I hope.

"But of course," she adds with a forced laugh, "you were always going to land on your feet, being Mr. Valmary's ward."

Boarding is announced and the woman turns away, but the damage is done. I can't look at anyone else as I carry my cabin bag onto the plane in silence. Maybe she said what everyone is thinking. Maybe she spoke the truth.

The tour company has sprung for business class seats and the whole front part of the Airbus must be filled with musicians. I find my seat, 7B, and I'm so sunk in unhappy thoughts that it takes me a moment to realize that Laszlo is sitting in 7A.

"Oh—Hello. Is this right? Is your assistant meant to be here or Marcus, or…?" I tail off because he's looking at me with one brow raised, amused. Is this a coincidence or did he arrange for me to be next to him? He gets up and stows my cabin bag and we settle ourselves into the comfortable seats, and despite the fact that there are people all around us it feels cozy and private in these two seats.

"Did you want to talk about my career or the tour or…?" I trail off, wondering why he arranged for me to be sitting next to him, because now I think about it I doubt it's a coincidence.

"No. I just like you close to me, Isabeau."

Butterflies riot in my belly, this time with pleasure. He's never said anything like that before. A flight attendant offers us a tray of champagne and orange juice. I take a champagne without thinking and swallow a large gulp. "Oh. Are we allowed to drink on tour? Sir," I add under my breath.

Again that gleam in his eyes. He takes one himself and toasts me. A memory of a drinks reception at the Mayhew when I was sixteen comes back to me. Laszlo holding a glass of champagne, me sidling up to him. *Can I have a sip, please? It looks so golden and pretty.* Laszlo passing me the glass and saying sternly, *Just one sip.* Tasting the dry, ashy wine, and then sneezing because the bubbles tickled my nose. Laszlo smiling and taking the glass back. I wonder if he's remembering that, too. Or if it's just occurred to him that this is the first time we're having a drink together.

I remember the way he stood so close to me in his office yesterday. How he's looking at me now. Properly looking at me. He's not the same Laszlo as he used to be. The last year we lived together he seemed to be afraid to look at me. I remember how evasive he was when I tried to be affectionate to him. Did he know how I felt about him? Did it disgust him and he just couldn't find a way to tell me?

And now? His hazel eyes don't slide away from my face any more. He's looking at me with an intensity that makes my heart beat faster. Watching him conduct I always knew that Laszlo was an intense man but he's never directed that intensity at me before.

I take another sip of my champagne, pretending to be more at ease than I feel. "Well, this is civilized. Does the RLSO always travel this way?"

"Preferably. I need you all well rested and limber when we get to our destination."

I smile to myself. I might have known that there'd be a practical reason for the expense.

"When we land there'll be time for a short sleep in the afternoon and then I'll need you all at the concert hall by eight so we can rehearse."

This will be my first professional performance…well, ever, really. I've never been paid to play in an orchestra before. I think of Hayley and the progress she's made with her orchestra and solo career. She's only one year older than me but she's years and years ahead. At twenty-one Laszlo was musical director of the Cambridge Symphony Orchestra. I'm so far behind it makes me feel sick. To distract myself I ask, "Are Singaporeans very passionate about classical music?"

"Yes. The city has two concert halls and their own symphony orchestra since 1979. A very good one."

Suddenly I feel worse. It will be an educated, unforgiving audience, and I'll be right at the front where they can see me. The champagne is making me feel dizzy and I put it down. "Do you ever get nervous before you perform?"

Laszlo studies my face. "Are you all right, sweetheart?"

"Oh, I'm fine," I say quickly. "I just…I suppose nerves are good, really. They mean you play your best."

I'm saved from more questions as the flight attendants begin their safety instructions, and I turn to listen as if my life depends on it.

Chapter Twelve

Laszlo
Then

"Laszlo, today I heard the most beautiful piece of music and I knew I had to play it with you."

Isabeau hurries into the lounge still in her beret and coat and clutching some pages of sheet music. She hands me a piano part and at the top I see that it's Rachmaninoff's *Vocalise*, a very beautiful duet about five minutes long. I don't think I've ever heard it performed by a piano and cello before. It could be quite lovely.

When I look up I see that she's taking off her beret and is shaking her hair out. It must be damp out as her hair's hanging in long auburn curls. I force my eyes back down to the page. "Would you like to play it now?"

THE PROTÉGÉ

"Yes *please*, Laszlo."

I smile to myself as I follow her up the stairs. She's seventeen now but she's always said it just that way since she was eight. Yes, *please*, Laszlo.

Though neither of us have ever played the piece before we get through it easily enough, but we both know we can do better. As my hands ply the keys I watch her between glances at the sheet music. I vastly prefer conducting to performing but this is one of my favorite things to do, playing with Isabeau. When she was younger it was *The Swan*, of course, but when she was feeling lively we'd play *The Royal March of the Lion*, our instruments doing battle with each other to sound the most prideful, the most regal, but getting less and less stately toward to the end, louder and faster, my hands crashing through the chords and her bow whipping across her cello until we finished the piece in a mess of notes, tempos and laughter. When we performed the piece in the youth orchestra I could see the smile glimmering in her eyes at the memory every time. It made me smile, too. We've played Elgar. We've played Brahms. But nothing has felt like it has playing this Rachmaninoff piece and I don't know why that should be. We get to the end a second time and Isabeau sits in silence for a few minutes, sunk in thought.

Finally she asks, "What do you think that piece is about?"

I don't know what I think and I don't want to search my feelings, either. Straightening the sheet music I reach for what I've heard about the piece. "It's said to be a love song, a sad one. One of the instruments saying *I love you*, and the other answering *I loved you, but I don't anymore.*"

She hums the cello part for a moment. "I don't believe that. I think it's a love song on both sides, but a love that's destined never to be."

I feel strange, my heart racing lightly. I think again about the music, the way the two instruments play together and yet seem to be very much alone with the emotion they're expressing. Maybe she's right, but I don't want to talk about it anymore. I close the piano lid and stand up. "Goodnight."

Isabeau lays her cello and bow aside, still smiling, still as happy as she was when she came toward me with the sheet music. She puts her arms around me and kisses my cheek, something she used to do all the time when she was younger. Lately I've been calling out goodnight from the stairs or while walking away from her so she couldn't hug me.

She rubs the tip of her nose through the bristles on my cheek. "Night, Laszlo. Mm. Your beard is getting long."

My body clenches and I don't hug her back. I pretend to have forgotten something in the lounge and pull away from her. As I walk down the stairs I touch my beard. She's right, I do need to clipper it. I rub the place where her lips touched me, not knowing if it's because I want to obliterate the memory or long to relive it.

Isabeau wants to play *Vocalise* just about every Monday night from then on. I want to say no but I've never said no to playing with her in nearly ten tears and I don't know how. A piece of music has never been too much for me no matter how emotional or stormy, but I feel like *Vocalise* is killing me every time we play it. It should be losing its power over time but it only gets stronger. We learn the parts by heart and she plays with her eyes closed, pouring her every emotion into the notes. I can't tear my eyes away from her. Who is this young woman playing so beautifully beside me? There's no coltish uncertainty about her now and in a few months' time she'll be eighteen. When did she get so grown up? When did she become so beautiful, inside and out? And loudest and most confusing of all: why does it cause me such pain to look at her when she's everything I hoped she would be?

Each time we play her cello sounds sadder and sadder, until one evening she stops playing abruptly halfway though the piece and puts her cello away without a word. I don't dare look at her. I stare at the piano keys, not moving, waiting until she's gone and it's safe to look up.

"Goodnight, Laszlo," she says behind me, a wobble in her voice.

"'Night."

She comes forward and clasps me around the shoulders, hugging me close, burying her face in my neck. She holds me like that for several long moments. I close my eyes, savoring her closeness. Paralyzed by the feel of her arms around me. Then she's gone, hurrying to her room. I put my hand up and touch my neck and feel wetness there, as if she's been crying.

I can't say goodnight to her unless I'm on the other side of the room. I can't say no to her when she asks me to play. I can never tell her how I feel and I can barely admit it to myself. I love Isabeau. I'm in love with a seventeen-year-old girl.

It gets harder and harder to be around her. I'm upsetting her with my coldness because she doesn't understand why I'm avoiding her and I don't know how to explain why I'm acting like this. I *can't* explain it. There's no one I can talk about it to, either, because I shrink with horror from admitting that I have tender feelings for a seventeen-year-old girl. If it gets out I'll be the Woody fucking Allen of the classical music world. Questions will be asked. *He's been living with her all this time, since she was a child. He wouldn't have…would he? To a child? But why did he take her in in the first place? Where did she even come from?*

Worse, what would they say about Isabeau? To Isabeau?

I dream about her at night, the feel of her soft lips beneath mine, her warm body in my arms. I want her as much as I love her and this sends bolts of guilt through my body like an electric current.

All the while her eighteenth birthday approaches, the date on the horizon both tantalizing and alarming.

Chapter Thirteen

Laszlo
Now

Isabeau falls asleep somewhere over Eastern Europe and I watch her face in sweet repose. The powerful protective instinct I've felt for her since she was sixteen unfurls in my chest. Jealously protective. Not like the tender protectiveness I felt for her when she was eight. This is something reflexive. Territorial.

What has she been doing the last three years? Who has been getting her laughter? Her music? Her kisses? I'll lose her amid the chaos of the tour over and over again so these moments when I have her by my side are precious. With a forefinger I smooth a lock of her hair back from her sleeping face. Her hand right hand is close to mine and I could take it, but that one light touch of her hair is all I'll steal.

A flight attendant leans over us and hands me two bottles of water, whispering, "For your wife when she wakes up." I take them silently, enjoying the mistake. Enjoying it far too much. Isabeau's left hand is hidden beneath the blankets but I imagine a diamond ring sparkling on the third finger. A ring that I've given her.

"You're all musical, aren't you? Are you in a band?" the flight attendant asks, indicating the business class seats around us.

"An orchestra."

She breaks into a smile. "How wonderful. Do you two play together at home?"

My chest feels tight, remembering ten-year-old Isabeau, her hair in a braid and wearing pink pajamas, giggling as we play Saint-Saëns; fourteen-year-old Isabeau practicing in the dusky pink dress I bought her so we can be sure it won't get in her way when she performs; seventeen-year-old Isabeau, astonishingly beautiful and graceful, her eyes closed as she plays Rachmaninoff while I watch her hopelessly from behind the piano. For three long years the music room has been empty of Isabeau. Empty of happiness. Then Isabeau just a few days ago, clutching her bow in a white-knuckled hand and asking to be my protégé again.

"All the time," I tell the attendant.

She smiles again, and moves on.

I don't sleep the whole flight. I don't want to miss a single second of Isabeau. I'm relearning her and she's coming back to me as effortlessly as a favorite piece of music.

When she wakes I'm reading a newspaper and I pass her a bottle of water. She smiles and pushes the hair back from her face, blinking sleepily up at me. I'm pierced with longing for a place I've never been. A place where she and I always wake together, and a ring sparkles on her finger.

At the airport we separate. Singapore is sultry and hot and everyone peels off layers of clothing as we stand in the cab rank. There's heavy cloud cover but it's ninety degrees. Isabeau finds her way back to the other cellists and I keep one eye on her as I talk with Marcus about the rehearsal tonight.

Everyone is rested and changed and at Esplanade Concert Hall by seven forty-five and we rehearse on stage in the empty, vaulted space, all golden lighting and honey wood. People used to build cathedrals like this, spaces that go up and up toward the divine, song used for worship. Now we build concert halls, the music itself deified and conductors as priests. My eyes drop to Isabeau, her long tresses curled in the humidity and her legs bare beneath her cotton dress. I want to kiss a benediction onto her mouth. *Beautifully played, my child.*

After, we all stand outside in the marina and look at the lights of the skyscrapers reflected in the water. Isabeau is smiling, looking from one sight to the next and breathing in the heavy, scented air. There are gardens growing in every spare corner in Singapore, even up vertical walls. I think there's jasmine nearby.

She's so close that it's an effort not to look at her beautiful face. So close and I still can't have her.

Later, back at the hotel, I fall into an exhausted sleep. Sometime around seven am local time I wake up, drink a bottle of water, and go back to sleep. I wake again at two in the afternoon and haul myself out of bed to make a pot of filter coffee. The hotel we're booked into is a grand colonial affair of white plaster, high ceilings, brass fittings and potted palms. I stand on the balcony overlooking a deep green garden and drink my coffee. And I notice Isabeau pacing up and down the garden, chewing her nail.

Nervous again. This isn't like her. What's happened in the last three years to undermine her confidence so much?

That would be you, asshole.

I sigh heavily. My support was yanked out from beneath her and she had to adjust to losing the person she was closest to along with beginning university life. Was I right to let her go without trying to contact her? The question keeps gnawing at me. I thought it was better that way because I wanted her too much and she was so very young. And before? Was I right to keep those secrets about her father from her? Am I still doing the right thing by keeping them? Did I encourage her to go and see him as often as I should have? Did I sound like I meant it when I said it?

I don't know the answer to any of these questions. All I can do is my best for her now.

Leaning over the balcony I call out, "Isabeau? Are you all right?"

She turns and looks up at me and the lost expression on her face makes my heart hurt.

"Can I talk to you, Laszlo?"

Chapter Fourteen

Isabeau
Now

"Room 305," Laszlo calls, and disappears back inside his room.

I go inside and climb the stairs to his room, still chewing on my nail, trying to sort my feelings out. The more I worry I will make mistakes tonight the more likely it is that I'll make them but I can't make my mind slow down. The violist's words cycle through my thoughts again and again. *But of course you were always going to land on your feet, being Mr. Valmary's ward.*

He opens the door before I can knock and stands back to let me in. In the silent privacy of his suite he puts his hands on my shoulders and asks gently, "Sweetheart, what's wrong?"

I swallow and look up at him. "It's tonight. I can't stop imagining that I'm going to let everyone down."

"What else?"

I blink, surprised. Isn't that enough? I take a deep breath and examine my feelings. There is more. Much, much more. "I think I've ruined my career," I say in a rush. "I haven't done any of the things I thought I would have by now. I should have a reputation as a soloist, any reputation as a musician, but I have nothing except what I get from being associated with you. And on top of all that is the horrible feeling that I'm only here because you took pity on me and that every mistake I make will be a disappointment to you and another reason I should just go home."

I slide into miserable silence, not looking at Laszlo. He knows everything now and I must be a huge disappointment to him.

"Isabeau. Look at me." I drag my face off the carpet and watch as he ticks off a list on his fingers. "First of all, you could never disappoint me. Ever. Second of all you're here because of your talent, and that's got nothing to do with me. And thirdly, if you played wrong notes all through the concert tonight I'd want to help you, not send you away."

I study his face, wanting to believe him. "That's not the Laszlo Valmary everyone knows and is terrified of."

"No. But it's your Laszlo Valmary."

My heart turns over. *My* Laszlo Valmary. Looking at his face I think he might mean it. But I crave something more from him today. I need that darker side of Laszlo, the part that seethes with strictness and can center me in seconds.

"Can you, um, do something?" He frowns at me, unsure of what I mean. I'm not even sure what I mean. "Can you do something, *sir*. Please. To help me feel less nervous."

Order me to go and practice. Tell me you expect the very best from me and nothing else will do. Give me something tangible to pull me back into line and make me focus.

Understanding dawns on his face. He seems to be considering something as he watches me. "Have you ever been spanked?"

I stare at Laszlo, barely comprehending the words, let alone the order in which they've come out of his mouth. "Spanked?"

"The pain releases endorphins. The heat. The submission. It helps with stress."

Mutely, I shake my head.

Laszlo seems to take my silence as horror and he goes on briskly, "It's something to think about. Meanwhile why don't you try some exercise? There's a gym on the fifth floor. A run would do you good."

But I don't want a run. I want to know more about what Laszlo just suggested. "Does it hurt?"

"Only if you roll your ankle."

"*Laszlo.*"

His eyes are sparkling darkly. "Not in a way that you would dislike. Not unbearably so."

I stare at him, my breathing shallow, unable to move a muscle. My eyes drop to his hands. I've always loved his hands. Large, square, strong hands that caress piano keys and scrub through his too-long hair. I've spent hundreds of hours watching them as he conducts, flips through a score, cooks us dinner. The thought of him using them on me is strange and arousing.

But this is a lot more intimate than we agreed.

"Only say yes if you're sure. It's something I can do to take care of you, to calm you down, if you want it and if you trust me to do it. But I'm going to need you to ask me, sweetheart, because I have to know for sure."

He's saying we can move the boundaries of our arrangement if I want. I picture myself face down over Laszlo's lap. *The pain releases endorphins. The heat. The submission. It helps with stress.* I definitely wouldn't be thinking about my nerves while that was happening. "Could you please, um, do that. Sir."

He nods slowly, his hazel eyes very steady. "All right. I can do that for you. But few things first. I'm going to go very easy on you, as this is your first time. No tears. No marks tomorrow. It's to make you feel calm, not a punishment."

Immediately my mind shoots off in several directions at once. He might do this again. He might do it as a punishment, so hard it would make me cry. Leave marks. Would I enjoy that as much as I think I might? What would he be like if he did that? Sweet, understanding Laszlo, mercilessly punishing me. A wave of heat rolls through me as I imagine his eyes black and severe as he hurts me till I cry.

"You can say stop at any time. Not just now. Any time. But you don't say stop, you say banana."

"Why banana?"

"Because you've been known to tease me in the past and I won't be able tell if *please no, sir* is your way of asking for me to be fiercer with you or asking me to stop."

The deeper part of my sex clenches as I imagine crying out *please no, sir* and him only spanking me harder. That shouldn't be such a turn-on.

He smiles faintly. "And I know how much you hate bananas."

I do hate bananas. He's known that for a very long time. Laszlo never laid a finger on me when I was a child that wasn't a hug, but I'm reminded now of the way someone might punish a naughty child. I feel like I need it for letting my life get out of hand. And Laszlo's the man to do it.

He looks down at what I'm wearing. "I need you to take your jeans off." He gives the order calmly as if he's done this hundreds of times before. As if he's used to taking nervous women over his knee and spanking them, sometimes till they cry. The thought makes my heart and mind race. Who is this man, really?

"And my, uh, underwear?"

"No, keep them on. I can work around those."

I wonder if he's going to look away like a gentleman but he doesn't, he just watches me, and waits. What about him, will he be taking any clothes off? I've never even seen Laszlo with his shirt off in all the years we lived together. Actually, that's a lie. At home he always emerged from the bathroom swathed in a bathrobe. Several times when I've woken him up over the years or brought him cups of tea when he was feeling poorly I've always found him sleeping in a t-shirt. I don't think that's what he would have done if he was alone. I think it was for my sake. I was the same, always getting dressed before I came downstairs, not wandering around in a towel or my underwear. We were very mindful of each other, and we never went to the beach or the pool together either.

But I have seen him almost naked, at a hotel pool in Edinburgh when we were on tour with the youth orchestra when I was sixteen. I wanted to take a swim early in the morning of our first day, but Laszlo'd had the idea first. I watched him through the glass wall as he swam laps, my towel over my arm, rooted to the spot. There was no reason I shouldn't join him and maybe I would have if there'd been other swimmers. But he was alone, slicing through the water with an unhurried freestyle stroke, muscled shoulders glistening in the water. As I watched he finished his laps and got out of the pool, water sluicing down him. I'd seen hints of his body over the years. His legs in running shorts, arms in t-shirts, or his shirtsleeves rolled back past his elbows. His throat in open-neck shirts. Hints of his chest when his shirt gaped as he reached for something or conducted. Every glimpse was burned into my memory and the sight of his whole body all at once was...mesmerizing. He didn't look how the boys my age looked when I saw them at the pool. Laszlo was more muscular. Hairier. And oh, how I liked that. The thick patch of dark hair at the center of his chest narrowed as it trailed down over his belly and disappeared tantalizingly into his swimmers.

I was watching him towel his hair dry when there was an obnoxious voice behind me. "Are you *perving* on Laszlo? Oh my god, he's like your *dad*."

I jumped and turned around, seeing two girls from the orchestra dressed in their swimmers, staring at me with delighted incredulity. Jaime and Ashley, a French horn player and a bassoonist.

"I wasn't perving," I snapped at them. "I forgot my goggles and I was trying to remember where I left them. And he's not my dad, he's my mentor." I didn't like reminding people he was my guardian. That I was his protégé felt more special. He'd chosen me.

"Since you were like, *eight*."

I can still remember the heavy emphasis of Jaime's words. Her playing was as overstressed as her stupid voice. Behind them, I saw Hayley watching me with a perplexed expression. Even then she knew there was something unwardlike about my feelings for Laszlo. *Why aren't you going out with Ryan? He's so cute and he thinks you are, too.*

Because Laszlo says I'm not allowed.

Okay, but it's weird you look so happy about that. Just saying.

I was angry and upset about the exchange and I came down late for breakfast, worried that Jaime and Ashley would have told Laszlo that they'd caught me looking at him. But Laszlo had just smiled and said good morning as he'd passed me on the way to get more coffee from the buffet.

I was out of sorts for the rest of the day and didn't really understand why. Later I realized it was because how I felt about Laszlo wasn't the way other people expected me to feel about him. And that it was definitely not the way Laszlo thought about me. And I worried that if he ever found out how I felt he'd be disgusted with me.

But that didn't wipe the semi-naked memory of him from my mind. Lying in bed that night I fantasized that I had gone to stand next to him by the pool and touched his hard body, wet from the water. Somehow we knew we'd be alone and he took me in his arms and kissed me, his lips cold and his tongue warm. Stripped the suit from my body. Lay me down on one of the long pool chairs and made love to me. It hurt, and after there was blood on the wet tiles, but it didn't matter because he was so gentle and sweet with me. I fantasized over and over again about Laszlo taking my virginity and it was beautiful every time.

The reality of me actually losing it in my second year of university was dismal. A boy I barely knew and didn't much like. Discomfort, the hospital smell of latex. The long silence afterward. I don't even know why I did it and I haven't wanted to go to bed with anyone since.

Anyone who isn't Laszlo.

As I look at him I see that he's got no intention of disrobing. It's just me who's going to do that, apparently.

Because it isn't sex. He's taking care of his protégé, that's all.

It's not sex, but it still feels sexual. Laszlo's been talking to me in the most understated yet kinky way for days in the full knowledge that it turns me on. Though he's not doing it to turn me on. He's doing it because it centers me, because I've asked him to, and because he likes making me happy. Now he's offering to put me over his knee and spank me because the submission will make me feel less nervous about the performance tonight. Being submissive to him, him giving me a safeword, it's all so sexually charged and yet bizarrely restrained at the same time.

A blush staining my cheeks I unbutton my jeans and wriggle out of them, remembering my white briefs as I do. Thank god they're newish as I have some that aren't in a major way.

He moves toward the sofa and holds out a hand to me, palm up. I put my hand in his and move closer, but then I freeze.

Laszlo looks at me questioningly. "Sweetheart?"

The last time I was this close to him we didn't speak for three years. I'd rather not touch him if I have to go through that again. "Laszlo," I manage in a whisper. "You won't get angry with me, will you? If we do this?"

He grips my hand tightly. "Sweetheart, I've never been angry with you. Not even that night. I promise."

That night. But he was angry that night. He was furious. When I keep chewing my lip he sits down and pats the sofa next to him, and after a moment I sit down next to him. I press my knees together, acutely aware of being in my underwear. Of how close he is.

"I know you said you wanted to go back the way things were but this is very different to how we've been with each other," he says softly. "I like doing this with you as long as it makes you happy. But only if it makes you happy, so you have to tell me if it doesn't. And I promise to be honest about my feelings, too."

I nod, unable to look at him. There are so many things I want to ask him, about how he feels about me. About that night. But I settle for something much less frightening. "Would it be all right…Could I have a hug, please?"

"Oh, sweetheart, of course." He wraps both arms around me and holds me tightly against his chest and I want to cry it feels so good. Like coming home. My Laszlo, hugging me the way he always used to.

"I don't want things to be like the way they were that last year I lived with you. I want these new things with you." My words are muffled in his shirtfront.

When I look up he strokes a finger down my cheek. "I want that too, sweetheart."

Relief pours through me. It's not like it was when I was a child, and it's not like that terrible time when he could barely even look at me. We're becoming something new together.

Taking a deep breath I let go of him, and then get on my hands and knees and slink over his lap, feeling exquisitely embarrassed, the blood rushing through my body. He doesn't seem self-conscious at all and is quite happy to arrange me in his lap, his hands on the small of my back and the fleshy part of my behind.

"Are you all right, sweetheart?"

I nod, and he strokes his hand up my back and into my hair, his long fingers rubbing over my scalp. He takes his time and it's so relaxing that by increments I feel my body go limp in his lap.

"How do you want it? *Dolce*? *Allegro*?" he asks. *Sweetly? Fast?*

I swallow, not knowing what I want because I don't know how it will feel. "You're the conductor, sir."

"So I am." One of his hands leaves my behind and he brings it down in a hard, stinging slap. There's nothing *dolce* about it. It's more like the hammer strike from Mahler's Sixth and my head rears up in a gasp of surprise.

"Ow! That hurt."

"You sound surprised, Isabeau." His voice is as smooth as melted chocolate, almost like a purr.

"You said you were going to go easy on me."

He laughs darkly. "I promise you I am. Does it still hurt?"

My ass doesn't sting anymore. In fact it feels tingly and sensitized beneath his touch. "It feels sort of hot."

"Good. That's what we're going for." He spanks me again, just as hard, on the other cheek, and I yelp. He keeps going, setting up a regular percussive rhythm that makes my skin burn without quite becoming unbearable. But it's close. Very close.

"Ah! It's very—*ah!*—loud. What if someone—*ow*—hears?"

"Stop squealing so much then. And hold still." He takes a firmer grip on my hips with his free hand, holding me tight against his thighs and belly. A bright, hot sensation shoots through my insides. I imagine someone walking past the door and hearing the rhythmic slaps of flesh on flesh. Someone who knows it's Laszlo's room. Someone who later sees me leave, pink-cheeked and flustered.

"It's not my—*ow!*—squealing that I'm talking about, it's your *hand*."

His voice somewhere over my head is unrepentant. "I can't spank you any quieter, Isabeau. This is what spanking sounds like. And I'm not going softer on you. This is meant to hurt just enough, otherwise it won't work."

Well, fine, but he needn't say that with quite so much relish.

"Would you like me to go on? It's up to you, sweetheart."

He waits, one hand hovering over my flesh, until I nod. I grab a cushion and push my face into it as his spanks grow fiercer. I flinch against each one, wriggling this way and that as he beats the same spot over and over, making it glow white hot before moving on.

He smooths the flat of his hand over my heated flesh, a long, hot caress as I pant into the sofa cushion, too spent to move. My heart is pounding and all the heat down there is making my sensitive parts tingle and I dearly want him to keep touching me, to move those fingers deeper. But he merely straightens the lace edges of my underwear and helps me up. I sit beside him on the couch, my ass burning, pushing a hand through my tangled hair. I feel hyperaware of everything. The lights are too bright. My breathing is too loud.

I reach for my jeans with a shaking hand.

Laszlo's arms come around me, pulling me against him, and the relief is intense. I curl into him with a little moan and he gets an arm under my knees and pulls them across his lap.

"Isabeau?" But I feel too funny about what just happened and hide my face in his shirtfront. He laughs softly. "Feeling shy?"

I nod without looking up. Shy, but not unhappy. I burrow into him, needing the warmth of his body, his strength, and he gives it to me without hesitation, like he used to do when I was younger. Proper big-hearted, tight-against-his-chest hugs, not like the stingy, tense hugs he gave me after I turned seventeen that left me feeling bereft. Except this is better because his hand is stroking the bare skin of my thighs and I know he won't make me let him go anytime soon.

His lips are against my hair. "You did so well, sweetheart. That was quite fierce, but I think you needed it."

I'm sinking deeper and deeper against his body, more relaxed than I can remember being in a long time. Laszlo's presence curls around me like a beloved melody.

"You're not going to feel nervous tonight. You're not going to be upset about your career or worry over it, either. You're a beautiful cello player and no one can take that away from you. We're going to figure everything out together, all right?"

I take a deep breath and close my eyes. "Thank you, sir." With that simple word, sir, I know that everything's going to be all right. If I can get through this then what's playing for a few hundred people in a concert hall?

He's holding me so close that my ears are filled with the thundering of his heart, the sound of his breathing. The cologne he always wears envelops me along with the scent that's just him. Laszlo. Masculine and comforting.

After a minute I notice he's humming softly, the vibrations deep in his chest rumbling against my cheek. It makes me smile because Laszlo always hums when there's silence, or taps out a melody on his leg or the kitchen counter or the steering wheel of his car. It was one of the first things I noticed about him. Sometimes I don't think he's aware that he's doing it.

I listen to him for a few minutes, just breathing him in and enjoying his warmth. Then I shift in his lap and look up at him. "Are you always thinking about music?"

He's surprised by my question and stops humming, and in the silence that follows he seems to realize why I asked. "Always. For as long as I can remember. I thought it was the same for everyone and I was shocked when I realized that wasn't the case. It used to drive me mad when I was young because I couldn't stop it. I used to bang my head against the pillow, trying to knock the music out so I could fall asleep. I think that's why I became a conductor. So I could take control of the music." His lips brush my forehead. "I like being in control."

"Does the music still keep you awake?"

He smiles, running his fingers through my hair. "Not anymore. It's still there, but quieter now because I'm doing what I need to do. The music doesn't need to be so insistent anymore."

Laszlo goes back to humming and watching my hair slide through his fingers like silk. He's never said so but I think he's always liked my hair.

I recognize the piece he's humming. "Dvořák's Ninth. Are we going to perform it on tour?" It's one of Laszlo's favorites. It's one of everyone's favorites really, sweet and pastoral at times, then piping and happy, then dramatic and strained, all winding up to the most joyful climax in the fourth movement. I don't need to ask Laszlo to know that he finds it a lot of fun to conduct. I can tell from his energy, the light in his hazel eyes. I love seeing him like that. We played the last movement in the youth orchestra the year I was seventeen and I remember what one of the percussionists said when he announced we'd be performing it. "Is that the one that sounds like *Jaws* at the beginning?" There were snickers, because the first few bars of the movement are a slow and ominous *dah-dunnn, dah-dunnn* that is very much like the *Jaws* theme.

Laszlo looked pained, as if comparing Dvořák's most famous symphony to the score of a horror film was too much for him. But he just nodded. "Yes, Mr. Baqri. It's the one that sounds like *Jaws* at the beginning."

"In Bangkok," Laszlo says. "The Seventh, Eighth and Ninth Symphonies. We have to do the Ninth. That's the big one."

"Oh, yes. That's the daddy." I say it without thinking. I didn't mean that sort of daddy, I meant it in the way he said, "the big one," the daddy of all Dvořák pieces. But of course I can't say *daddy* to Laszlo without it meaning something very different.

Do you like that, daddy?

I feel a blush creep over my face. He holds my gaze, long and intense, his expression unchanging. "Yes, Isabeau. The daddy."

I shift a little on his lap, not breaking his gaze. *Please can I call you daddy, sir?* I still want to, despite everything. It expresses all the complicated feelings I have for him. That I want to submit to him. That I want him sexually. That he makes me feel safe and small and sweet. I want to call him daddy because it's respectful and submissive and beautifully screwy at the same time. When I was eighteen I hadn't thought about it particularly hard, I just knew that it was something you might call an older man in bed, to inflame, to tease, to make him put his hands on you with a little more tender roughness than he normally might. And because he always made me feel safe and secure and loved, like a father would. Almost, but not quite. Because I don't love him as a father, I love him as a man. As my mentor. As whatever he is now. I think he might be my dom but I'm not sure and I'm afraid to ask. If we put a label on this it might be too much, and I'm frightened I'll scare Laszlo away. I don't think he likes being reminded of the fact that he's known me since I was a child. I think he's decided to compartmentalize me into Isabeau then and Isabeau now and the only reason he's able to separate the two is because we spent three years apart.

    I don't want to push Laszlo too far. I need him.

Chapter Fifteen

Laszlo
Now

I lift her chin up to mine, looking into the deep green of her eyes. "Are you feeling more relaxed, sweetheart?"

Isabeau nods, sucking her lower lip into her mouth. Christ, I want to kiss her. I don't think I'll ever get how she looked when she slunk over my lap out of my head. She's so close to me and her arms are around my neck, and by moving just a few inches I could press my mouth against hers. I could do even more, and lay her out on the sofa beneath me and find out whether the spanking I gave her made her wet. My fingers were so close to the soft folds of her pussy and I dearly wanted to spread her open and feel for myself. Even better than a spanking for nerves is a spanking and an orgasm, but I'll have to just use words instead.

Fixing her with a stern look I say, "You're not going to be nervous tonight, all right?"

She nods, and when I raise a questioning brow at her, she says, "Yes, sir."

"Good girl." I help her up and go to pour her a glass of water while she gets back into her jeans, and she drinks it before going back to her own room, casting a final, slightly flustered, but happy look at me.

As soon as she's gone I strip off and turn on the shower. I'm still hard, something I hope she didn't notice. I don't think she did. I wait, watching the water start to steam but picturing her red ass in her tiny white briefs. I consider watching some porn but it's no good. I'll still picture Isabeau. The shy way she wriggled out of her jeans. The eager yet uncertain way she splayed herself over my lap. Her cries as I spanked her. The heat from her red, plump flesh. How I wanted to grab fistfuls of her and spread her open and bury my tongue in her pussy and ass.

I really need to come, now, and it's going to be while thinking of Isabeau because there's no way I'm getting her out of my head after that. I can think about having sex with her without actually initiating anything, even when she drapes herself half naked over my lap and begs me to spank her. I groan and get under the water, taking myself in my hand, letting myself think every lurid thought about her naked body that I've never allowed myself to indulge in. I picture her over my lap again but this time she's naked. It's so easy to imagine slipping two fingers into her pussy while spanking her with my other hand; the sounds she would make as I finger-fuck her. All the while I'm picturing this I'm pumping my hand up and down my cock, eyes closed, one hand braced against the tiles. It feels so good thinking about her that I want to draw it out, but then I imagine that she's sucking on my cock at the same time as I'm driving my fingers into her, her whimpers muffled because her mouth is so full of me, and I lose it, coming in a rush. *Sweet fucking girl, swallow me all down, that's right.*

I shake the water off my face and open my eyes, blinking to clear my vision. The release is intense, and with the memory of her sprawled in my lap and imprinted onto my hands it feels almost as if we have just fingered and sucked each other to orgasm. Is she doing the same thing right now in her own room, getting off while thinking about me, her ass still red from my hand? Is this some sort of comedy of errors where we're both pretending we don't want each other while we simultaneously self-immolate from desire?

Maybe. But maybe that's just wishful thinking.

THE PROTÉGÉ

As I dress in my tuxedo I find that I'm humming the joyful part of Dvořák's Ninth and that I'm actually in a very good mood. Lighter and happier than I have been in a long time. I was able to make Isabeau happy. We're performing together, tonight. Life, unexpectedly, is very good indeed.

When I'm dressed I head out and I smile at Marcus as we wait for the elevator to take us down to the lobby. He's in black tie as well and gives me a sharp look.

"You seem cheerful. Over your jetlag?"

"Something like that." The doors slide open and I start to whistle as we get into the elevator.

At half-past seven I'm in the wings, watching the orchestra on stage tuning up and the audience waiting patiently for the performance to begin. I take a deep breath and stride out in stage, shaking Marcus' hand and then bowing to the audience. They applaud, and then settle into silence as I take my place at the podium.

Isabeau, sitting just a few feet away, glances up at me and her face doesn't change, but a pink blush blossoms in her cheeks and a smile threatens to break over her face. Fuck, she's too perfect. I watch her glance at her sheet music, the blush still bright in her cheeks, the smile still hovering at the corners of her lips. She's thinking about what we just did together and she's calm, not nervous in the slightest.

I look out over the orchestra, all my musicians with their instruments poised. I love this moment. The perfect silence and stillness of a thousand souls behind me, waiting. I raise my hands and give the first downbeat and the music begins. Out of the corner of my eye I can see Isabeau. My Isabeau, her bow whipping across the strings of her cello.

We play three dates in Singapore and they're all superb. I couldn't be prouder of the orchestra and I couldn't be prouder of Isabeau. She's getting to know her fellow musicians and there's a smile on her face everywhere she goes. Seeing her so radiant takes my breath away.

On Thursday morning we have a short flight to Kuala Lumpur, the capital of Malaysia. The string and woodwind sections have to check their instruments with the airline due to space restrictions with our local courier and we all wait in a long queue. I wait with them rather than swan off to the business class lounge, talking to Marcus about the program for the coming weeks.

A few feet in front of us Isabeau leans sleepily against her cello case. She's tired today, the pace of the tour and the early start catching up with her, and seems to prefer standing quietly rather than talking to the others. Her gaze wanders and she spots a piano forte a few feet away, one that anyone can play. Isabeau wanders toward it and her fingers trail idly over the keys. *Plink plink plink.* Then she frowns and plays a short melody. My heart starts to pound as I recognize it. A few people in the queue turn to look at her.

Isabeau plays the gentle melody again and then turns and sees me watching her. "Laszlo, play *Vocalise* with me?"

I look at her with a dry mouth. The piano is right there, waiting for a pianist, and she has her cello. What better way to pass the idle minutes than to play something beautiful? Except that she doesn't understand this song causes me as much pain as it does pleasure.

A few orchestra members around us have overheard her request and they add their voices, amused by the idea of their conductor actually sitting down and playing some music for a change. My eyes lock on Isabeau and I know I can't say no to her, even now. It will hurt me, but make her so happy.

We don't have the sheet music but we don't need it. This piece is burned into my soul. I could never forget it, not if I lived for a thousand years.

I sit down at the piano and regard the ebony and ivory for a moment. It's a clean, well-kept instrument and when I play scales I find that it's perfectly tuned. Isabeau sits on her cabin bag with her cello between her knees, bow poised, and looks at me expectantly, her eyes eloquent with feeling.

She knows.

Not the pain I feel, but she knows how special this song is to us. That it always was and always will be something that connects us on a deeper level than mentor, mentee; guardian, ward. That we pour our feelings into it when we're unable to find the right words to say to each other.

I play, and she joins me, and everything else falls away. There's just the piano beneath my fingers, and her. I watch her as I play, her eyes closed as she plies her bow across her mother's cello, lost in the music, every one of her notes twining around mine. It's as close as I've ever got to her, playing this piece. Closer even than when she's snuggled in my lap in her underwear, cheeks flushed, behind reddened by my hand. Because this is the only way I get to tell her how I really feel.

We finish playing and those around us applaud. A woman with tears in her eyes comes forward and embraces Isabeau, and whispers in her ear. When she draws back Isabeau gives her a quick smile and shakes her head, and starts to put away her instrument.

I take her cello from her and look toward the check-in queue and find it has shortened dramatically. I don't see the people around us as she stands quietly by my side. I'm still lost in the music we played. When she performed it alone in the Mayhew I heard only sorrow in the notes she played.

Now there's not quite so much grief, but I still hear its echoes. I've always thought that music is a far superior medium than words when it comes to communication, but for the first time in my life I feel that it's not enough.

Tell me, Isabeau. Show me everything you're feeling.

But I know it's not fair to ask her to confide in me when I can't do the same for her.

When we're through check-in and security and heading for our gate Isabeau pulls me aside, moistening her lips as she looks up at me. "Laszlo. It's very special to me, that song. I can only ever play it with you."

I want to reach out and touch her, but I'm conscious of everyone around us. "It is the same for me, sweetheart. Always has been."

She looks at me for a long time, words hovering just behind her lips. What does she want so badly to tell me? But I don't find out because she turns and hurries away.

That afternoon we arrive in Kuala Lumpur and not long after we've checked in there's a knock on my hotel room door. I open it and see Isabeau wearing a tank top with a plunging neckline and a bra that seems to be pushing her breasts up. Her red hair is in a long plait hanging over one shoulder and there's a faint pink bloom in her cheeks. She looks like a juicy peach and I want to sink my teeth into her.

"Sir," she says, as softly as a bow barely touching cello strings. She's biting her lip and smiling. "I feel nervous again."

Chapter Sixteen

Isabeau

Now

We haven't even got a performance tonight. It's a rest day. I wonder if I should elaborate on my supposed nervousness but Laszlo merely takes me by the hand, leads me to the couch and waits for me to get over his knee.

I catch his hazel eyes when he looks up and a blaze of desire shoots through me. I don't feel nervous in the least. The last time he spanked me I touched myself thinking about him, my hand inside my damp underwear the moment I got back into my own room, back against the door, fingers working my clit furiously. I came in under a minute. I didn't even have time to scrape together a coherent fantasy. Just *hands — chest — strong — heat — Laszlo.*

I slide down over him, wondering if Laszlo thinks that way about me. If he can, now I'm older. He pushes the skirt I'm wearing up to my waist and both his hands squeeze my behind. I feel something akin to a groan deep in his chest against my thigh. He takes a moment to unbutton the sleeves of his shirt and roll them back, and I wait, my body humming with anticipation. I crave how much this will wind me up sexually even as it calms me down emotionally. I watch him out of the corner of my eye as he pushes his cuffs past his elbows, and the anticipation is making me wet. He's got beautiful forearms, lean and strong and veiny. I used to watch them openly at youth orchestra rehearsals, wondering why I found them so fascinating. Admiring their strength, the dusting of dark hairs, the way the muscles in his arms move.

"Longer this time, I think," he murmurs, and the first strike of his hand catches me by surprise and I squeal. He works me over thoroughly until I'm a sweaty, panting mess, my behind and the backs of my thighs on fire. He goes on and on, and the pain recedes behind a wave of heat and arousal that makes me melt across his lap. I don't care if people can hear as long as he doesn't stop. My shirt rides up and I'm almost bare to him as I squirm in his lap.

He smooths the flat of his hand down over my flesh and I know he's finished. When he helps me up I'm smiling woozily. He pulls me tight against his chest and I burrow into him, his shirt cool against my hot cheek.

"That feel good, sweet girl?" he asks, and I mumble my assent. Taking me by the shoulders he sits me up and looks sternly into my eyes. "What do you say?"

I feel another surge of wetness between my legs. That dark glimmer is back and I lick my lips. "Yes, thank you, sir."

"That's better," he says, sleek satisfaction in his voice as he pulls me against him. *Mine,* I think, burrowing my face against his chest, drunk on this surfeit of the man I've always wanted. His hand slips beneath my shirt, caressing my back. When he hums to himself his lips are against the top of my head and I want to cry from happiness.

"Good girl," he murmurs softly.

The next afternoon I'm back. And the next. I can't help myself.

Laszlo doesn't question why, or exclaim over how nervous I'm pretending to be. He just lets me in and gives me what I'm asking for. Thoroughly. Harder by increments each time, making me cry out against the sofa cushions and squeezing tears from my eyes. The harder he gets the more I want, and more again. Then he strokes me and murmurs loving words and holds me in his arms. I've never known anything like it. The longer and harder he spanks me the more he fusses over me afterward. Stern, fierce Laszlo being soft and buttery with me, his cool fingers smoothing the hot tears from my face and telling me I did so well, what a good girl I am. I can't get enough and I want to feel even more vulnerable as I'm prone across his lap.

Standing close to him while he holds my hand to lead me to the sofa one afternoon, I say, "I'm worried about people walking past and hear me crying out. Will you gag me, sir?"

"Of course, Isabeau." He finds a handkerchief in his suitcase that came with his tuxedo, puts it between my teeth and ties it behind my head. He reminds me that I can still use my safeword when I'm gagged this way and he'll understand what I'm saying.

The next time I want to be gagged again, but I also add, "Sir, I think I squirm about too much on your lap and I don't want to. Will you tie my hands together?"

I'm not worried about the noise. I don't think I squirm too much. If he knows what I'm doing he pretends he doesn't. When I'm gagged and he's tied my hands behind my back he rakes me with a long, heated look but doesn't say anything, just moves past me to sit down on the sofa. This time when he spanks me he hooks two fingers into my underwear halfway through and yanks them up. I give a muffled moan as the fabric rubs tightly against my clit and sensitive parts. He pretends not to notice. He doesn't remark on my underwear being wet, either. Because I am wet. I'm very wet.

Later, at a drinks reception hosted by the patrons of the concert hall we're playing in, Laszlo comes and stands beside me. "Good evening, Isabeau. Do you like my tie?" he asks, stroking his fingers down the silk.

My eyes widen as I see it's the same one he bound my hands with a few hours earlier. "It's ah, very nice."

Before he moves away he murmurs in my ear, "I like that you like it, very much. It's important to me that you're happy." I watch as Laszlo takes a glass of champagne from a waiter gliding by and then he turns away to talk to Marcus.

He likes that I'm *happy*. He must know that what we're doing doesn't just make me happy, it makes me aroused and wet. Why is he pretending he hasn't noticed? Is it so I don't get embarrassed? Or is he letting me know that he knows what I'm doing when I ask to be bound and gagged, that I'm finding new ways to be submissive to him?

There are things I pretend not to notice, too. That the knots Laszlo binds me with are practiced and neat and nothing ever needs to be retied. That there's a hungry glint in his eyes when he looks at me, bound and gagged. And that when he spanks me, Laszlo gets hard.

Chapter Seventeen

Isabeau
Then

"Can't we play it just the two of us? Please? Like we always have."

Laszlo's slicing vegetables for a stir-fry and doesn't look up. "And leave the whole orchestra sitting silently? Sweetheart, that would be a waste of their talent."

I take a piece of carrot from the chopping board and chew it, thinking. In just over a month's time I'll be eighteen and too old for Laszlo's youth orchestra, a thought that makes me feel horribly sad, like being told I'll never go back to Narnia. I and three other members will be graduating at the upcoming Summer Concert and we'll each be performing a solo piece. I want to play *The Swan*, of course, and I want to play the arrangement for cello and piano and perform it with Laszlo. "I just think it should be special, that's all."

He smiles down at the chopping board. "It will be special because you'll make it special. I'm the conductor, not the pianist. What am I supposed to do, boot Celeste off her instrument?"

"She'll do whatever you tell her to do."

He eyes me from beneath the lock of sandy hair that's fallen into his eyes. "Now, is that fair on Celeste?"

I suppose he's right, but I'm just going to miss being in the orchestra so much. I'm going to miss living with him even more as in a few months I'm going up to Durham to study music and I'll be living in halls. I'll only see Laszlo during the holidays and on weekends. I'll take the train up to London as many times as possible, and he's promised that during the week when he's not performing or rehearsing he'll come and visit me.

Three long years away at university. Away from Laszlo. But after that—excitement fizzes through me—I'll be a properly trained cellist. "Can I join your orchestra when I graduate?"

Laszlo presses the point of the knife into the cutting board and regards me. "I've been thinking about that. Not just lately, but many times over the years. I want that so much, sweetheart."

But. I can see the unsaid word written all over his face and panic makes me stop chewing. He doesn't think I'm good enough for his orchestra?

"Remember all those times you've talked about being a soloist?" he asks.

I start chewing again, thinking. "Well, yes. I want that too, but I just love playing with you so much. I'll still have to play with an orchestra behind me a lot of time as a soloist, so why not yours?"

I remember what he said to me all those years ago when I debuted at the Mayhew with his orchestra. *Solo pieces are a collaboration between the soloist and the conductor. You bring your own vision for the piece and I interpret it for the rest of the orchestra.* I love that sense of collaboration between us. He knows me better than anyone. I don't want any conductor but him.

Laszlo nods. "And you will, but you'll be so famous that I'll have to beg you to come back and play a show or two at the Mayhew with my orchestra. I *want* it to be that way, even though I..." He trails off and goes back to chopping.

I feel bereft at the thought of all the performances he's imagining for me that aren't with him.

"What about Jacqueline du Pré and Daniel Barenboim?" I ask. "They were always together. Why can't we be like them?" Du Pré was a famous cello soloist in the sixties and Barenboim was a conductor and her husband. Everyone wanted to see them perform together with his orchestra until her career was cut savagely, painfully short by multiple sclerosis. Her biography was one of the books that Laszlo gave me to read when I first came to live with him and I've never forgotten her. I've reopened that book many times over the years and run my fingers over the many glossy pictures of them smiling at each other, working alongside each other. *They're perfect together. Cellists and conductors were meant to be.*

Laszlo slices a chili in half. "Not always together and du Pré was famous in her own right before she met Barenboim." He looks up at me. "You're going to make a name for yourself, Isabeau, without my help."

Laszlo wants to be sure this is what I want, and that people will value me for me and not because of his reputation. He wants me to stand on my own two feet.

Fine. I can do that. I will do that. When I've graduated I'll be such a famous soloist that Laszlo will ask me again and again to play with his orchestra.

I bite savagely into a sugar snap pea, thinking of the eight cellists in his ensemble who sit close by him night after night, and I'm green with envy.

"If one of your cellists is sick and it's the weekend or I'm on holidays can I please, please fill in for them? I'll jump on that train the second I get your call. You know I can play anything."

He thinks about it, turning up the heat on the wok. "All right. If you're not busy with your studies and you feel confident about the piece we're performing then of course you can. You'd be very welcome." Laszlo smiles at me, though it's not a smile that reaches his eyes.

I watch him as he cooks, and think of how he hasn't hugged me for such a long time. The smiles that slide off his face too quickly. Is he sad? Because of all this talk of me going away?

I say in a husky whisper, "I'm going to miss you so much."

Laszlo stills, and when he looks up at me I see my own pain in his expression. He reaches out and strokes the backs of his fingers my cheek, his eyes running over my face. "I'm going to miss you, too, sweetheart. I won't know myself without you."

We just look at each other and my eyes grow blurry with tears. Ten years. More than half my life, but it's gone past in the blink of an eye. I've been so happy with Laszlo and once I leave this house I don't know how I'm going to be happy without him.

Unless...whispers a little voice from deep within my heart. *Unless we become lovers on one of my trips home.*

It could happen so easily. A late night together, hands drifting closer in the back of a cab, or walking on the heath, so close that we're touching. A late night supper in Covent Garden after a performance, tucked away in a little candlelit booth. I imagine standing together in the wings at the Mayhew, him kissing me slowly, wonderingly, because he's seeing me with new eyes. It might even happen the night of the Summer Concert. There's no reason why not. I'll be eighteen.

Laszlo looks down at the counter as if he's trying to remember where he was with our dinner. "So, *The Swan*. The harp and strings arrangement? Make your conductor proud and the audience cry again?"

I pull myself reluctantly out of my daydream. "Yes. All right, Laszlo. And thank you for scheduling the performance on my eighteenth birthday, it's the most wonderful present."

A smile skirts his lips. "The dates happened to match up, that's all."

I can't resist a little teasing and bat my lashes at him. "So it's not because I'm your favorite?"

He opens a tin of coconut cream and doesn't look up. "Now, Miss Laurent, you know I don't have favorites."

"Yes, *maestro*. Can we play *Vocalise* after we eat?"

There's a millisecond hesitation and then he gives me that quick, not-quite smile again. "Of course, sweetheart. We can play whatever you like."

A few weeks later Laszlo shows me the printed program and halfway down I see,

The Swan, Saint-Saëns

Isabeau Laurent, cello; strings

He doesn't say it but I see the unsaid words in his hazel eyes. That this is the way it has to be. That piece should be played properly, beautifully, and for that I needed the orchestra behind me. He's the conductor. I'm the musician. But I still feel heartsick at the thought that it could be the last time I'll ever be on stage with him.

It won't be. I won't let it be.

Further down the program, right at the bottom, is simply, *Be/ethoven*. It looks like a typo but it's actually a visual pun that we're counting on no one getting. I grin. I can't wait to see the audiences' faces when we get to the finale.

THE PROTÉGÉ

On the morning of my eighteenth birthday Laszlo puts a flat red velvet box next to my plate of pancakes and bacon and kisses my cheek, the bristles of his beard rasping gently against my skin.

"Happy birthday, sweetheart."

I stroke the box with my fingers, enjoy the soft feel of the velvet. I don't even care what's inside. It's a present from Laszlo so I know I'll always treasure it.

He sits down opposite me and picks up his fork. "Aren't you going to open it?"

I look up at him, smiling a watery smile. Feeling so happy. So full up with happiness, like the overture from *The Marriage of Figaro*. "I don't think I'll ever be happier than I am right now. Thank you, Laszlo. I don't know what would have happened to me if you hadn't talked to me in the street that day."

Laszlo just looks at me, his eyes full of feeling. He takes a deep breath and I think he's going to say something else, but he goes back to his seat. "Open your present, sweetheart."

I do, and inside I find a beautiful silver pendant and earrings. "To go with your dress tonight," he explains.

They'll look beautiful with the red satin gown hanging in my wardrobe. As I'm a soloist tonight I don't have to wear black. "Thank you, Laszlo, they're perfect."

He watches me close the box and stroke my fingers over the velvet some more. "You could call your father. You can do anything you want. You're eighteen now."

But I don't want to spoil the day by dredging up that awful part of my life, the time after my mother died and before I met Laszlo. I've done such a good job all these years of pretending those months never happened.

One day I'll see Dad. One day. Just not now.

There's a full house at the Mayhew for the concert that night and the four of us who are graduating stand out, bright and colorful, against the sea of black as we wait backstage. Laszlo has a white shirt on beneath his black suit, open at the neck. I love seeing him this way. No bowtie and tails for youth orchestra performances. He scratches a hand through his long hair, his eyes bright with excitement as they always are before a performance.

He puts a warm hand on my shoulder before I head upstairs with the others to tune up. "You look beautiful. Happy birthday, sweetheart."

I go up on tiptoe and kiss his cheek, happiness flushing through me, and his hand clasps me briefly about the waist.

As we play through the program I look up at him often and smile, and he smiles back, just a glimmer each time but so much for a man like Laszlo who is always so focused while he's working. When we finish *The Swan* and I open my eyes he smiles properly at me as the applause rolls over us. Hayley's in the front row of the audience wiping tears from her face and when I catch her eye she waves frantically at me and gives me two thumbs up.

Soon it's time for the finale. Laszlo has his back to the audience and they can't see what he's doing, but we can. We all struggle to keep straight faces as he puts something around his neck and over his face. Behind him, the audience are shifting curiously, trying to see what's going on. Laszlo raises his hands, as he would before the introduction to any piece, and they settle again. He gives a downbeat, and the first famous eight notes of *Symphony No. 5* by Beethoven sound from the string section.

Da-da-da-dunnn. Da-da-da-dunnn.

Laszlo ends the last beat with a flourish, his index finger pointing into the air. There's a pause, the orchestra silent, and he pivots slowly toward the audience so they can see that he's wearing a pair of dark glasses with mirror-ball rims. He's undone two more buttons on his shirt and a gaudy gold medallion is glinting on his chest. He tries not to smile but as the titters break out in the audience he grins, pointed canines showing. Still looking at them, he gives another downbeat and we start to play, but instead of the tense, insistent notes of the famous symphony a disco beat breaks out. Laszlo sweeps back around to us, and the audience begins to cheer and whoop as we play *A Fifth of Beethoven* from *Saturday Night Fever*. Laszlo has rearranged it for a full orchestra, giving the synth parts to the woodwinds and the drum machine to the percussion section. The string section is almost the same as the original symphony.

It sounds fantastic. Most of the audience probably know that Laszlo's in the middle of conducting performances of Beethoven's original symphony on this very stage and hearing us play the disco version with the same solemn, talented conductor while he's wearing mirror-ball sunglasses is too much, and they go mad. We do three reprisals. The cello part is delicious to play, all dark, deep notes that build and build beneath the bright woodwinds and steady drums. This is what I love about playing with an orchestra, the way all the parts coalesce into something with a huge force of energy and emotion behind it. This is why I don't want just to be a soloist.

Laszlo hugs me long and hard when we get off stage and I wrap my arms around him as tight as I can. It's our last performance together for some time at least and we both know it. He buries his face in my neck, holding me closer than he has in a year, his breath warm against my throat. It brings tears to my eyes how close he is and I realize how much I've missed him even though he's been at my side every day.

"I'm so proud of you," he whispers fiercely. "Do you know that, sweetheart?" I look up at him, breathless. I want to tell him now, that I love him. That I've always loved him. I open my mouth to speak.

Someone calls out to Laszlo and he pulls away. A photographer from one of the daily newspapers has come backstage and wants a picture of him with the four soloists.

Laszlo puts one arm around me and gathers the other three to us. All the orchestra is there, whistling and yelling out to us as the photographer raises his camera and we can't stop laughing. I'm looking up at Laszlo as the flash goes off.

"Mr. Valmary, what do you think Beethoven would say if he knew his symphony was being played on the same stage as a disco remix?"

Laszlo starts to laugh at the journalist's question, but then quashes it. "My orchestra is happy and the audience enjoyed a great show. That's all I care about." He turns his back on the photographer and calls out to everyone, saying that it was the most fun he's ever had onstage at the Mayhew and we did the place proud.

It takes a long time to pack up and get changed as no one seems to be in a hurry to go home. We're all high on the performance, laughing and giddy. Everyone wants to say goodbye to me and the three others who are leaving the orchestra after tonight. I'm going to miss them so much. Finally I peel myself away and find Laszlo outside by the stage door, talking to the handful of waiting parents. The mirror ball sunglasses are still on top of his head, glinting in the darkness.

I glance at them and grin. "Suits you."

"Do they now?" he asks with a smile, slinging an arm around my shoulders and giving me a squeeze before hailing a cab. I feel higher than ever. He hasn't touched me this much in months.

When we get home he flops on the sofa and I make us coffee, my back to him as he talks about the performance. I try to listen but my heart is hammering in my chest. I remember what he said this morning.

I'm eighteen now. I can do whatever I like.

"You performed so well, sweetheart," he says as I put a cup of coffee next to him and sit down, butterflies rioting in my belly. I need to say something. Do something. By tomorrow morning the magic of tonight will have passed and I won't have the courage to speak up for months. Maybe even years. I can't let us grow apart while I'm away at university.

I lean closer to him, tucking my feet under myself. "You never say *good girl* anymore."

Laszlo frowns and swivels to look at me. "Don't I?"

I don't have to hide what I want from Laszlo. I don't have to call him just Laszlo or Mr. Valmary. I can call him what I've heard girls my age call handsome older men. *He's such a daddy.* I like the sound of that so much. *Such a daddy.* Big, strong men with stern faces but sweet smiles, and hands that look like they could caress, could smack, could give pleasure while you sit in their lap. Who would call you sweetheart and baby and little one as you called them daddy. Laszlo already calls me sweetheart. Laszlo is big and strong and stern, and his sweetest smiles are only ever for me. I might be a virgin who's never been kissed but imagining calling Laszlo daddy makes me so wet and weak.

"No, you don't. Daddy."

His face transforms in shock, but I think I see something else flicker in his eyes. Just for a second, and it gives me courage.

"What? Don't call me that."

But I liked calling him that. He's sitting so close to me, his shirt still unbuttoned and I can see his chest, the dark hair there that I want to nuzzle with my nose, run my nails through, press my cheek against. "Why not?"

"Because I'm not your father."

"I know. I didn't mean it like that." I close the foot of space between us, slipping into his lap and pressing my palms against his chest. My knees hug his hips. He feels better than a cello between my legs. I want to hold on tight while he plays me like a musical instrument. Laszlo and his skillful fingers can play anything. His hands go to my waist and I reach up to touch the bristles of his beard, running my nails luxuriously through them, like I've always longed to do. Not just for a moment, but for as long as I want, drinking my fill of him. I've imagined doing this as I've watched him scratch his cheek sleepily in the morning or rub his chin as he pores over a score. He feels as good as I thought he would, soft yet prickly at the same time.

"Do you like that, daddy?"

His eyes are locked on mine and he's barely breathing. My finger slides over his full lower lip and his mouth parts. Laszlo. My Laszlo. I press my lips to his and it feels so right. I've always loved him and he's always loved me. It took ten long years for me to grow up and for him to see me as a woman. I felt it earlier when he put his arms around me. He knew at last. I'm all grown up.

And he kisses me back. His arms tighten around me and he pulls me close against his chest. I don't know what I'm doing, but Laszlo does. He deepens the kiss by increments, his tongue flicking out to taste my lips, and I open my mouth to invite him in. My fingers rub through his beard as I kiss him and he bites down gently on my lower lip.

Moaning, I arch against him and feel something against my sex. Something hard. *He's* hard. He's hard because of me. He feels the same way I do about him. He *wants* me. I rub against him, back and forth, and the friction sends wildfire sparks through my body.

He breaks the kiss, watching me with heavy-lidded eyes, and when he speaks his words are roughened with desire. "Good girl," he murmurs, licking my lip with the tip of his tongue. Those words send as much pleasure through me as rubbing my sex against him does. His hands caress my hips, helping me move back and forth. Coaxing me onwards. I pant against his mouth and my eyes close as I feel an orgasm swiftly approaching. I rub harder against him, my arms locked around his neck. I'm so close. I'm going to come for him. I'm going to show him how much I want him and how good he makes me feel.

But a moment later he pushes me roughly away and I find myself sitting on the cold sofa cushion, his hands gripping my upper arms.

"No. Isabeau. We can't."

I don't understand what he's saying. He releases me and sits back, pushing a hand through his hair. Powerful emotions are warring in his eyes. But there's no reason why we shouldn't make each other feel good. I want to make him feel as good as he makes me feel. "What's wrong, daddy?"

But he doesn't seem to hear me. My frustrated orgasm is waiting in the wings and I reach out and touch him, try to get back in his lap where we both feel so good, but he grabs my wrist in a painful grip and growls, "Isabeau, what the fuck are you doing?"

It's as if he's slapped me out of a dream. I've never seen him look at me as he's looking at me now, with such naked fury and revulsion.

I revolt him.

A panicked sob rises in my throat and I jump up off the sofa and run from the room, shame and horror pouring through me. I get to my room and slam and lock the door. What have I done?

"Isabeau!" Laszlo pounds up the stairs after me. He tries the handle and then starts knocking on the door. I'm pressed back against it, one hand to my mouth as I shake with silent tears. Laszlo keeps talking through the door but I don't know what he's saying. The blood is roaring so loud in my ears. He doesn't think of me in that way at all. He watched me grow up and he thinks of me of his daughter, and I just kissed him and called him daddy.

What the hell is *wrong* with me?

Years of hope and love and adoration have warped my brain and I've just done the most disgusting thing I could have ever done to Laszlo and now he hates me. I saw it in his eyes. I sink down onto the floor and press my hands over my ears, begging for this all to be a bad dream.

I take it back I take it back I take it back.

Sometime later the knocking stops, but he's still in the house. I'll have to face him if not now, then in the morning.

I can't. I wipe the tears from my face and look around the room. I need to get out of here, just for a while, until he stops being angry with me. Until I figure out how angry he really is. Cello. Overnight bag. There's nothing else I need. I force my mind into silence as I hastily pack some clothes and sneak downstairs. All is quiet. Laszlo must be in his room. I think about leaving my key on the hall table, like the day I left my father's house forever. But I clutch it convulsively as I close the front door quietly behind me. *I'm coming back. I'm not going to lose Laszlo.*

Three streets away I order a ride with an app on my phone and when it arrives it takes me across London to Hayley's flat. Several times I try texting her to let her know I'm coming but I don't know what to say. I just pray that she's home. She was at the concert tonight, in the audience, and maybe she went on somewhere for drinks afterward.

Twenty minutes later I buzz the flat, and wait. There's a light on in her living room window and a few seconds later she sees me through the video com and buzzes me up.

Seeing my disheveled appearance and bags her eyes go wide. "Isabeau, what's happened?"

I don't know what to say. It's like a waking nightmare. Did I really kiss Laszlo? Did he really look at me like he's never been so disgusted in his life? In a choked voice, I manage, "I had a fight with Laszlo."

Hayley motions me into the flat. "Oh, shit. I'm so sorry. Do you want to talk about it?"

I shake my head, my eyes burning. I just want to be alone. Hayley puts me to bed in her flat mate's room, as she's away on holiday.

Automatically, I undress and get into bed and lie there, my eyes wide open in the darkness. Everything's so surreal. My phone's silent. If Laszlo's realized I'm gone by now he's not calling me, and reality begins to sink in. I'm eighteen and I'm going to university in a few months' time. I don't need a mentor or a guardian anymore so there's no reason for him to come after me. I'm an adult and he can just cut me lose.

Staring at the bedroom ceiling I realize everything's over between Laszlo and I, forever, and I start to cry.

Chapter Eighteen

Laszlo
Now

Bangkok. Riotous, hectic, filled with flowers and color and spice. Even the occasional wafts of stagnant air from the canals are welcome because they remind me that I'm a world away from stately, quiet Hampstead. I burn my mouth on a curry filled with unidentifiable vegetables and I feel more alive than I have in months; happier too, my shirt clinging to my back in the humidity as I walk down Khaosan Road, eyes grazing the stalls.

We're more than four weeks into a five week tour that has encompassed much of Southeast Asia. I'm so proud of the orchestra and what they've achieved. I've pushed them more and more in each city and they responded beautifully.

This is what it means to be a musical director, having the proper control in order to tailor a performance to an audience and drawing on the strengths of my musicians. I want more of the receptive audiences like these in Asia. I'm tired of playing it safe.

Isabeau is a few meters ahead of me, sandals on her feet and a long skirt draped around her hips. I watch as she scoops her heavy red hair up and fans the back of her neck. She must remark on the heat to her companions as one of the violinists passes her a tie and she pulls all her hair up into a messy bun on top of her head. A member of her group points at something hanging from a stall and I see her laugh, her green eyes lighting up.

Beautiful girl.

I feel a throb of need and wonder when I'll get to touch her again. I remember the feel of her heated flesh beneath my hands yesterday afternoon, the sharp intake of her breath around the gag as I spanked her. The burn of my hand and the way she melted into my lap as I worked her over, all her tension flowing away, my arousal growing the more she surrendered to me.

How, I wonder, bemused by the soporific heat and my sheer delight as I watch Isabeau, did we get here? It's as unexpected as it is welcome after missing her for so long.

THE PROTÉGÉ

The morning after her eighteenth birthday I opened the paper as a distraction and found myself staring at a photograph of her in the Arts section. A photograph of me, as well, and the other youth orchestra members. My fingers touched the small, colored square in despair: Isabeau in her red satin dress and the birthday jewelry I gave her. Her whole being lit from within as she gazed up at me. I stared at her face, so tender and innocent, and grabbed my phone.

Call her.

No. Give her space.

Fucking call her, she's upset.

But guilt always stopped me. Did I want to call her for her sake or for mine? And, more cowardly, would talking to her mean that I would have to confess my feelings for a girl who was only just eighteen? I cringe inwardly even now at the thought of telling her.

One of the viola players approaches Isabeau's group, trying to get closer to a stall but not able to find a way through them. Instead of getting the attention of one of them and asking them if she can pass, she pushes through, knocking Isabeau aside and muttering something at the same time. The smile is wiped from Isabeau's face and she watches the viola player pay for her purchase and leave, a hurt expression in her eyes.

Isabeau's group seem to be exchanging annoyed words about the woman as they move off down the road. Suddenly they all laugh. Curious, I draw a little closer and hear the tail end of what my protégé is saying. "...into a dumpster without hitting the rim."

The cellists and violinists laugh again, and I feel my eyes narrow. She better not be doing what I think she's doing.

Isabeau speaks again and my suspicions are confirmed. She's telling viola jokes.

Viola players have been the butt of orchestra jokes for hundreds of years, probably because viola parts have a reputation for being simple, though the instrument itself is no easier than any other to master. All the same, violas are demeaned and viola players have a reputation for being less than intelligent. I've heard all the jokes. *What is the definition of perfect pitch? Throwing a viola into a dumpster without hitting the rim. How can you tell if a violist is playing out of tune? The bow is moving.*

Isabeau's opening her mouth to tell another joke when I clear my throat behind her. She jumps and turns to me, and the smile dies on her face.

"Miss Laurent, may I speak to you privately?"

Everyone in her group slinks away, stifling nervous laughter. I watch them till they're out of hearing distance. Then I lean down, put my face close to Isabeau's and say in a low and seething voice, "That is not how I expect a member of my orchestra and especially not my protégé to comport herself with her fellow musicians. Snide little jokes? If I hear one more unprofessional thing out of your mouth I will pull your underwear down in the street and spank you right here, do you understand?"

Her lips part in shock and she breathes in sharply. "Sorry, sir."

But I'm not finished. "If you're having problems with someone in the orchestra you go to your section leader or you come to me. You do not sink to their petty level."

Swallowing visibly, she manages, "Yes, sir."

I watch her for a long moment, driving my point home. She doesn't try to excuse her behavior and I'm glad. Even though the viola player was exceedingly rude to her Isabeau's not trying to shift the blame for her own bad behavior onto someone else. "All right. You can go back to the others."

"I'm really sorry, sir," she whispers again, more emphatically this time. Her face is flushed and tight with remorse and she can't quite meet my gaze.

In a softer tone of voice, I say, "It's all right, I believe you. Now off you go."

"Can I just—walk beside you for a minute?"

I nod, and we start to move down the street. As we walk I keep an eye on her, and there's something wrong. Her eyes are on the ground, her lips are parted and her breathing's shallow. I stop and tug her gently into an alcove, out of the view of the others up ahead. She won't meet my gaze even when I gently lift her chin to mine. "Hey. Sweetheart. What's wrong?"

She shakes her head, her eyes confused.

"You don't know?"

She nods.

"Is it what I said before? The way I said it?"

She thinks for a moment, then nods. She still hasn't said anything and she looks dazed and perplexed, and I suddenly realize what's wrong. After I spank her she becomes like this, pliable and quiet and unable to talk a great deal, but we're alone then and she's safe and able to come back to me in her own time. This time she's dropped into subspace on the street. Shit. I didn't mean to do that. I just wanted to pull her quickly and sharply back into line.

"It's all right, sweetheart. You come back when you're ready, I'm right here." I watch her, my hand on her shoulder. She stands quietly while people move past us and I know she's not aware of any of it. She's only aware of me so I keep myself very still, close to her, letting her know she's safe.

Isabeau takes a deep breath and blinks several times, finally meeting my eyes. They're so large and green and vulnerable that my heart catches in my throat. I can only look at her, helpless, her lips close to mine. It's not just me who has an effect on her. She affects me, too, knowing I've made her feel this way.

"Laszlo..." She trails off. Her green eyes are mesmerizing and I can't tear my gaze away. She raises her chin, tentative, and kisses me. Her lips are soft and full and she presses them against my mouth, and then again. Her tongue flicks my lips and the whole world around me evaporates to nothing. There's just her body pressed closed to mine, her lips against mine. A bold kiss. Inviting me in. Inviting more. I kiss her like I've wanted to kiss her since she was seventeen and I knew I was the worst kind of man for wanting her in that way. It's still wrong because even though she's twenty-one now I have too much power over her. And I like that power too fucking much.

She whimpers in my arms as I kiss her harder. I can't seem to stop and she opens her mouth, needing me. But I have to say something and I make myself pull away, cupping her face between my hands and breathing hard. "Isabeau. I didn't mean to do what happened just now. I didn't realize I could do it just like that. I'm sorry."

She reaches up hesitant fingers to touch my face, that punch-drunk look still in her eyes. "What is this feeling?"

"I put you into subspace."

She traces the outline of my lips with a forefinger. "Oh, is that what it is? I like it. I feel like I'm floating."

I capture her fingers in mine. I like it, too. I like it very much and that's why it's dangerous. She seems to know what I'm thinking and a woozy smile crosses her face. She presses herself closer, her lips just a hair's breadth from mine. "You like me being in your power. You like it when I slink over your lap and beg you to spank me. You like putting me into that place with just a few sharp words. Don't you, daddy?"

My breath catches. Daddy. A few years ago if a woman had called me that I would have thought it was cute, but told her that I preferred *sir*, or *master*. Master is very pleasing, so close to the *maestro* I'm called on stage. *Get on your knees for your master. Show me I'm your whole world.* I would have said that *daddy* is silly. Pouty. Sugary. I'm not a silly, sugary sort of man. But when Isabeau first called me daddy three years ago it didn't sound silly. It sounded fucking delicious and caused thumping, pounding arousal to course through my body. I want it from her again. I want it only from her, my sweet little Isabeau who wants to rub herself against me in my lap while she calls me daddy. I've never wanted anything so much in my life.

"Can I tell you a secret?" she whispers, her eyes searching mine.

"What's that, baby?" The words slip from my mouth as if I'm the one who's been put in a trance. I think maybe I have, by Isabeau and her deep green eyes and her plush kisses. I know only my hands on her waist, her breasts pressing against my chest.

She goes on in that soft tone of voice, pressing kisses to my lips between words. "You pretend you're so disinterested all the time. So in control of yourself. But you're not, are you? You try to hide so much from me but I see things in your eyes. I hear them in your voice, because I'm older now. I've learned things."

I can only stare at her, my heart starting to pound. How much does she know? Isabeau's never talked to me like this before and I don't know what to do. She's still close enough that she doesn't need to speak above a whisper. I notice every little detail about her. The tendrils of hair sticking to her damp neck. The swell of her breasts in her thin shirt. She lets go of me and steps away, her chin raised and her eyes challenging. Focused. She's come back into herself and I'm the one who's adrift.

"I adored you when I was eight. I wanted to be yours when I was twelve. I thought about you touching me when I was fourteen. I touched myself thinking about you when I was fifteen. Sixteen. Seventeen. Only ever about you, Laszlo. I kept it to myself until I was eighteen because you're a good man who couldn't touch me, would *never*, when it wasn't right. I was so very patient."

Isabeau slinks close to me again and tilts her mouth up to mine as if she's going to kiss me, but doesn't quite. "And I'm still waiting. I feel you hard against me as I lay across your lap. When I go back to my room I make myself come, over and over, thinking about you fucking me. You want me, too. You make yourself come thinking about me. Don't you, daddy?"

She kisses along my jaw until her mouth is very close to my ear. I can only listen to her, paralyzed by her closeness and the things she's saying. All those years she thought about me in that way. *Only ever about you, Laszlo.*

Isabeau keeps whispering in my ear. "You're not a closed book to me anymore. You're a piece of music I can read as easily as a symphony. I've realized that there are two Laszlo Valmarys. The Laszlo Valmary who took a sad little girl off the street and gave her a life of music she'd only ever dreamed of. Kind, clever and patient Laszlo. Generous and sweet Laszlo.

"But there's another Laszlo Valmary and you try to hide him from me. He's the Laszlo who told me I was a good girl as I rubbed so sweetly against his lap on the night of my eighteenth birthday. The Laszlo who looks at me like he's never heard anything so delicious as when I say *yes, sir* in my best, most obedient little girl voice. The Laszlo who looks like a starving wolf when I ask him to tie me up. I want to get to know this Laszlo Valmary. I want him very much. Did you want me then, too, daddy? Is that why you're so conflicted, because you wanted me when I was only seventeen?"

I feel myself nod stiffly.

She doesn't seem shocked by this admission. "I used to make myself come thinking about you taking my virginity. I wanted that so badly. Did you do the same?"

"It was just once." I hear the defensiveness in my own voice. Once is too many times when she was a teenage girl.

Isabeau puts her hands on my chest and then slides them up around my neck, slinking closer. "Did you make yourself come thinking about me, daddy? What did you imagine?"

"I don't remember."

She rubs a forefinger over the bristles on my chin and my eyes close briefly. I can't do anything, say anything but drink in the sensation of being so close to her. "I hear you, Laszlo. I hear all the things that you try to hide from me because you think it means you're not a good person because you wanted a seventeen-year-old girl. I can still see that fear in your eyes but I'm here to tell you that it doesn't matter anymore. You never laid a finger on me. You never did one thing that you should feel remorse for. If you still want me, I'm yours." She presses her lips against my ears and breathes, "And I'll let you do whatever you want, daddy."

Isabeau plants a slow, tender kiss on my cheek, achingly sweet and innocent in a way that belies her seductive tone.

Whatever you want, daddy.

She detaches herself from me and saunters back in the direction of the others, as serene as one of Tchaikovsky's swans. As if she hasn't just taken all my beliefs that I've held dear for so long, snapped them one by one in front of my eyes and thrown them to the ground.

Chapter Nineteen

Isabeau
Now

I walk away, willing my legs not to shake. I can't believe the things I've just said to Laszlo. It was that...place he put me in. I felt vulnerable and powerful at the same time, like there wasn't anything I couldn't do, because he was there.

Did you want me then, too, daddy? How had I known? I look sightlessly at a young woman cooking noodles amid clouds of fragrant steam, remembering all the odd little things from the last year that I lived with Laszlo. How he pulled away from me physically, denying me his big, generous hugs and kisses goodnight. How he seemed afraid to look too long at me, or tell me I'd done well. His fleeting expression of pain when I asked him to play *Vocalise* with me. Then, the tight grip of his hands on my hips the night of my eighteenth birthday. The way he kissed me and said *good girl*.

My eyes graze stacks of colorful silk and carved wooden elephants. I was so preoccupied with his angry rejection that I never wondered why he seemed so conflicted that night. Why he kissed me so hungrily.

I spend the rest of the afternoon browsing the stalls with my fellow musicians and then we all head back to the hotel to rest and freshen up for that evening's performance. At the concert hall I'm getting out my cello to begin tuning when I feel my phone buzz in my pocket. It's an email from Laszlo and the subject is, *I lied. I remember.*

I frown. He lied? What about? Then I remember our conversation. *Did you make yourself come thinking about me? What did you imagine?*

I don't remember.

I open the email with a shaking finger and start to read.

You in that white lace t-shirt you used to wear. Pulling it up and seeing your breasts spring free. Ripping off your underwear. Getting my mouth all over you. Licking your clit and hearing you whimper my name. Spreading your legs open and watching as I penetrated your sweet little cunt and feeling how tight you are. Pulling out and seeing your blood glistening on my cock, and then pushing slowly back in as you clung to me and cried out. Being so, so gentle as I pushed every hard inch of myself into you, taking my time and seeing that you were well fucked your first time. I knew you were a virgin because you never let any man get close to you but me. I don't think you're a virgin now and I don't give a damn, I even prefer it because now I don't have to hurt you and if some other man had managed to make you happy you wouldn't be here, would you? Wanting me.

I take a shuddering breath and read his words through again. And again. Laszlo fantasized in lurid detail about taking my virginity. How did we get it so wrong when we both wanted each other so much?

I turn off my phone and start to tune my cello, playing scales but barely knowing what I'm doing. When the time comes I file out onto the stage and sit with the orchestra, dimly aware of the rumble of the audience in the enormous concert hall as I continue to tune up under the lights. Finally Laszlo walks out onto the stage and the audience applauds. He bows to them and takes his place at the front of the orchestra. The baton is held in his fingers just so, and he gives the first downbeat. We play, all the instruments in harmony with each other. I wait for Laszlo to catch my eye and I mouth, slowly and carefully, *Please fuck me, maestro.*

He swallows and looks away, his eyes darting over the second violins. Then he comes back to me and pins me with such look of naked lust that it makes my knees clench tightly on my cello. He doesn't stop the precise movements of his hands but he holds my gaze for several bars, his gaze hard and unrelenting.

Of course no other man has managed to make me happy. How could they, when there's no other man for me. There's only Laszlo.

As I pack up my cello after the performance I marvel at how outwardly normal I am. I switch my phone on and find a text from Laszlo from just a few minutes ago.

My room at half past twelve

That's in an hour's time. My heart races as I type, *Yes, sir*

Yes what?

Yes…I'm not sure what

You know what. Call me daddy

I whimper and clutch my phone. Does he really want me to call him that? I think I called him daddy in the street earlier because that's what he is to me, my sweet, stern man I want to be so very good for.

Yes, daddy

There's a good girl

I feel my toes curl. I'm not even sure how I get back to the hotel as the next thing I know I'm walking through the lobby on the way to the elevator, pretending to listen to the others talk about that night's performance. I see Laszlo in his black tuxedo and bowtie just as the elevator doors close. Something dark and lustful flashes in his eyes when he meets my gaze and my stomach swoops in response.

I go back to my room and change into a t-shirt and jeans, and then pace up and down, thumbnail between my teeth. Twenty minutes until half past twelve. Ten minutes. Five. I remember what Hayley said, about me not really knowing what Laszlo's like, as a man.

I guess I'm about to find out.

I close my door behind me and walk quickly down the hallway. Despite my nerves, I want to laugh. Hayley knew exactly where Laszlo and I would end up.

Laszlo's in his shirtsleeves when he opens the door and he stands there for a moment, just taking me in. Like I'm something he's waited a long, long time for. His face is unguarded for a change and I see his desire for me. All of it, and it takes my breath away.

He takes my hand and pulls me into the room, and then his mouth descends on mine. It's a fierce, hungry kiss and he presses me up against the closed door, desperate for the taste of me. My hands rove over his back as I open my mouth to invite him in, my body knowing what to do even though a man has never kissed me like this. *More. Take me over. Overrun my senses until there's nothing but you.*

Laszlo breaks the kiss, still holding me close, his hot breath against my mouth. "I want you over my lap."

I whimper in his arms. "Are you going to spank me like before?"

He smooths his hands up beneath my t-shirt, large and warm and caressing, and squeezes my nipple through the lace of my bra. His soft touch belies the darkness in his eyes. "Better than before."

I'll let you do whatever you want, daddy. Desire and trepidation flicker through me. But I don't need to be afraid. This is Laszlo. He pulls my t-shirt up and over my head and for a moment he just looks at me, drinking in the sight of what he's never allowed himself. With a forefinger he traces my collarbone, my throat, and then down to the cleft between my breasts.

"Beautiful."

For a moment the darkness flickers and he just looks as if he can't believe this is real. I don't think I believe it either. I wait, breath held, for the moment to break like a bubble. But he goes on touching me with his large, warm hands, fingers tracing over the lace cup of my bra and circling my nipple. My flesh puckers under his touch and my breath comes back in a gasping rush. It's real. This is my Laszlo, touching me, at last.

I watch him unbutton my jeans and he slips a hand down to cup my sex with his fingers. A victorious smile curves his mouth as he feels my underwear. I'm soaking wet. I've been wet all night, since I got his email, my pulse pounding hard between my legs. I gripped my cello like a lover all through that performance, imagining it was him.

"Do you know how much daddy loves your little cotton briefs?" He rubs his fingers back and forth, stroking my clit through the slick fabric. "Such a sweet little girl, aren't you?"

I bite my lip and nod, knowing my sweetness is coating his fingers, knowing how much he loves it, reveling in how good this feels. He's standing so close that I can feel his thickening cock pressing against my thigh.

He goes on, his voice rich and indulgent. "A good, obedient girl who would never disobey daddy."

Daddy. There's something so arousing about hearing him call himself that. Oh, yes, I'm a good girl for him. I'll do anything for him as long as he goes on touching me like that. I need the release of him so badly. His strokes become firmer, right where it feels best, but I need more. I need him to pull my underwear aside and touch my bare pussy. I whimper and nod. "I'll always be good for you, daddy. Always."

Please, please let me come and show you how good I can be for you.

"Always good for me. Like when you tell jokes in the street like an unprofessional, bratty little protégé?"

My breath catches and I open my eyes. There's a hard, unforgiving expression on his face and he pinches my clit between his thumb and forefinger, not enough to hurt but just enough to make a very clear point. *You've been a bad girl.*

I squirm in his embrace but he's got me pinned against the door.

When he speaks his voice is as cold as flint, and ice water floods my veins. "Don't think I've forgotten that, little girl. Don't imagine that you can twist me round your finger with a few kisses and I'll let you get away with behavior like that. Have you forgotten who I am?"

In the excitement of having him at my mercy in the street I did forget. That he's Laszlo Valmary, a man no one dares to disobey. "I'm sorry, daddy," I manage in a whisper.

Laszlo pulls his hand from my underwear and lets go of me. The shock leaves me cold and trembling. Is this how he will punish me, by bringing me here and then turning me away?

"Please," I whisper brokenly.

"Please, what?" He folds his arms and his expression is black with reproach.

I take a shuddering breath. "Please let me make it up to you, daddy. I want to show you how sorry I am. I'm sorry, daddy." *I'm sorry, daddy. I'm sorry, daddy.* The words are a shattered mantra in my head. I want so badly to show him how sorry I am that it's an ache worse than the one between my legs. "Make me sorry, please. Just don't turn me away."

Laszlo traces the path of a tear that's slipped down my cheek, satisfaction gleaming in his eyes. "Don't cry, baby." But he's smiling, a victorious curve to his lips. He goes to sit down on the sofa and gazes up at me with hard, implacable eyes. "Take your clothes off and get over my knee."

It's not going to be like before, a spanking to relieve my stress. This is going to be a punishment. This is going to hurt.

He watches me wiggle out of my jeans. I hesitate a moment, and then slip off my bra as well, wondering what he sees when he looks at me. Does he like my breasts? Does it turn him on seeing me like this? I feel my cheeks burn as I reach for my underwear because even though I'm not a virgin I've never really been properly naked and scrutinized by a man before.

Laszlo stops me. "Leave those on and come here."

His voice and expression are still hard and menacing. I get over his knees wearing only my briefs and his large hands settle me down where he wants me, my stomach pressed against his thighs, my ass up in the air. All the other times he's spanked me he's been so careful about where he touches me, but now his fingers go straight to the slick, damp patch of underwear between my legs. He slips his fingers inside the fabric and rubs my pussy in circles with his fingers. His touch is confident, practiced, homing in right where it feels good, leaving me no opportunity to feel embarrassed because the blood is heating my skin for other reasons. I press my face into the sofa and moan as he rubs my clit in tight circles.

"There," he breathes. "Aren't you being such a good girl for daddy already?"

I moan into the cushion. I think I could come just from the caress of his voice. With his other hand he cups my breasts, squeezing and then gently twisting my nipples. A moment later his hands draw away and he fits the handkerchief between my teeth and ties it behind my head, and then reaches for a tie and binds my wrists together behind me. I feel that sensation I felt so powerfully in the street, that floaty headspace, steal over me again: of being at Laszlo's tender mercy. *Make me sorry, daddy. I deserve it.*

In one movement like the sweep of his arm as he conducts, Laszlo strips my underwear down to my knees and leaves them there. He spreads me open with his fingers and I feel him looking at my most intimate parts, his chest rising and falling against my hip. He leans forward and spits on me, and the warm liquid runs down between my ass cheeks and over my sensitized pussy. I groan against the gag. That's such a weird thing to do. His fingers slide through my slick folds and I wriggle in his lap, desperate for him to touch my clit again. He raises his hand and spanks me hard, a warning to keep still and I half-moan some muffled words. I don't even know what they are. *Yes, daddy* or *please more* or *touch me I'm dying*. But I hold still, trying my best to be patient. He circles closer to my clit, and I jump in his lap when he finally reaches it, rubbing the hard little nub with not quite enough pressure. With his other hand he slips a finger into my pussy, but not deep enough to bring me satisfaction. He teases me slowly, the movements of his hands increasing in intensity and then easing off again. He plays me like a musical instrument, perfectly in control.

One of his slick fingers traces higher, to the tight pucker of my ass and I feel my eyes go wide because no one's ever touched me there.

"Sweetheart. Daddy wants to put a finger in your ass."

I don't know what it feels like to have anything in your ass but it's supposed to feel good, doesn't it? It feels good to be stroked there. Good but strange. I nod, my face sweaty against the sofa cushion, wondering what sort of punishment he has in mind. He presses firmly with his wet finger and I feel my flesh give against his, and he slides in just a little bit and I stretch around him. *Oh, god that's weird.*

He hooks a finger into my gag and pulls it down. "Tell me how that feels."

I pant for a moment, thinking. Bizarrely good. I don't know if I want more or less. He presses deeper and I groan. *More. Definitely more.* "Strange, daddy."

"Strange how?"

His voice is hard and demanding but I still feel too shy to speak how I feel out loud. "Good strange."

He spreads me open and pushes his finger deeper, spitting again to ease the way. Then he slides a second finger into my ass, the one slick from my pussy, and my head rears up with a gasp. He fucks me with his fingers, working them deeper by slow increments, his other hand rubbing my clit, more intense now, no longer teasing. "How about that?"

I'm beyond words but manage something like *oh, god yes,* into the sofa cushion as I moan low and loud.

"Does it feel like you couldn't move if you tried, and you really don't want to? Like the only thing that exists for you in this moment is my two fingers deep inside you and the sound of my voice? That you're more vulnerable than you've ever been in your life?"

How does he know so perfectly how I'm feeling? I swallow and manage to pant, "Yes. Yes, all that."

"Good. Because I fucking crave that feeling from you like air." He take his hand from my clit and strokes my hair back from my face. "Just look at you. Stretched so tight around my fingers and unable to move. Say, *thank you, daddy*."

"Thank you, daddy."

"You're welcome, you little slut."

My mouth drops open in surprise and I look round at him.

He gazes back, unapologetic, rubbing firm and fast on my clit in a way I know is going to make me come if he keeps it up. "What? You are my little slut, aren't you? Asking me to fuck you on stage in front of thousands of people. Some of them saw you, you know, asking for this. I wish they could see you now, ass up with your underwear around your knees while I finger-fuck you right in the ass."

I've never heard him talk like this before. I didn't know he *could* talk like this, my kind, sweet, patient guardian.

"Beg me not to stop." When I take longer than a second to answer his hand comes down hard on my ass and pain explodes across my flesh. "*Do it.*"

I unstick my tongue from the roof of my mouth. "Please, please don't stop. I'm so close, I'm so close." I'm going to come any moment, hot and strong and tight around his fingers and I don't even understand how.

"You don't deserve to come, do you?"

"Please," I half-whimper, half-sob.

"But you still hope I'll be merciful. You want me to give into my panting, slutty girl who's barely even able to think right now. But listen to this. Really fucking listen." As his words get harder his touch on my clit grows more luxurious, drawing out and heightening the sensation. "My benevolence is given when *I* choose. I control when you get to come and when you don't. Even if I give you that satisfaction, this is never over. My control. My praise. My punishment. My comfort. I bestow them, and always on my terms, little girl." He drives his fingers deeper into my ass to illustrate his point.

This is how he wants me to feel. Completely vulnerable to him. At his mercy and on the precipice of something he can so easily withdraw.

"Do you understand now?" he growls.

I thought he was going to hurt me to show me he was in charge, but he doesn't need to do anything so crude. I'll be good for Laszlo out of fear, but I will walk to the ends of the earth over red hot coals and broken glass for his generosity.

I understand everything now. "Yes, daddy."

"Yes what?"

"Yes, sir."

"Yes *what?*"

But what else is there? Then I remember. "Yes, *maestro*."

"There," he says with a purr. "Good girl, Isabeau. All three. Daddy. Sir. *Maestro*. I rule you in all three parts of your life and don't you fucking forget it."

He turns his attention to his fingers and the sensation he's rubbing into my clit turns golden. Each circle of his fingers is accompanied by another thrust into my ass and he works me closer to the brink with slow deliberation.

"Your pussy is dripping for me you love this so much." His voice has that melted chocolate quality again, as if he's savoring every second of this.

I'm high on sensation and gratitude and I come like a wave crashing into shore, feeling myself clench rhythmically round his fingers as he thrusts short and fast into my ass, firm and unrelenting. I didn't even know I could clench there. He makes a sound deep in his chest as he feels it, a hard groan of satisfaction, as if he's enjoying this as much as I am.

I lay gasping like a fish in the aftermath, my heartbeat thundering in my ears, and I know that nothing is ever going to be the same again.

"Well, aren't you just fucking perfect? But I always knew you were, babygirl." Laszlo withdraws his fingers and wipes them clean on a t-shirt, and then pulls me up so I'm sitting astride his lap. His eyes run over my flushed face. "You're so fucking beautiful. Did you like that, sweet girl?"

But I can't say anything. I can only stare at him and feel the after-effects of the things he's said to me churning through my body. He unties me and I press my hands against his chest. Like it? I feel like he burned right through my soul and woke up parts of me that I never knew were slumbering.

I swallow and manage in a whisper, "I understand now." He's everywhere, thrumming through my consciousness, but he doesn't make me feel imprisoned or afraid. I feel alive and hopeful. Strong.

Laszlo's eyes run over my face. "I know you do, babygirl. Something in me matches something in you. When I hold you in my arms I feel everything that you are, and this is how I cherish you. You make me feel free."

"Free?"

"Yes. Free." He's still clothed and I explore his body with my fingers, rubbing my hands up his chest, his strong shoulders. It's heady, being allowed to touch Laszlo, and I want my fill of him.

He looks at me with his clear hazel eyes. "Being a conductor is all about power and command and I have to rein myself in all the time from going on a massive power trip. I don't like to rein myself in with you. I want to push you down onto your knees before me. I want to say the filthiest things to you. Tell you that you're my little slut.

Make you be my little slut. Make you feel more vulnerable than you've ever been in your life. Strip you bare until there's nothing left for you but me and the power I have over you. But all that can be very overwhelming and you may not like it. I wanted to give you a taste so you know how it feels. I will rein myself in as much as you need me to because as much as I like this, I like you much, much more."

I squeeze my knees around him even tighter, rocking against him and clasping my arms around his neck. I've seen what Laszlo's capable of when he's working. He can make a hundred people produce the exact sound that he's looking for and they enjoy doing it for him. He exerts total control but in such a way that makes people thankful.

I want to be pushed down by him. Be overwhelmed by him. And I will say thank you every time. "Please don't rein yourself in, daddy. I want you like this. I want all of you."

But he shakes his head. "Don't answer now. Later, when you're not so defenseless. Just listen to me and remember what I'm saying. The way I want to talk to you is crass and unpleasant. My sweet fucking Isabeau. Daddy's little slut." He takes hold of both my nipples and begins to twist them, firmly but slowly, his voice a low, harsh growl. I whimper, my gaze locked on his. "I want to drive you deep into subspace and keep you there while I fuck you, hurt you, choke you, make you come again and again and then bring you back out again and see you smiling and happy, holding onto me so tightly like you can't ever let go. It's a difficult and challenging thing for me to do to you but that's why I like it. I *like* difficult. I want that if you want it, too. If you trust me to do that to you, over and over, and keep you safe. I wouldn't do it if I didn't think I could keep you one hundred per cent safe because it can go very, very wrong. I didn't mean to put you into that space in the street and I will be much more careful now that I know I can. I don't want to make you feel vulnerable where you don't feel safe. It's something just for us, baby. Just you and me."

I might be defenseless right now, but even through my orgasm haze I know one thing for certain. "I want that, too, daddy. I've only ever wanted you and me."

Laszlo looks even more vulnerable than I feel all of a sudden. As if everything he's ever tried to hide from me has been stripped away. "It's always been you and me, babygirl, one way or another. Even when we were apart my heart has always been with you."

I close my eyes and press my forehead against his, tears shimmering in my eyes. I feel like my heart will burst from all this happiness. I want to go back in time to the girl crying her heart out in Hayley's flat and tell her it will be all right in the end. That though the pain is terrible it will be worth it.

"Does what we do make you feel different, too?" I whisper against his mouth. "Is there dom space?"

Slowly, he nods. "I thought I was used to it, but..." His arms come around me tightly and he breathes hard. "I never want to lose you again, Isabeau. No matter what we become to each other. It will kill me if I lose you."

I press my lips against his mouth. He might be satisfied with friendship but I can't be. I need this. I need Laszlo. "I'm yours. I only want to be your Isabeau, your slutty little girl and all the other tender, filthy things you want to call me."

"Shh, baby. Not now." There's delight burning brightly in his eyes, even though he tries to hide it from me.

I put my head down on his shoulder and close my eyes, feeling my body rise and fall on his chest as he breathes. My mind drifts in a warm, gentle place. When I feel him start to hum I smile, because I know it means he's happy.

His fingers trail through my hair. "Who was he?"

I open my eyes and look up. "Who was what?"

"The man you went to bed with."

I try to detect jealousy in his voice but he just sounds curious. "How do you know it was just one?"

"The way you touch me. It hasn't really changed since that night you were eighteen."

I make a face, embarrassed. "Am I rubbish?"

"No. You're incredibly sweet and tentative. Incredibly horny, too. It's wonderful."

I giggle, scratching his nails through his beard, because I am so very needy for him. "He was just someone in my second year. I regret it."

Laszlo looks pained, as if he hates the idea of me regretting anything, and I go on quickly, "It was impersonal and unpleasant and I did it for all the wrong reasons. I was lonely. I missed you."

He presses his forehead against mine and cups the back of my neck, a rueful twist to his lips. "I'm sorry, baby. For all those long years apart."

But we needed this time apart, to figure out what we truly wanted. I tilt my head and kiss him, still unable to believe I can do this whenever I want. That it won't make him angry. I reach down and stroke my fingers along the shaft of his erection through his trousers, hard and hot and thick. I'm fascinated by him. He watches the path of my fingers, his breath hitching.

I hesitate, and then look up at him and whisper, "I want to rub myself against you like I did that night. You felt so good, daddy. Can I, please?"

Chapter Twenty

Laszlo

Now

"Oh, Christ. Yes baby," I groan. My hands slide around her hips and I pull her sex tightly against me. She wraps her arms around my neck and begins to rub back and forth, back and forth, and I drink in the sight of her naked body as she moves against me. The gentle curve of her waist. The pale buds of her nipples. The redness of her bitten lower lip. She's so beautiful, but it's not that which is entrancing me.

It's that she's mine.

She wants me how I want her. I could feel it in the way her body responded to my voice, could hear it in her plaintive, *Yes daddies* she cried as I finger-fucked her ass. My beautiful Isabeau wants to submit to me, please me, be good for me. When I kiss her deeply she sucks the tip of my tongue, making me groan. Her fingers stroke through my beard and I remember how good this felt the first time. How good it feels to give into it completely now. To slide my fingers around the curve of her ass and squeeze tightly. Possessively. *Mine.* I've waited so fucking long for this.

"Do you like that, daddy?" she pants against my mouth, a pink blush over her cheeks. She's still shy and uncertain and oh so fucking sweet, and I nod and let out a moan as she rubs her bare slit along the length of my cock. I can admit it now. Yes, I like that. It's more than good. It's magical, watching her show me how turned on she is.

"Did you like it that night, daddy?"

"So fucking much. You have no idea how many times I thought about it since, sweet girl." The wet heat of her pussy is making me ache with the need to be inside her but I just watch her, enraptured. Her breath is hot against my mouth and there's a look of sweet supplication in her eyes that I remember so well. I have a strong urge to push her down on the couch, to get my mouth on her, to make her come myself, to take control, but I make myself keep still. We've both waited three years for the culmination of this moment.

The movements of her hips become small and rapid and the pressure of her sex against my cock is driving me crazy.

Her fingers clench my shoulders, her cries coming short and fast. *Come for me sweet girl*, I urge silently, drinking in the needful look in her eyes. *Show me what I've dreamt of so many times.*

Isabeau's body flexes against me and her head tips back as she comes. She's like a swan, her neck elongated as she flies high.

"Good girl," I say roughly, feeling her sex pulse against me through my trousers. Her pussy is so strong and responsive and the ache to bury myself inside her surges afresh.

When Isabeau comes back to me she presses panting kisses to my mouth. "I wanted to do that for so long. I love rubbing against you and…and showing you and…" She looks down into my lap and strokes her fingers along the hard rod of my cock. Then she looks up at me, uncertain. "Can I touch you?"

I nod, and watch, barely breathing, as she undoes my belt and zipper and tugs my length free. She strokes my cock gently with her fingers.

"How do I feel, baby?"

She blushes and lowers her eyes, her lips curving into a smile. "You feel…hot and stiff. Soft, too. I like the way your breath catches as I touch you." She trails her fingers down my length, the fingers I've seen so often playing her cello. "I like the veins," she whispers, curling her hand around me and squeezing. "I like how thick you are."

Isabeau strokes me up and down and it's sweet torture, the way she's touching me.

"Daddy, I want you properly."

If it hadn't all gone to hell that night maybe this is how it would have played out. Tight, delicious lovemaking with Isabeau on the couch. But I would have felt terrible in the morning, knowing that she hadn't been ready for this.

She's ready for it now.

Isabeau unbuttons my shirt and I watch her, letting her lead, wanting her to feel safe, unpressured, trying to hide how urgently I want her. I can feel her growing confidence in the way she's touching me, how she pushes my shirt back from my shoulders. I might like to be in charge but sometimes it's even better to sit back and let someone show you what they need. I'm learning Isabeau inside and out.

I reach down without moving her off me and fumble inside my cabin bag for a condom, and she helps me roll it on. When she squeezes her fingers around me I groan, needing more of that tightness. I glance at the bed and then back at her, but she shakes her head.

"Here. I want it to be here." She wants to know what it would have been like with me that night. I'm not her first, but I'm her first who counts.

I put one hand on her hip and wrap the other around the base of my cock, keeping myself steady as she raises herself up on her knees and then slides against my cock. She fumbles back and forth a little, thoroughly wetting the head of my cock. I feel myself slide into place against her and pull her down. She gives a few inches and cries out, her eyes going wide. I wait, giving her time to adjust, to work herself back and forth on me. She feels like fucking heaven I don't want to wait but I have to, and I make my hand unclench on her hip.

She rests her elbows on my shoulders and bears down, whimpering, trying to force herself around me.

"Easy. Take your time, baby." Isabeau works me deeper into her tight, wet heat with her tentative movements. My eyes run over her naked body, her full breasts with their pink nipples, the curve of her hips. I let go of my cock and wrap my hand around her throat, holding lightly but firmly, feeling her pulse thrum beneath my fingers. I grit my teeth, making myself hold still when all I want to do is push her onto her back and thrust into her hard, over and over.

She seems to notice my struggle and puts a hand over mine, the one holding her throat, and her eyes are glittering. "Daddy? Make me feel you. I want to feel you."

Make me feel you. Oh, yes, I can do that for her. I hold tight to her waist and pull her down roughly on my cock at the same time I thrust my hips up, penetrating her deep and fast. She cries out, her tight flesh yielding to mine. I don't give her any time to recover. I pull her up and then thrust again, even deeper this time, and then again, watching her with a narrow, heated gaze. Her pussy is clamped around me.

But it's not enough. I need more.

I turn her and push her against the arm of the sofa and get out from beneath her. She braces her hands while I take hold of her hips from behind and when I penetrate her she cries out. I pound her hard and she presses back, needing every inch of me. She feels like heaven and I'm so greedy for her. To hear each and every one of her whimpering cries. To keep going until I burst.

But I stop and pull out, going down on my knees so I can lick her, lovingly, thoroughly, working her clit with my tongue. Isabeau's breath comes faster and faster and I know she's almost at her peak. Almost. I pull away and she cries out in dismay, but then I take my cock into my hand and find her tight sheath and I'm thrusting into her again. I wrap her hair around my hand, to keep her still, keep her aware of me, and so I can enjoy the lovely silken feel of her vulnerability. I want her to come like this but I don't know if she can, if it's too soon, if it's enough for her, and I'm about to tell her to rub her pretty little clit for me when she gives out a long, low moan and I feel her clench around me.

"Fuck, babygirl." She feels so good rippling along my length that I come a moment later, pressing deeper and holding tight to her hair and waist, feeling myself spill into her, pulsing slowly as we breathe hard.

I gather her up into my arms, holding her tightly. She gives a soft cry and turns to face me, burrowing against my body. I know she feels it too. This need we have for each other, this connection that has withstood so much and grown into something new and wonderful.

I half-carry, half-walk her over to the bed and after I get rid of the condom we lay down together, naked bodies pressed close. Isabeau looks up at me, her fingers trailing through my chest hair. I smile and kiss her softly, feeling so at peace. It's a strange thing when you're a man who's used to driving your own destiny to open your eyes and see the thing you were too afraid to hope for in your arms.

"I'm so grateful to you, Isabeau. For this, and all the years with you. I always got to smile when I was with you."

Her fingers move up to my brow, smoothing the frown lines there. "You know, for years and years I thought you were the same with everyone as you were with me. I thought everyone knew you as sweet, indulgent, smiling Laszlo."

I pull her closer, the only person I've ever wanted to be sweet with. To indulge. "No, baby. Only with you."

I remember her so clearly as a child with a pink lunchbox. Half a cheese sandwich, half a marmite sandwich. A bunch of grapes. I used to like making her lunch and holding her hand as we crossed the street. It felt so wonderfully grounding to have her to look out for. It was a simple time, and so very happy.

I want that feeling again. To be able to look out for her and keep her safe.

"Daddy," she says tentatively. "Will you tell me about that last year that I lived with you? About why you weren't the same Laszlo with me anymore?"

I don't want to tell her, because I'm not proud of any of it. But I have to. "I could feel you slipping away from me and I hated that, but at the same time I knew I had to let you go. That it wasn't right, the way I felt about you. How possessive I felt, and how viciously pleased I was that you didn't want to date anyone. I'd had you to myself since you were eight but I was going to have to watch someone else take you from me."

She presses her soft, plush lips against my mouth. "No one was ever going to take me from you, Laszlo."

I kiss her fiercely and roll her beneath me. The urge to declare that no one ever will is so strong but I make myself stay silent. I'm conscious of not saying too much. Being too much. I don't want to push her or smother her when I've only just encircled her in my arms. I press my forehead against hers and whisper, "I knew I was screwed when we played that piece."

"*Vocalise*," she guesses.

I nod. "You were so beautiful when you came to me with that piece. A woman just about grown up, and yet you weren't. I couldn't tell you how I felt. I couldn't tell anyone."

Isabeau looks pained and starts to speak, but I put a finger over her lips. "I'm not asking for sympathy. It was my responsibility to deal with. I'm glad you didn't know how I felt at the time, though I'm sorry I was cold to you and it upset you. It wasn't on purpose, sweetheart."

She nods sadly, remembering. "You started to pull away from me that year. You stopped saying good girl. Giving me hugs just because. I wondered if it was because I was going to leave and you didn't think there wasn't any point to us being close anymore."

I hold her close, as greedy for her as a parched man in the desert is for a drop of water. "No. It was because I liked doing those things too much."

"You kept playing *Vocalise* with me," she points out.

I remember all those hours in the music room together. The turmoil in my heart. The longing as I watched her play.

"I made myself give up a lot of things, sweetheart, but I couldn't give up that."

Her hands move over my throat, my collarbone, my shoulders. I love her touching me, her fingers moving lightly, exploring my body. Her hands are fine and pretty against my thicker bones and muscles. As I watch her those instincts to protect and dominate surge up. Such a pretty little thing she is. How I love to feel her fluttering like a bird in my merciless grip.

"Did you ever date, Laszlo? While I was living with you?"

It takes me a moment to drag my mind out of the dark place it's delved into and I have to repeat her question in my mind. "Date. Not exactly. I had, ah, friends."

She smiles. "You mean those women who used to come round late at night and you'd sneak them up to your bedroom?"

I feel my face transform in horror. Isabeau knew? But I was always so careful to get those women into the house quietly and to keep them quiet once they were there. The gags I like to use served two purposes back then. I didn't want Isabeau hearing anything and it just felt unseemly for a child to know I had casual female company in my bedroom every other week, and rarely the same woman for longer than a few months. "God, you didn't hear—"

"No, no," she assures me quickly. "Just a woman's voice sometimes. Some laughing. There was one who sounded like a goose."

I grin. "Oh, her. Do you know she was one of the most talented sopranos I'd ever met? And with a laugh like that."

Isabeau giggles in my arms. "But why didn't you date? Properly I mean. You...you seem to like company."

I enjoy "company", but dating, there's a difference. When Isabeau was younger I didn't have the time—or rather, the time I wanted to invest was in Isabeau. Her schooling, her tutors, playing music with her. Later, when she was more independent, I did have the time, but I kept myself busy with the youth orchestra and my work. When Isabeau wanted to spend her free nights with me it was easy to tell myself she needed me. "I don't know," I hedge. "I didn't find anyone I wanted to date."

But she's too perceptive for that. "It was because of me, wasn't it?"

I clear my throat. "In a way. I had you, I had music, I had my orchestra. I didn't want anything else. I was happy."

Isabeau sits up, her expression bright and urgent. "All that you're saying, it was the same for me. I only wanted to be with you. I was happiest when I was with you. I don't want you to have any regrets, Laszlo. Promise me."

In this moment with my arms around her my happiness is complete. My beautiful girl, the only one I will ever want. But I'm silent for a moment, thinking. "I have one regret."

She looks distressed by my confession.

"I wish I could have spared you your pain," I tell her. "I regret making you feel like you'd done something shameful by kissing me. I know I did and I'm deeply sorry for that, sweet girl."

Isabeau threads her fingers through my hair. "I know you are. I'm sorry, too. For running away."

"But you came back." I'll never forget the sight of her in the Mayhew, a vision with auburn hair, clutching the cello that I'd watched her grow into.

Isabeau smiles. "I came back." She props her chin on my chest, thinking. "Laszlo? What are we going to tell people once they start finding out about us?"

I feel my face harden and in that moment I hate every person in the world who isn't Isabeau. Why can't they just leave us alone? I can feel them pushing at the boundaries of our happiness, eager to spoil it.

She strokes my bristly cheek thoughtfully. "People might think terrible things about you. I hate the thought that this could damage your career."

It's sweet of her to be concerned for me but I'm more worried about her. It's not new to me, worrying about

Isabeau. The worry has become an old friend nestled deep in my heart, right next to my love for her. As long as she's not hurt by any of this I don't give a damn what people say about me.

But she could be hurt. She could be hurt badly.

The year she turned seventeen I started having terrible dreams, about Isabeau turning to me with loathing in her eyes and telling me she wished she'd never met me. I seemed to have the dreams every other month and they became more frequent as her eighteenth birthday approached. I feel that witching hour dread fill my heart now, because my feelings for her could still hurt her.

I'm silent for a long time, thinking about her questions, not wanting to pierce the happiness of this moment but also needing to prepare her for the worst.

"Isabeau. It's not a case that people might think bad things about me, or us. Some people will. I want you to be prepared for that. That there might be a cost for us, being together."

Chapter Twenty-One

Isabeau
Now

I stay all night in his bed, sleeping in Laszlo's arms. I wake several times and see him in the dim light, his handsome face softened by sleep and the bristles on his chin making him look like a rough angel. I close my eyes with a smile on my face and fall back asleep.

At ten minutes to six he kisses me awake so I can go back to my own room before too many people start to stir. We agreed that while we're finishing the tour we should try and keep our relationship quiet. But I can't go right away, not when he's right there and we're both naked. I draw his hands up to my breasts and his gentle, chaste kisses swiftly become deep and heated. I feel his hard length against my thigh and I pull him closer, opening my legs beneath him. I gaze up at him, scratching my nails through his beard, unafraid. Happier than I think I've ever been. He fumbles for a condom and then eases himself into me, and it's even more delicious this morning, feeling his weight upon me and the incredible heat from his body. His movements are languid, one large hand on my inner thigh, pressing me open. We watch each other as we make love, our mouths very close together, panting breaths mingling, and as I come he groans *good girl* in my ear. He pounds me hard, watching his thick cock sliding in and out of me and then looking up into my eyes. His brows draw together as he comes, his eyes tightly closed and my nails buried in his back.

I press my face against his chest, breathing him in. I don't want to go but I know I have to, and I finally manage to extricate myself from his arms and the tangled bedsheets. Before I open the door Laszlo catches me in his arms and kisses me. "Think about what we talked about last night. Take your time. There's all the time in the world to decide what you want, sweetheart."

I nuzzle his beard with the tip of my nose. "Yes, daddy. What about you, though, and what you want?"

He smiles down at me. "Just you, baby. That's all I want. And whatever you give me will make me a happy man."

Everything doesn't encompass what I want to give Laszlo. I wish there was more than everything.

There are just a few staff in the corridors as I make my way back to my own room. I let myself in, my head full of memories of last night. I remember how different it was the first time we kissed, the fleeing and the tears. The cold and lonely days that followed. The email from the agent asking me to audition...

My back against my door, I frown. I haven't thought about that in years: the day after the concert an agent who'd been at the showcase emailed me about representation. Amid all the heartache and confusion I put off replying and put it off some more, until I just never replied.

I make a pot of coffee in my room and boot my laptop up, and in the morning light from my open window I find the agent's email and read it again.

Dear Ms. Laurent,

I want to congratulate you and the rest of the Royal London Symphony Youth Orchestra on a wonderful performance last night. I was particularly captured by your playing of The Swan.

I represent United Kingdom-based soloists and work comprehensively with musical directors across Europe and beyond. If you are considering representation at this time I would love to hear your audition tape...

I stop reading and sit back and look out across Bangkok. It's been three years since this woman—Paloma Sanchez, her name is—sent me this email. She's long given up on me and probably even forgotten who I am.

I consider again what I want from my career. If this email arrived in my inbox today, what would be my first impulse? Well, to panic, because I've never recorded an audition tape. But putting that aside, would I be excited to be offered the possibility of representation as a soloist?

Yes.

My heart beats a little faster and I reach for my phone to text Laszlo. Then I stop myself. I need to think first, about a lot of things, and the space he's given me within his embrace is as special as his embrace itself. I can feel the ghost of his body against mine and it makes me braver. I want to figure this out on my own, but knowing Laszlo's there if I need him is everything. I glance toward my cello standing expectantly next to my bed. I have all day before I need to be at the concert hall for tonight's performance. I need to think and I'm going to do it with my cello in my hands.

I have a quick shower and put on fresh clothes and then take out my cello and start to play. But I stop almost immediately, wincing. The notes sound terrible in this tiny, carpeted space. I pick up my instrument and head down to the lobby where I speak to the concierge at the front desk.

He's helpful and understanding and points me to the mezzanine level. I go up and find a large, wooden floored conference hall standing empty and silent. There's a stage at the far end and I take a folding chair and my cello and walk up the stairs.

The acoustics aren't wonderful but I have space and peace. I play from memory, and I really listen to myself. I play the way *I* want to play, not in any the styles I've been taught or the way that people expect. I play *The Swan*, and I pour all my grief over my mother and father into the notes, but also all the love I have in my heart. There's so much love. I feel it radiating through me as the strings tremble beneath my bow. I play Bach, Elgar and Brahms. I play all my favorite pieces like I used to do, experimenting with the sounds, inflecting them with my emotions.

And as I play I think. This is really why I went to the Mayhew five weeks ago, to face the three most difficult things in my life: losing Laszlo, being stuck with my music, and my grief over what might have been with my parents. They're all connected, and if I want something real with Laszlo that means being real myself and facing the things I've done, stretching back to that day thirteen years ago.

As the music swells around me I let everything rise up. I remember the first time I saw Laszlo, the kindness on his face as he hunkered down before me and showed me that newspaper article. *That's me, Isabeau. I have an orchestra filled with musicians like you. Only the very best people, and I think one day you might be one of those people.* I looked at the page and I looked at him for, what? Three seconds? I wanted what he was offering so much. A strained note enters my playing. I left my home, my life and my father, for a complete stranger and the jewel-box offer of a life of music. I was a child, and I don't think I knew what *forever* meant, or what my father must have felt losing me. But I feel it now, the pain I must have inflicted.

I don't know if a child can be held responsible for making thoughtless decisions. I don't know if I can—or should—regret what I did.

Regret what Laszlo did.

I don't want you to have any regrets, Laszlo. Promise me.

When I finish I put my bow aside and open my eyes, breathing hard through my nose, in and out, defiant tears in my eyes. This is what I want people to hear when I play. I don't know if it's good enough and I don't know if it's what people will want. But it's all I have. People might think I'm strange or uninteresting or just plain wrong. I might make people angry with what I do. It's scary, the thought that *everything I have* might still not be enough. But what if just one person wants to hear it? Really *needs* to hear it? That will be enough. I may not become the great soloist that I dreamt of but I won't exhaust myself trying to be something I'm not, only to be left in the end with the ashes of my misguided efforts.

I get up and start to put my cello back in its case. It has to be *everything* from now on, or nothing. I won't hold back just a little in case I fail. No more holding back. I look down at my cello laying so snug in the black velvet lining. My playing might be nothing to strangers' ears, but it's exactly what I want.

And that means it's not nothing. It's everything.

Back in my room I write an email to Ms. Sanchez, apologizing for never replying to hers and telling her that I'm looking for representation if she's still interested in me. I feel a huge sense of relief once I've sent it off.

But my mind seems determined to dwell in the past today and my thoughts turn again to my father. Is there anything left for us to rebuild from, or is he too sick and addicted?

He never even tried to get better, I think defiantly. *He never reached out to me. He didn't want me. He was probably relieved when Laszlo took me away.*

And, I remember, anger racing through me, I tried, once. So if my father and I don't have a relationship now, it's not my fault.

Chapter Twenty-Two

Isabeau
Then

The house looks strange after all these years, as though while I wasn't here it gave up. I almost turn around and leave because if this is what the house looks like what sort of state will my father be in?

But I keep walking right up to the peeling front door and I knock. I at least need to try. I made excuses all throughout my childhood and high school years for not seeing my father. But I'm not a child anymore. I'm nineteen and it's time I started acting like an adult, and looking difficult things squarely in the face. If I was writing an essay about my journey through my second year of university I would call it, *Losing My Virginity and Other Crappy Things*.

There's no answer so I knock again, louder this time. I hear a sound through the door like a snort or a snarl. It's hard to tell with the road noise behind me.

"Dad?" I hammer on the door then stop and listen. Nothing. Trying the door I find it's unlocked and I go in. A familiar stale aroma engulfs me, but everything looks different. Worn. Deflated. The hallway has a depression in the middle and the skirting boards are scarred with scrapes. At the other end of the hall I can see the kitchen. The sink is filled with dirty dishes and there are takeout containers open on the table. A fly buzzes indolently around the room.

I call out again and then head into the living because that's where he slept. The mattress is on the floor with its tangle of sheets. Discarded clothes are draped over the furniture. And dad's there, asleep on the bed. Or passed out, I can't tell which. There are needles and a battered, scorched spoon on the carpet, and my heart sinks.

"Dad," I call, going over to him. "Dad, it's me. Isabeau."

He awakens with a snort, his eyes startlingly green. It's the heroin. It turns your pupils to pinpricks.

Dad looks around the room and then his gaze falls on me.

"Issy?" He sits up and fumbles for a packet of cigarettes and lights one. There's an overflowing ashtray on the carpet and I nudge it closer with my foot. Then I just stand there, my hands deep in my coat pockets, watching as he smokes.

"Look at you. All grown up." But he doesn't say this like it's a good thing. "Never bothered to come till now, did you, to see your old dad."

The smoke coils up toward the ceiling. Outside a truck grinds past. "I was afraid."

"Of what?"

It might sound harsh but it's the only thing I can say. "You."

He takes a long, deep drag of his cigarette and exhales slowly. "Bullshit. Ashamed, more like." Angrily he stubs the cigarette out. "You've done your duty and seen me and now you can just piss off. Go on, get out."

I don't even know what I want. I feel guilty about leaving him on his own all these years. I feel guilty about what I said to Laszlo. *Do you like that, daddy?* I flinch and look down. What a gross thing to have said. No wonder Laszlo was angry with me. No wonder he's never called me.

"I thought we could talk," I venture. Isn't he a tiny bit curious about what I've been doing all these years?

Dad lights another cigarette, not looking at me. "About what? How I get my hits?"

"About Mum. About what she meant to both of us. About how you're still my father, even though..." *Even though I never looked back and you never tried.*

That makes me the angriest. He's addicted and in pain, but he never tried, ever, to get better, so that we could have some sort of relationship.

"He told you to come see me, didn't he?" Dad's voice is hard and bitter. I suppose he hates Laszlo, the man who took me away. The man who never stops trying.

Until now. The pain is as fresh as it was on my eighteenth birthday.

Laszlo wanted me to see my father when it would still have meant something. Now it's too late. Guilt and shame aren't a foundation for anything and the absolution I seek isn't here. It isn't anywhere. I just have to live with the things I've done.

I take a deep, shuddering breath, and leave without another word.

Chapter Twenty-Three

Laszlo
Now

"You're just so cheerful lately, Laszlo. It's weird. I don't like it."

Marcus hands me a tumbler of whisky. We're in the hotel bar and it's gone midnight, but we performed Stravinsky tonight and this particular composer doesn't lend himself to a relaxed after-show feeling.

I give him a dry smile. "Sorry. Shall I try to be grumpier?" It's true, I am happy; happier than I think I've ever been. How could I not be? Triumph burns brightly in my chest and I gaze around at the people dotted here and there. Everyone in the world is all right by me tonight.

Marcus examines me, eyebrows raised. "What's caused this change in our famously deadpan conductor? Or rather, who?"

I take a sip of my whisky and shake my head innocently. "Must be the change of scenery. London was getting to me, I suppose."

He gives me a knowing nod. "Ah, of course."

I don't like people prying into my business and Marcus should know that by now. But it seems he can't help himself because he says, in the same innocent tone, "Isabeau Laurent is a very pretty young woman."

I set my glass down hard on the bar. "How the fuck did you find out?"

Marcus gives me a withering look. "Laszlo, you idiot. You were kissing her in the street."

My heart sinks. Of course, in the market on Khaosan Road. I thought everyone was ahead of us but it seems I was wrong. I don't even remember who kissed whom first. I just remember how perfect it felt, and now our tentative relationship has been thrust out into the open for people to titter about. I pass a hand over my face and sigh. "How many people know?"

"Oh, everyone," Marcus says cheerfully. "You know orchestras."

My heart sinks. I do know. Gossip spreads through an orchestra faster than a replicating virus. I want to swear but I clench my jaw on my angry words and knock back the rest of my whisky. The bartender notices and comes over to pour me another measure. I bloody need it.

"You needn't be angry or worried," Marcus says, serious now. "From what I understand people think it's either the juiciest piece of gossip they've ever heard or the most romantic thing that can happen in an orchestra."

I swallow more whisky and glare at him.

Marcus nods. "All right, it's a shitty way for it to come out. But no harm done, and people respect you, Laszlo. You're a fair man. And they like Isabeau."

I tilt my glass, looking into the amber liquid. "I'm a lot older than she is, and there's her…past. Our past."

Marcus shakes his head. "That's your business, old man. If it doesn't bother you and Isabeau then that's all that matters."

It's good of him to say so but that's not how the world works. If our jobs weren't in the public eye things would be different, but I meant it when I told Isabeau there could be a cost that goes beyond being gossiped about. It's easier for me as my career is solid and I'm a man with a reputation for being intimidating. Isabeau's just starting out and people can be cruel to women who draw attention to themselves through scandal. The fact that she's so much younger than me and used to be my ward could disgust people. Their disgust is out of my control and I hate it. I don't want Isabeau or her career—which hasn't even begun yet—to be tarnished with this.

After she left my room this morning, cheeks flushed with sex and emotion, I fantasized about getting off that plane with her at Heathrow in a few days' time and taking her straight home in a cab. To our home. Where I need her. I take another swallow of whisky and try to temper my possessiveness. I have to think about what's best for Isabeau, not what I want.

"What about that viola player?" I ask, thinking in terms of damage control over the next few days. "She doesn't like Isabeau and I want to know if we're going to have a problem with her. The tour's nearly over but as you said the gossip's out."

He raises his eyebrows. "How do you know about that?"

"I caught Isabeau telling viola jokes."

Marcus grins. "Which ones? Wait, I know a good one. 'What's the difference between a viola player and a vacuum cleaner?'"

"You have to plug a vacuum cleaner in before it can suck," I finish impatiently. "Yes, I know all the viola jokes."

He snorts with laughter, but when he catches my eye he finishes seriously, "If Isabeau was telling jokes on stage or during rehearsal I can have a word with her about being more professional."

"I already have. That's what I was doing on Khaosan Road, telling her off about it."

Marcus stares at me. "What, when you were kissing her? Bloody hell, she's got you twisted around her little finger already."

Despite myself, I smile broadly. I am thoroughly twisted around Isabeau's little finger. I've never been burdened with a soft heart but it's a delightful affliction to have. It's wonderful being stern with Isabeau but it's even better telling her what a sweet little girl she is for daddy. And she is. Fuck me, she is.

Marcus' eyes widen. "You don't even mind."

I don't, but I realize we're getting distracted. "I'm serious, Marcus. Are we going to have a problem in the orchestra? Not everyone is going to take this merely as good gossip."

He muses on this for a moment, tilting his glass back and forth. "I shouldn't say so. Miss Laurent isn't staying beyond the tour, is she?" I hesitate, and Marcus' eyes spark with interest. "Oh?"

"It's complicated. I don't know. I just…" I want her to have the career she deserves. If the worst happens and she can't find work then she'll have a place in my orchestra until the scandal passes. And it will pass. People have short memories these days.

"You just like her very much," he finishes.

I can feel myself being pulled in so many directions, by my desire for Isabeau, by my need to see her achieve all the things she wants. I wish I could tell if I'm doing everything I can for her, unselfishly and objectively. "She's a wonderful cello player," I hedge.

Marcus gives me a long look. "Come on, Laszlo, she's more than that to you. It's not just the kissing in the street. I saw the way you two were looking at each other in the Mayhew the day she turned up out of the blue. As if the last time you saw each other you two had a quarrel." He hesitates, and then adds, "A lovers' quarrel."

He must suspect how old she was the last time I saw her. I can't bear the thought of people whispering dirty things about her, that I touched her while she was underage. "I never—"

He cuts across me. "I know you'd never. That's why you fought, isn't it?"

I scrub my hands over my face. I wasn't ready to talk about this with anyone but it seems like I have no choice.

"Yes. She caught me by surprise on her eighteenth birthday and I panicked."

He nods, understanding. "And now?"

I take a sip of whisky, giving myself time to think. "I don't care what people think about me but I worry what people will say about her. And I think it would hurt her if people are horrible about me."

Marcus thinks for a long time, and then he claps me on the shoulder. "It'll be all right, old man. You'll see."

I wish I could share his optimism but I have a terrible feeling in my belly that everything is about to go wrong. I'm so used to being in control of everything in my life and it's more important than ever now that I have Isabeau back. But I can't control this.

In the morning there's a knock at my door and when I open it I see it's Isabeau, smiling up at me. I feel my own smile break over my face just looking at her and I gather her into my arms, closing the door behind her. "Good morning, baby. Sleep well?"

She rises up on her tiptoes and kisses me, the vanilla scent of her shampoo filling the air. Just having her in my arms is enough to drive away all my gloomy thoughts from the night before.

"Very well, daddy. I'm better than I have been in a long time, actually."

I smile again, hearing her call me daddy. I've got a sweet tooth for Isabeau. I stroke the backs of my fingers over her cheek. "You are, kitten?"

She tells me about practicing her cello in the conference room and how she thinks she's uncovered her musical voice, the quality in her playing that will make people want to go to see her rather than any other soloist. All I've wanted since the first day I met her is for Isabeau to be happy and looking at her now I can see she is. Sincerely happy. Only she can play music in her unique, beautiful way. I've heard it for the longest time. I can't wait for other people to hear her, too.

"And as soon as we go back to London I'm going to see my father," she says.

Her words catch me by surprise. It's been nagging at me these past few weeks, the things she doesn't know, and I've wondered if I've been right to keep them secret. Maybe I won't have to break my promise to Isabeau's father after all. Piers Laurent and I have both wanted to protect her but she's not a child anymore, and surely the danger of false hopes are long gone. I could tell her myself but I gave my word, and I'm a man of my word. It should come from Laurent.

"Sweetheart, that's wonderful," I say. And I mean it.

"But I have a confession to make," she says, her happiness dimming. "I did something foolish. Bad for my career."

I study her face and she looks so afraid, as if I'm going to tell her off. "Tell me, baby. It's all right."

"An agent emailed me after the Summer Showcase, the day after my eighteenth birthday. She was at the performance and she wanted to offer me representation but in the... Well, I never replied."

I understand. She was in too much pain to think about auditions and agents.

"I emailed her back yesterday apologizing and asking her if she was still interested in me and she's replied. She wants to see me when I'm back in London but she also wants me to send her my audition tape." She chews her lip, still looking worried. "I don't know if she'll think I'm too flakey to work with now."

I kiss her forehead, holding her close. "She's still interested, baby. That's what's important."

"I hope so. Laszlo, will you please help me make an audition tape? The agent has asked for one and I'd like to get her something as soon as possible."

This is something concrete I can actually do for her. I dig out my phone. "Let me call the general manager of the symphony hall. We can make the recording on the stage." The acoustics are perfect and they'll have all the equipment we need. "You go and change into one of your gowns. Let's make a proper video. She should see how beautifully you play as well as hear you."

She smiles excitedly at the suggestion. "All right, but give me forty-five minutes to get ready. I'll have to put some makeup on as well."

I kiss her swiftly before she heads back to her room. Once I'm alone I find a recent email from the manager and call the number in her email footer. She speaks excellent English, thankfully, so I'm able to communicate what we need and she readily agrees. Before I hang up she adds, "It's serendipity that you called me, Mr. Valmary. I was going to call you today. The owner of the concert hall wants your opinion about an idea, something very close to your heart and his."

"Oh?"

She asks if I can meet with him after tonight's performance and I agree and end the call, wondering what the owner could possibly have to ask me. Maybe they want my opinion on next season's program. Maybe they even want the RLSO to be part of the program. That would be very agreeable.

But I push that aside for the moment. My priority right now is Isabeau.

Chapter Twenty-Four

Isabeau

Now

It feels strange to be on the bustling day-lit Bangkok streets in a gown with a face full of makeup. The locals look at me and smile as Laszlo hails a cab. I like the Thai people. They're friendly and seem to love our music. It's a pleasure to play for them.

As we're driving through the city Laszlo points out a construction site. "See those cranes? They're building a state-of-the-art concert hall, twice as big as the one we're playing in. It's going to be quite something."

Quite something is understating it. Even unfinished the building looks modern and striking, and perched a dozen or so floors up it will command beautiful views of the city.

The concert hall we're going to record in is quite something itself. I sit down on the stage and tune my cello while Laszlo and the stage manager sort out the lighting and the recording equipment. A few minutes later Laszlo nods at me from the stalls.

"Whenever you're ready, Miss Laurent."

"Yes, Mr. Valmary," I reply innocently, though I'm sure he can see the glimmer in my eyes as I raise my bow. I play my favorite cello pieces by Brahms, Elgar and Bach, and I play them how I feel them and want them to be heard. I forget about the recording equipment, the agent back in London, Laszlo and the stage manager watching me. I don't think about anything but the music and what it means to me.

Finally, I want to play *Vocalise*. There's a grand piano to the side of the stage and I glance at it and hesitate. I see Laszlo shift on his feet, and when I look at him he gives me a nod of understanding. It's a good thing for a soloist to show that they can play with other instruments as beautifully as they play on their own. But beyond any of that, this piece defines me like no other. Even more than *The Swan*, because I chose it myself.

Laszlo sits down at the piano, and when I hear the opening phrases of the piece I close my eyes and imagine we're back at home in the music room, just the two of us, playing together.

I want to move back in with Laszlo. I want to be in that house with him and have everything we once had together, and all these wonderful new things, too. I want us to have that life of music and happiness and I pour that need into the piece, playing with all the longing in my heart. I open my eyes several times as we play to look at him and find he's watching me, an expression in his eyes that I think I've felt before but not seen. As if he looked at me like this when we used to play together, but he just never let me see.

Laszlo arranges for the stage manager to edit the recording and send him a copy that evening. In the afternoon I'll compose the email to the agent and send it off after our performance tonight.

But first I want something else.

Once we get back to the hotel I put my arms around him and kiss him in the elevator. "All those things that you offered to me yesterday," I whisper against his mouth, kissing him between words. "I want to be your good girl. Your sub. Your sweet Isabeau. I want you to be dark and wicked. I want you to enjoy the power you have over me. Let yourself off the leash with me."

He looks down at me with dark, hazy eyes and I know he wants this too. He craves it as much as I do, this heady blend of sex and need and control. And in the end, when we've burned hard through each other and into each other, all that will be left is us. As we are. Forged like steel together.

"Put the leash on me, daddy."

The elevator pings and I let go of him, standing demurely beside him, one hand on my cello case in front of me. Two people get in and turn to face to the doors, pressing the button for the rooftop bar.

I glace at Laszlo as the doors close and there's a dark flicker in his eyes. He puts his lips close to my ear and murmurs, so quietly, "Do you want to be mine, Isabeau?"

In all the ways. I want everything he's offering me and I need it to start now.

His lips are warm against my ear as he breathes, "Do you want to be a little slut for daddy?"

I stifle a whimper and nod again.

In a normal tone of voice he announces, "Oh dear, you've dropped your bracelet." Laszlo kneels down and pretends to feel around by my cello case for a piece of jewelry I wasn't wearing. With his other hand he reaches up beneath my long satin skirt, grasps the back of my thong and pulls it down.

I pretend to look around on the floor while stepping out of my underwear, which tangles on my heels. We attract the other couple's attention and the woman half turns to us as Laszlo straightens up.

"Did you find it?" the woman asks.

"Oh, she wasn't wearing any after all," Laszlo says, surreptitiously pushing my underwear into his pocket. I choke on my laughter. The woman gives us an odd look but Laszlo announces that this is our floor and we get out. I want to hurry, aware of my nakedness beneath my skirt, but Laszlo holds tightly to my hand, making me walk slowly to his room.

When we get inside he puts aside my cello and turns to me. "Do you know how beautiful you sounded on stage? I'm so proud of you."

Gently, lovingly, he takes off his belt and loops it around my neck. Holding the straps tightly in one hand like a collar he kisses me, his tongue invading my mouth. I whimper as he tugs gently on the belt, bringing me up onto my toes.

Still kissing me, he puts a heavy hand on my shoulder and forces me down onto my knees. Breaking the kiss he looks at me with flashing eyes. "Perfect, baby. That's just where I like you."

I gaze up at him, my breath shallow, savoring the sensation stealing over me, watching how it's spreading through Laszlo, too. This deep connection between us, exposing us to each other. Raw, fundamental, primal.

THE PROTÉGÉ

"Tell me what you want, Isabeau."

I arch my neck against the leather tight about my throat. "Please be my dom. Show me all the ways that we can make each other feel so very good. Please, daddy."

His lips curve into a smile. "Open your mouth."

I do, and he places two fingers on my tongue, which I obediently suck. He groans. "Do you want to be good for your daddy, baby?"

I nod, still sucking his fingers, letting my need for him fill my eyes.

"How can I say no when you ask so very, very nicely." The belt tightens slightly and I feel the pressure around my throat, constricting, but I go on sucking his fingers. I like the sensation of his fingers in my mouth so I reach up and unzip his trousers, taking out his cock. I look up at him as I take a first, slow lick. I grow bolder, taking him into my mouth and closing my eyes. He fills my mouth, hot and smooth and delicious.

"Let me see you play with your pussy, baby."

He wraps his hand around the base of his cock, holding it steady for me while I use my hands to lift my skirt. Opening my knees wider, I let my fingers play over myself, feeling the wetness there, rubbing over the swollen folds, my clit. I rub the tight bead of nerves with my middle finger, going on sucking him, long languorous strokes of my mouth and tongue, moaning as the sensations beneath my fingers grows. Laszlo pushes his length deeper into my throat and hisses with arousal, squeezing the belt even tighter.

"Pretty girl," he murmurs, his breathing as hard as mine is labored.

He releases his grip and pulls away from me, leaving me gasping at his feet while he undresses. My eyes rove across his body hungrily. I love his body, the rough hair, his heavy limbs, his broad chest, the muscles across his shoulders and his strong throat. He takes a firm fistful of my hair and compels me up and over the arm of the sofa so I'm bent double, my ass in the air.

"I'm in a leather mood today, babygirl." He's still got his belt wrapped around one hand, the straps hanging loose. His grip is menacing.

"But I've been so good," I say, realizing what he means to do, my toes curled tight into the carpet in anticipation.

There's an indulgent smile in his voice. "I know, baby."

Laszlo draws back his arm and the leather cracks over my flesh. I cry out, seizing the cushion, and he traces the red marks lovingly with his fingers. When I'm bad he makes me come. When I'm good he hurts me, because he likes it. I plant my feet more securely and let my body go limp, waiting for his next lash. Craving that feeling he gives me.

It comes a moment later white hot and fast as lightning. I squeal and tears leak from my eyes. I sniffle loud enough for him to hear. Wanting him to hear. Suspecting he'll like it.

He strokes my hair back from my face, making a sympathetic noise deep in the back of his throat, and I know I'm right. "Babygirl. You're so pretty when you cry. Can you cry a little more for me? Let me help you."

He's more than helpful, he's thoroughly vicious about raising welts on my backside and every time he touches them his breath is harder and more roughened. His fingers find my pussy and bury themselves in my slickness.

"So tearful, and so wet. That's just beautiful, sweet girl." He rolls a condom down over his cock while I'm still gasping softy against the sofa cushion, and then his length is thrusting into my heat. He pinches the stinging flesh of my ass, the pain heightening the pleasure of his thrusts.

"Are you my good girl?"

"Yes—" I start to reply but he wraps the belt around my neck again, choking off my words. I hear his satisfied groan and a moment later he loosens his hold on the leather.

"What was that, baby?" he asks, that dark chocolate indulgence in his voice.

I take a deep breath. "Yes, da—" But he tightens his grip, and when my words are cut off he makes that satisfied noise again. He holds on longer this time and pounds me hard. Not long enough to make my lungs burn but long enough to make it clear he's doing this deliberately.

"Breathing is a privilege, baby. Do you understand?"

I nod, and he laughs softly and then loosens the belt so I can take a gulping breath. As I do my orgasm rushes up, sudden and strong. He clenches his hand around the belt, tightening it on my throat. I barely seem to need air as my orgasm goes on and on. I feel his finger slide through my wetness and then push into my ass, and I welcome the sensation.

Next thing I know he's pulled out and I feel the blunt tip of his cock where his finger was. He pauses, just rubbing himself against me. I understand the question, and I want it. I push back against him, feeling myself give around the first inch of him.

Laszlo grips the belt to hold me still. He leans his weight into me, slowly, slowly, his other hand making my back arch for him.

"Do you like shedding tears for me baby?" he asks, moving his hips, working himself deeper, each stroke of his cock making my body sink down into the sofa.

"Yes, daddy," I murmur, rubbing my cheek against the cushion beneath my cheek.

"Do you like feeling totally at my mercy?"

He knows I do, and I turn my head, letting him see my smile through the tangles of my hair.

"Do you like being my slutty little girl?"

I arch my back and push back tightly against him, feeling the length of him inside me. "Best of all, daddy."

He's tender now, the belt falling away as he holds me with both hands around my waist, thrusting with firm, deliberate, strokes. The sensations are making my clit tingle and I reach between my legs to touch myself.

"Beautiful girl," Laszlo says, his voice tight. "Melt for me again and I am going to burst."

And I will, for him, because he makes me believe anything is possible. His fingers scratch over the raised marks on my ass as I rub tight circles on my clit, the glow deep inside me growing.

"Laszlo, please," I moan, needing more, and he fucks my ass faster, the rhythm of his cock lighting up my insides. My orgasm is fast approaching and he must feel it, and he murmurs words of encouragement under his breath. *That's it. Come for daddy. Good girl.* He's so generous with his affection and it makes me cry out with happiness and release as I come.

I hear the groan of his release, feel his rhythm stutter as he presses deeply into me.

We stumble to the shower and clean up, the hot water blasting our skin. I feel heady and I'm rushing high and he holds me tight in his soapy arms.

Later when we're clean and drying and back on the bed we're both still smiling. I rub my forefinger over his lower lip. "I've always loved your teeth."

He smiles, amused. "My teeth?"

"Yes. Those pointy canines of yours. You're like some sort of good-natured vampire or something."

Laszlo nuzzles my neck, growling and nipping me with his teeth. "All the better to eat you with, my dear."

I giggle, shifting myself closer in his arms and running my fingers over his jaw, his cheeks, through this hair. I can't seem to get close enough to him. I think it must be that place he puts me into, subspace, he called it, and I hold him back, hard. I feel so close to him in my mind that I need his body even more as I start to come out of it. I think that's how he feels, too.

"Have you enjoyed the tour?" I ask when I'm able to unclasp him a little.

His face splits into a grin. "God, I have. So much. It's been a challenge but the audiences in Asia are so much more receptive to experimentation than they are in the London. There's opportunity here for more. I'd bring the orchestra back in a heartbeat. In fact, I have a feeling we're going to be invited back before we even leave the country." He gives me a mysterious look but won't say anymore. "What about you? Have you enjoyed the tour?"

I think back over the doubt and nerves, the hot stage lights and the riotous applause. And Laszlo. "I have. In all the many and varied ways. So much has happened for me in these past few weeks that it's hard to tease it all apart, but I can say it's been wonderful, discovering all these things with you." I take a deep breath. "I'm so happy you're my dom. My lover."

He looks at me for a long time, like he's trying to figure out what to say. It's there, hovering at the edges of our cozy little nest. *I love you.* I feel it so keenly and I want to speak it out loud. I'll continue to fight, to reach for the things that will make me happy. But for now I hold back the words. It's not that I'm afraid, but I'm learning patience. The moment will come when I will tell Laszlo how deeply I love him, and he will say it back. There's no need to rush.

"I'm so happy too, baby. With all my heart."

Chapter Twenty-Five

Laszlo

Now

After the performance that night the owner of the concert hall greets me backstage, a man in his early forties called Mr. Niran Anumak. We shake hands and he takes me up to his office, which looks over the sparkling lights of Bangkok.

"Do you like the view, Mr. Valmary?" he asks me, hands clasped behind his back as he smiles out at the vista of skyscrapers lining the Chao Phraya River. The roads are filled with moving cars and scooters and pedestrians line the sidewalks of the night markets and restaurant precincts. Bangkok is an intensity of light and color, especially after dusk.

I watch him narrowly for a moment, catching a meaningful tone in his innocent question. "It's very beautiful."

"Very different from the gray London streets, hmm? There'll be an even better view from the musical director's office at the new concert hall."

I keep my tone as casual as his and say, "Yes, I imagine there will. I've been past the construction site many times."

Mr. Anumak turns to me with an appraising look. "I suppose you know we're looking for a musical director for the new concert hall."

My face doesn't change but my heart starts to pound. "No, I didn't."

He smiles at me broadly and then gestures to his desk. "Why don't we sit down, Mr. Valmary. There are some things I'd like to discuss with you."

It's gone three in the morning when I leave the concert hall but I feel wide awake. Musical director of the new state-of-the-art Bangkok concert hall. A chance to handpick every member of the orchestra myself. Control over what the orchestra plays. Greater freedom to experiment and innovate, to invite world-class soloists.

I look around at Bangkok with fresh eyes. This could be my city. Mr. Anumak wasn't merely offering me the chance to apply, he was offering the job to me. All I have to do is say yes.

I consider hailing a cab to get back to the hotel but the evening is warm and fragrant and the lights of the city are bright. There are plenty of people abroad and I stroll along the sidewalk, thinking. There's lots to think about. Isabeau is foremost in my mind, because wherever I go in the world I want her with me, but I also know that London is the best place for her.

Asia, though. Asia could be good for her career, too.

All I know is that I want to say yes to Mr. Anumak. I want to shape the new Bangkok symphony orchestra with my own hands. Me. Not anyone else.

The scent of flowers reaches me. I want to tell Isabeau how I feel, how I *really* feel, but there's a correct way for things to unfold. You can't have the finale before the overture, even though we've skipped straight to the crescendo. It's time for things to be returned to their proper order, and that means Isabeau knowing everything that happened after I took her into my house when she was eight years old. I could tell her now, putting a finger under her chin and drawing her face up to mine. *"Sweetheart, there's something I need to tell you. Several somethings."* Will she be angry with me? With him? I've wondered this so many times over the years and I don't know the answer. Her feelings are hard to gauge because Isabeau's always refused to talk about her father. The heroin frightened her and the loss of her mother was painful. I wonder if that's why her sub tendencies have manifested in the way they have. I'm not afraid of the power I have over other people. Power can be benevolent. Power can support, uplift. That's all I want, to see Isabeau and my orchestra thriving in my care, and I swear by every star above me in the night sky I will have it.

Patience, Laszlo, I caution myself. *You will have it, but you need to be patient.* When the tour is over and we're back in London I'll set things in motion for her to learn the truth. I'll be there to deal with the fallout, to hold her as she cries if she needs to cry.

And to offer her my heart at the end. Forever.

I want to see a diamond ring sparkling on her finger, a ring I've given her. I want her to be my wife. Everything else, Bangkok, London, orchestras, performances, can fall in around that most important thing: having Isabeau as my wife.

I'm awoken by my phone ringing and see that it's eight-fifteen in the morning. I groan, wishing that whoever it was could just let me sleep. I don't recognize the number but it has a +44 country code, which is the United Kingdom.

I press the answer button and mutter, "Laszlo Valmary."

There's a short silence, and then a woman's voice comes on the line, as if she didn't hear me. "Mr. Valmary?"

I swing my legs over the edge of the bed and sit up, rubbing my face. If this is a journalist or musician wanting to audition I will give them a piece of my goddamn mind, though that seems unlikely as it's the middle of the night in London. "Speaking."

The woman goes on in slow, empathetic manner. "I'm very sorry to disturb you while you're out of the country. I spoke to your assistant earlier and I understand you're traveling at the moment. My name is Astrid Clark."

My assistant. She must mean the office assistant at the Mayhew because my PA is here in Bangkok. There must be an important booking, some fussy manager who doesn't like to do things over email. "It's fine, Ms. Clark. What can I do for you?"

She hesitates. "I'm calling regarding Mr. Piers Laurent. I'm afraid I have bad news."

Chapter Twenty-Six

Isabeau
Now

The first thing I do when I wake up is check my email and I'm disappointed to see I don't have a reply from Ms. Sanchez yet. Then I laugh at myself, as she only received my reply and the recording less than a day ago. Anyway, it's the middle of the night in London. She might not even have seen that I replied to her yet.

But she will reply. I don't know if I will be what she's looking for but if not there are other agents who might be interested in me. I won't crumple under a single rejection.

I make coffee and drink it looking out the window across Bangkok, wrapped in a bathrobe. Tonight is the final performance of the tour. Soon I'll no longer be in Laszlo's orchestra which makes me a little sad as I've loved every moment playing alongside them. They have welcomed me and been kind to me. Even the silly incident with the viola player doesn't smart any longer and she's left me alone since then.

There's a knock on my door and when I open it I see Laszlo. He wasn't with us after we left the concert hall last night I didn't get a text letting me know how his meeting went. "There you are! I was wondering what happened to you last—"

But I stop myself, seeing the tense look on his face. He comes into the room, shutting the door behind him and taking my hands. "Sweetheart. I need to talk to you."

Laszlo leads me over to the sofa by the window and sits down with me, holding both my hands in his. "I've got some difficult news for you. It's about your father. He's very ill. He's in a hospice in London."

Something cold and hard comes loose inside me and begins to fall. A hospice. I've heard that word before. It's where people go to die. My father's dying. I try and get my head around it, my father dying, my father being dead, but then realize that Laszlo's still talking.

"...admitted two months ago but he refused to allow the hospice to notify his emergency contact until yesterday. His liver is failing and he was refused a transplant." Laszlo looks at me, perplexed. "Do you understand, sweetheart?

"Who's his emergency contact?"

He frowns, as if that wasn't the question he was expecting me to ask. "I am."

I want to ask why that should be but Laszlo goes on talking quickly. "My assistant is booking you on the first flight back to London and I'll follow you as soon as tonight's performance is over. Are you going to be all right? If you need me I'll come now. You're more important to me than the performance."

But I tell him not to be ridiculous, that of course he needs to stay and that I'll be fine in London for twelve or so hours by myself. I stand up to go. Packing. That's what I should do. Suitcase, airport. See my father. Logical and right. I should probably feel something about the fact that I'm seeing my father before he dies, but there's nothing there.

Then as I head for the door it does hurt. Oh god, it hurts. But not for the reason it should.

I turn back to him, needing to say something, now, before I'm torn away from his side. "Laszlo, there's something I need to tell you."

Laszlo puts his arms around me and holds me close, all gentle assurance. "I'll be right behind you, I promise."

But I have a terrible feeling that if I don't say it now I might never get the chance. Look what happened three years ago when I left him suddenly: I lost him for years and years. "My plane might crash or you might get hurt or I could…could just *lose* you. I have to say it."

Realization dawns on Laszlo's face. He puts his hands on my shoulders, fingers digging in. "Isabeau don't, please—"

But the words are clamoring to get out. Whatever he thought I was going to say, whatever is making him so afraid, it's not that, it's something much better.

"I love you, Laszlo."

His eyes close and he just stands there, his body braced as if there's a truck barreling down on us at a hundred miles an hour and it's too late to get out of its path.

When he opens his eyes there's so much pain in them, and he can barely speak above a whisper. "Isabeau, you have to go."

I shake my head, not understanding, wondering what I've done that's so terrible. "No, you didn't hear me. I *love* you."

In the ringing silence that follows I realize that he did hear me, perfectly. And he's not saying it back. It's the night of my eighteenth birthday all over again, me thinking that my feelings will be welcomed by him and Laszlo meeting them with horror.

"I…"

My heart leaps and I anticipate the words. *Say it. Say it, please.*

"I need you to go, baby."

Hope comes crashing down. I've ruined everything again, except this time I don't understand what I've done.

"Please, sweetheart," he whispers. I pull away, hoping he'll stop me, but his hands fall to his sides. I take another step and he watches me go, his eyes bleak. He's not going to do anything. He's not going to stop me.

Anger rises up and I rush at him, screaming, *"Tell me what's wrong. Don't do this again."*

His arms come around me as I slam a fist into his chest. He holds me, gently but firmly, as I do my best to hurt him. "Laszlo, tell me what it is."

Somewhere over my head his voice is fierce and bleak. "I can't, baby. It's not your fault, but I can't. Not right now. There are things—"

Can't, or won't? He wouldn't tell me all those years ago that he wanted me and there's something he's not telling me now. I wrench myself out of his arms.

He watches helplessly, speaking quietly but breathing as hard as I am. "You need to go now and see your father or you will regret it. That's what is important now, and I'll be with you very soon. I need you to trust me on this, baby. Will you trust me, please?"

I don't understand any of this. What is Laszlo not telling me? He thinks he has to protect me from everything, against my will. "How can I when you won't talk to me? I don't think you understand how much you're hurting me. Hurting *us*."

But he doesn't say anything and he's not going to change his mind. This is the Laszlo that everyone else sees. Cool. Remote. Unreadable. And the most painful thing about this is that I never thought he would turn this blank face on me.

I rake my hands through my hair, wanting to scream again. I feel like a piano that someone's hidden a bomb inside, and striking one more chord will set me off. I need to pull myself together through all the pain like I did that night and just go. Go to London. See my father. That's what's important now, my duty to him, not Laszlo and his distance.

I look at him one last time, giving him another chance to explain, but he just stands there silently, and I run from the room.

Later, when I emerge with my suitcase and cello, he's there and he takes them from me. We walk downstairs in brittle silence, suddenly strangers again. He hugs me before I get into the waiting taxi but my arms are too heavy to hold him back.

As I get into the car I feel the weight that started falling when Laszlo told me my father was dying. It's still in freefall, plummeting down and down, and I don't know if it will ever stop falling.

Seventeen hours later I arrive at the hospice, straight from the airport. The flight passed in a blur of restless thoughts and knots in my stomach. I think I forgot to drink any water and I know I didn't sleep.

When I tell the nurse on duty who I am a doctor takes me into a private room.

"Your father is in the latter stages of liver failure," she tells me when we're sitting down, her manner matter-of-fact but gentle, as if she's used to doing this sort of thing. Which I suppose she is. Who decides they want to become a doctor in a hospice, shepherding people into the next life, knowing there's nothing you can actually do to heal them? Or is it more something you fall into, by seeing an ad or being referred by a friend?

I realize my mind is wandering and I make myself listen to the doctor. The jetlag must be clogging up my brain.

The doctor tells me that many years of using street heroin cut with all sorts of chemicals damaged the blood vessels in his liver. The damage has progressed slowly over many years but, because of his addiction, he wasn't a viable candidate for a transplant.

Anger rolls through me. He put this poison into his body day after day and he never tried to get better.

"I'll take you to see your father. He might be confused or incoherent at times," she warns me gently. "As his liver is failing it's causing electrolytes to build up which hinder brain function."

How much brain function? I wonder. *Why did he finally let them tell Laszlo he was dying? Did he want to see me one last time?*

The doctor takes me to Dad's ward and leaves me sitting by his bedside. He's asleep, or unconscious. I can't tell which. I sit and watch him as he breathes. I watch the machines measuring his heartrate. The drip with the long, clear cord going into the back of his hand. The waxy pallor of his face, roughened by gray whiskers. I remember the photograph of my parents on their wedding day that used to sit on the mantelpiece, my mother in a lacy white dress and my father in a gray suit and tie. Both so young and healthy. Both beaming with happiness.

What did he really feel about her death? Why did he have to get hurt, too? And as I look at him I wonder, what hurt more, the pain in his back, or the pain of losing her? Because it hurts, losing someone. It hurts like cold wire stitching your organs tightly together, squeezing, mercilessly shredding your insides.

Hours pass and I must fall into a doze, my head resting back against the wall, because the next thing I hear is, "Issy."

I snort into wakefulness and look around, confused. Dad. The hospice. I stand up and go to him. He looks so small in the bed, his eyes yellowed and watery, his skin yellowed. I have my mother's nose, I remember, but I have his eyes and chin. Even through the sickness I can see the resemblance.

"The doctor said this has been coming for a long time," I venture at last. "Why didn't you let them contact Laszlo sooner?"

"Didn't want to disturb your tour. Got one of them internet alerts set up for your name. Saw you was with him again."

"Again? How did you know I wasn't?"

But he closes his eyes and takes a few breaths, as if these sentences have taken a lot out of him. I pull the chair up and sit down, wondering how long he's had an internet alert set up for my name.

"Did you finish the tour? In China or whatever."

"Southeast Asia. Almost. We had one more night, but there are lots of cellists." Maybe Laszlo found another to fill in for me or maybe they went on with only seven. It hurts so much to think about Laszlo right now. I want only to think about Dad, but then I remember something. "He was always urging me to come and see you. On my birthday. Near Christmas. I always said no." I examine Dad's face carefully, looking for condemnation, but his expression of blurry concentration doesn't change. "I think I was afraid. I didn't understand why you were the way you were. Later Laszlo explained."

There's a few seconds' lag, and then Dad's eyes narrow and he asks, "What did he tell you?"

"That you took heroin because it was the only thing that took your pain away."

His expression eases. "Good of him to tell you, once you were old enough to understand."

"But I didn't understand." The anger rises up again. Thirteen whole years in which we were absent from each other's lives. What would it have looked like if he'd reached out to me? If I hadn't been such a coward? "I still don't."

"You were a kid. Don't matter. Better this way."

It doesn't feel better. My mind is filled with what-ifs. "I haven't been a child for years," I whisper. "What's my excuse now?"

He fumbles for my hand and I give it, looking at the IV needles taped to the back of his. "You don't need one, love. You're here."

But I'm here at the end. There's nothing to be done at the end.

He closes his eyes but keeps talking in short, mumbled sentences. "I'm right proud of you, Issy. So much like your mum. Do you still play her cello? I never saw a sight so beautiful as your mum. Sitting at that instrument playing that song. Filling the air. I could even see the bird. Do you remember, Issy? 'member how she sounded…"

He lapses into silence and I see it too, the white swan on the water, almost painfully bright in the sunshine, swimming, swimming.

Chapter Twenty-Seven

Isabeau
Now

The funeral is held at a church in South London, not far from where Dad lived most of his life. There aren't many people there to pay their respects and I recognize none of them. He was an only child and my mother's side cut ties with him a long time ago. Hayley wanted to come with me but I made her stay at home. I don't know how to bring people into this part of my life.

The salary I was paid to tour with the RLSO was very generous and I see to it that there are lots of beautiful flowers inside the church and on the coffin. I feel like it's what my mother would want. She loved him, once.

THE PROTÉGÉ

I stand dry-eyed outside the church shaking hands with the dozen or so mourners who enter for the service. They look like people from Dad's neighborhood. I try not to judge when I see track marks on some of their arms. I don't know their stories. Maybe they were in pain like Dad was.

I've been in freefall ever since I left Bangkok. I can't seem to stop falling and I don't think I want to. Because it's not the fall that kills you. It's the landing.

I'm about to go inside when I see a car draw up, and Laszlo gets out. He's wearing a somber black suit and tie and his hair is neatly combed back. I haven't spoken to him since I left Bangkok. I know he arrived back in London not long after my father passed away, and he's called me dozens of times but I didn't have the strength to pick up. Finally I texted him to let him know what had happened, but of course he knew already. He was Dad's emergency contact, not me.

As he walks up the path of the church toward me, his hazel eyes on my face, I finally stop falling. He catches me in his arms as I hit the ground at terminal velocity and I sob, my face buried against his chest. "I forgot that he called me Issy."

Laszlo holds me tightly and strokes my hair. "It's all right, sweetheart. I've got you."

But it's not all right. I shake my head and pull away from him. "I've done a bad thing, and I think I might regret it for the rest of my life. I could have fixed it so easily and now it's too late."

Laszlo looks at me, his hands on my shoulders, not understanding what I mean. It's all I've been able to think about since Dad died. What if I'd tried harder to know my father? What if I'd reached out to him? What if we'd sat down and talked about my mother, even once? What if he'd tried, too?

I can see Laszlo desperately wants to take this pain away but he can't. He glances to the front of the church and I think the service is about to start. "I know you want to play but you don't have to. I'll tell the priest you're not feeling up to it."

He moves to go inside but I stop him. "No. I want to." I push my hands through my hair and wipe my face. I can do this one thing.

We go in and sit down on a pew, and I take gulping breaths, trying to compose myself. I can get through the next hour and later I can fall apart. Hayley's promised to be at home waiting for me. I've been staying with her and she's helped with everything. The best thing she's done is not ask too many questions. When I'm strong enough I'll tell her what happened between Laszlo and I. Again. She's too good a friend to say *I told you so*.

"Are you ready, sweetheart?"

I look up at Laszlo and realize it's time. I stand up on shaky legs and walk to the front. My cello is already set up there, to one side, along with a chair. I take my seat and arrange my instrument between my knees. Then I take a long, slow look around the church, at the mourners who don't know me and don't know what I'm doing. Laszlo taught me this. That a soloist should take her time. That the audience waits on her.

I know hardly anything about my parents, but *The Swan* meant something to both of them. At least I have this.

I take a deep breath and put the bow to the strings and close my eyes. I've played this piece at the most significant moments of my life. My first professional solo piece. My graduation piece. It's only right I play it at my father's funeral. He never got to hear me play it but I know he remembers how it sounded when my mother played Saint-Saëns.

The long, keening notes pour through me, beautiful and sad, a dirge in the gray chill of the church. There's only silence after.

I go quickly back to my seat, my head down. Laszlo reaches for my hand but I pull away.

After the service people come up to me and tell me how beautiful my playing was, how they didn't know that Piers had a daughter, that he must have been so proud of me. I can't find any words so I just nod, my eyes fixed somewhere over their shoulders.

The church empties out, and we leave. It's a gusty day and Laszlo and I walk quietly side by side through a nearby park. Finally he stops and turns to me.

His tone is even but his face is uncertain. "I've got some news for you, Isabeau. I've been offered an opportunity for my career. A very good one."

It's easy to smile a little because I'm glad for him. Laszlo works hard and he deserves to keep moving onwards and upwards.

"But it means going a long, long way away, and soon. So I'm going to turn it down."

I shake my head. "No, you can't. I know you're restless at the Mayhew. It's the new concert hall in Bangkok, isn't it? They've asked you to be the musical director."

He doesn't say yes but I know I'm right. And I'm glad for him.

I keep walking but he stops me with a touch on my arm. His eyes are pleading. "Come home with me, sweetheart. Please? Let me take care of you. You old room is there, just as you left it."

Just as I left it. I cringe away from the memory. Laszlo's home belongs to another Isabeau, and she fled years ago.

"Hayley's waiting for me," I manage, and I pull away. Hayley's flat is uncomplicated by regret, or love, or pain, and I'm feeling too much of all three right now. I love Laszlo even through all the guilt and pain, but he doesn't love me back. We were given one chance to try and make this work and it didn't. We'll never find our way back to each other now.

But I have to ask him one more thing before I go.

"Did we do the right thing? The day you offered me the whole world and I took it without looking back."

Laszlo steps toward me and his voice is low and urgent. "If there was any fault that day it was all mine, not yours. I will never, *ever* let you regret what you did. Not for one hour. Not for one *second*. I take it all upon my shoulders."

I can't look at him. I'm already feel myself pulling away because I can never see him again after this. It will hurt too much.

"No one and nothing can judge me except for you. Only you, Isabeau. If you think I did wrong I will spend the rest of my life trying to put it right." His voice becomes choked and his fingers touch my chin, as if he wants me to look up at him but he doesn't want to force me. "Please let me put it right, Isabeau."

Chapter Twenty-Eight

Isabeau
Now

When I left my father's home at eight years old it was the work of a moment to fill my schoolbag with a few personal things. I look around at nearly two decades of my father's cluttered belongings and feel overwhelmed by the job ahead.

All right, I think. *I'll approach it like a piece of music.* You don't just launch into playing a new symphony from the opening bar. First you study the piece, getting a feel for it as a whole and where the trickiest parts are. I walk from room to room, identifying personal possessions and valuable items—very few of either—that could be donated to a charity store, and what needs to be thrown out. I'll need to hire a truck or a skip or something.

There are a load of shoeboxes under the couch by the mattress my dad slept on and I hook them out and start going through them. They're full of letters, dozens of them, the paper crinkled as if they've been taken out of their envelopes and read many times.

They're are all addressed to my father in a slanted, spiky script I've seen on hundreds of scores over the years. Shock pierces the fuzziness in my head.

Laszlo's handwriting.

Letters with postmarks from five years ago, eight years ago, thirteen years ago. Right back to the time I came to live with him. I didn't know that he wrote to my father.

I choose a letter at random dated two and a half years after I came to live with him, when I was ten.

Laurent,

Isabeau had her Grade One cello exams today. The examiner gave me a copy of her performance and I pass it on to you.

Valmary

There's a CD with the letter and I play it, and that day comes back to me so vividly that I can see it. The hot room, the examiner scratching out notes. My father listened to this recording, and I wonder what he thought. Was he pleased to know I was still playing the cello? Did it make him proud? Why didn't Laszlo tell me he was writing to my father?

I turn to the next letter, another short missive, this time with the addition of my school picture, a skinny redhead with the biggest grin on her face.

Laurent,

Isabeau's teachers tell me she's a bright, kind and conscientious student. They don't tell me anything I don't already know, but it's good to have one's high opinion confirmed by others.

Valmary

I find myself smiling at Laszlo's words, and reach for another letter. This one is longer.

Laurent,

Last night Isabeau had her solo debut with my orchestra at the Mayhew. She played The Swan *on her mother's cello, her first performance with this instrument. Sometimes I look at her and I realize what I've taken away from you. I want you to know how proud I am of her. There's so much pride in me that it feels like I'm being proud for both of us.*

I burnt a DVD of her performance that an acquaintance recorded on their phone.

Valmary

I go to the television in the corner and put the DVD in the player. I see myself in the pink dress and hear my playing, the gentle sound of the strings behind me. It always made my father upset to hear me playing the cello after my mother died. I look at the box of letters, positioned so close to his bed where he could reach them, and wonder if it still hurt after I'd gone, or whether he found it comforting.

I read the letters in chronological order and as I progress I feel Laszlo's prickliness toward my father thawing with each one, and I wonder why. Perhaps my father is writing back. Maybe there are more letters.

One dated around my fifteenth birthday provides some answers.

Laurent,

I'm sorry about your relapse, for your own sake but especially for Isabeau's. I've done as you asked and I haven't told her that you're trying to get clean. I suppose you're right. This cycle of hope and failure would be hard on her and I want to protect her from life's disappointments as much as you do. But I won't stop asking her if she wants to see you. I would never keep her from you and if she ever asks I will bring her to you immediately.

I found another clinic online that has had great success treating patients such as yourself over an intensive three-month program. It's more expensive than the last one but I'm willing to cover the costs again. Please consider it.

Isabeau has learned to play...

I stop reading and look up. Dad tried to get clean. Dad tried to get clean several times, and Laszlo paid for the treatment. My heart is pounding so loud in my ears I feel like I'm inside a drum. Did Dad not trust he would get better? Was he afraid to hurt me with shattered hopes?

I feel my face crease with tears. All this time I thought he never tried, but he did. He tried for me.

I sit on Dad's bed long into the night, reading every word that Laszlo wrote him. Listening to every recording. Watching every performance. I'm stunned by the number, and there's not only these, but also descriptions of what I'm doing, how I laugh, what's interesting me. Laszlo wrote pages and pages about me, giving my father everything he was missing out on. I thought he hated my father but I feel that I'm reading kindness, even friendship, in the handwritten lines.

There's a letter around my sixteenth birthday that has angry, spiky lettering and I sense that Laszlo was in a temper when he wrote it.

Laurent,

I don't care that you failed again and that the money was "wasted". The money doesn't matter. Tell Isabeau soon, please. She can at least take comfort from the fact that you have tried to get better, that you want *to get better, for her, even if you can't. Because right now she has nothing and I can't help but think that this is worse. Shouldn't she at least know that I have kept you appraised of her life all these years? That you read my letters again and again? That you listen to her playing when the pain is at its worst to help you fall asleep? It feels wrong to lie to her through omission, day after day. I hate keeping this secret from her.*

If you could only see her face when I ask her if she wants to see you. She won't admit it but she's hurt that you have never reached out to her and I feel like the smallest olive branch from you would make all the difference. Every time she says she doesn't want to see you I'm sure she feels guilty. There's no need to protect her from false hopes anymore. She's sixteen, not a child.

But yes, all right. I know what you'll say. She's your daughter, not mine, and I respect your decision to keep this from her. Even if I think it's the wrong decision.

The letter lays in my lap and I stare at the dark window. Night has fallen while I've been reading. I remember Laszlo's face in Bangkok when I screamed at him to tell me what was wrong, what I'd done, what he was keeping from me.

I can't, baby. I can't. It's not your fault, but I can't.

I look down at the dozens of letters spread all around me. This is what he was keeping from me, at my father's request. My father tried to get better, for me, but was ashamed that he couldn't. Even on his deathbed Dad was too proud to tell me the truth.

I pick up the next letter. And the next. I read and read. There's a letter around the time I'm seventeen with a three-page description of me sitting at my cello while we play together. The paper is smudged with fingerprints and the folds are wearing thin, as if this letter has been read many, many times. Between the lines I can read all the longing that Laszlo had for me, and hid from me.

Tears fill my eyes. We want each other so much, but we still can't make it work.

Sometime around three in the morning I find Laszlo's last letter, written, I'm shocked to see, a few days after I fled his house. I read it, and I feel my heart break.

Chapter Twenty-Nine

Laszlo
Now

I thought losing Isabeau when she was eighteen years old would be the worst thing I'd ever experience in my life. Losing her a second time is far, far more painful. She's in terrible grief and I can do nothing to help her. She won't let me help her. I've stopped calling but I message her every single day. *I'm here if you need me. I'm always here for you sweetheart, no matter what. Please talk to me.* My messages go unanswered but I will keep sending them until she comes back to me. Or until she tells me to stop.

She loves me. Or, she did. I don't know how she feels about me now. Maybe she hates me. The confession took me by surprise and like last time it was guilt that made me silent. How could I tell her I love her, too, when she doesn't know about the letters? It wouldn't have been fair. Do I tell her now, against her father's wishes? Did he already tell her on his deathbed and she's too angry with me for hiding things from her to speak to me?

I'm still struggling with it. I don't know.

Meanwhile I work. I tell Mr. Anumak in Bangkok that he has to be patient, that I can't decide on his offer just yet. That I need time to think. The orchestra is back together at the Mayhew but I'm just going through the motions. None of this feels right without Isabeau.

Two days after the funeral I'm rehearsing with the orchestra at the Mayhew when someone walks out onto the stage.

Isabeau.

Her face is pale and her eyes dark green with some strong emotion. The orchestra falls silent as I turn to her. I want to crush her to me, to tell her how sorry I am. To beg for forgiveness.

She looks tired, like she hasn't slept all night. There's a piece of paper in her hand.

A letter.

My handwriting. My letters. Laurent kept my letters, all these years, and Isabeau has found them. She's read them.

"I wanted to tell you," I whisper.

Isabeau just stares at me. I search her face, trying to discern what she's feeling. She knows what I've been keeping from her. She has every right to be furious with me that we went behind her back all these years and denied her the comfort of knowing her father knew everything she was doing. That he was trying, for her.

It can make all the difference in the world, knowing that at least someone tried.

Beside us, the orchestra are all still and silent, watching us. Isabeau lifts the letter in a trembling hand and starts to read aloud.

Laurent,

I'm writing this sitting on her bed in her empty room. There are still clothes in the wardrobe. An empty teacup on her bedside table with cold dregs at the bottom. Lipstick on the dresser. Sheet music spread on the floor.

She's gone. This is the last letter I will ever write to you because Isabeau has left, and I drove her away.

When I took her from you all I saw was a vulnerable child in a terrible place, and I had a way to lift her up out of it and give her everything that she deserved. I didn't think about the woman she would become. The questions that would haunt her. The answers she'd lack.

I never imagined the way I would grow to feel about her.

I've never told anyone how I feel, not even Isabeau, but I've fallen in love with my protégé. She's only eighteen. I can't tell her. She looks to me for support and comfort and it would be so, so easy to convince her that she's in love with me, too. I've enjoyed influencing and protecting her all these years. I've kept her jealously close to me, just me, all mine, and I worry that my protection has become something insidious. I've always thought of myself as a good man but I don't know if I'm good man around her anymore. I tell myself that I only want what's best for her and fool myself that it's a coincidence when her wishes align with mine. That she doesn't want to see you. That she doesn't date. That she wants to kiss me. She's never been rebellious or gone against even a single one of my wishes and now I wonder why. As I look back over our years together I don't know if I've walked with her down this path or forced her onto it.

I'm jealous of every man who enters her orbit. All the times she said that she didn't want to see you I was always so fucking happy. I didn't want her to love you. I wanted her to love only me.

I can't trust myself around her so I'm letting her go.

The one thing I'm thankful for is that I don't think she suspects my feelings for her. She thinks I'm angry with her and it's terrible to cause her pain but the truth would be worse. My love would be a curse to her, leaden as it is with guilt and poisoned with all the things she doesn't know. A love that's good for no one at all.

THE PROTÉGÉ

I miss her. This house is silent now she's gone. I won't hear the music of her footsteps on the stairs anymore or smell the melody of her hair when she presses herself into my arms; see the notes of happiness in her eyes when she looks up at me from her cello. She's easy to adore when she's playing and it was the music that showed me how much affection I have for her. But I fell in love with Isabeau in between the music. Over all the days she gave me that were never enough.

I still want more, but I'll have to be content with what's left. With all that you were left with. No Isabeau. Just the music.

Valmary

There are tears on her cheeks when she finishes. No one in the orchestra moves but I'm barely aware of them as I look at her. She knows everything now. All my heart. All my secrets.

"I never knew that you loved me, Laszlo," she says in a tight whisper. "Why didn't you tell me? Why didn't you tell me about my father? About any of this?"

I shake my head, helpless, because I know even now that I couldn't have said such things to an eighteen year old girl. The things I said in the letter, about my love for her being poisoned with guilt, I feel the truth of that all over again. It would have ruined us.

"I couldn't, sweetheart. I just couldn't tell you how I felt. And the letters, all the things about your father, he made me promise not to tell you."

Her eyes search my face, fresh tears sliding down her cheeks. "And now?" she asks, a wobble in her voice. "Do you love me now?"

I take a deep breath and lay my baton aside. I put my hand in my pocket and draw something out. I bought it in Bangkok before I flew out, knowing that there was only ever going to be Isabeau for me. I should get down on one knee but I'm paralyzed by fear and hope, holding the white-gold diamond ring in clumsy fingers like a tiny talisman. "You asked me on the day of your father's funeral if we did the right thing, and my answer is still the same. If there was any fault I take it all upon my shoulders. I won't ask for forgiveness from anyone but you. I don't care what anyone else thinks of me. I only care about you."

I can say this to her, openly and truthfully, as I couldn't before. She knows everything now. All that I am. All that I have done.

"I've always loved you, Isabeau. I'll never stop loving you. And I'm asking you to love me too, always, now that you know the truth."

Isabeau lets out a strangled sob and runs into my arms. As her body thuds into mine my eyes close and I'm pierced with love and happiness so strong that I can only clasp her tightly against my chest, my eyes closed, thankfulness pounding through me.

My mouth seeks her lips and they're soft and salted with tears. We've found our way back to each other for the final time. "My love," I murmur between kisses. "My Isabeau."

I fumble for her fingers and she holds out her left hand for me while I slide on the ring. She turns her hand in the light, marveling at the sight of it sparkling on her finger. It looks better than I imagined. Isabeau Laurent is going to be my wife.

She reaches up and strokes her fingers through my beard, tears shining in her eyes. "I loved you since the moment I saw you looking back at me on that cold London street. I was only a child, but I knew. And I never want to lose you again."

A violin starts play. It's Marcus. Another joins him, and then a cello. Then more instruments until all the string instruments are playing *Vocalise*. I wonder how they know before I remember that Isabeau and I played it at the airport. I've never cared what people think about the things I do, but all the same the sound of their playing is like a blessing. These people at least are happy for us.

"No one's taking you away from me. Not ever."

She slips her arms around her neck and her voice drops to a whisper only I can hear. She gazes up at me, eyes shining. "Do you promise, daddy?"

I smile as I look down into her green eyes. "I promise, sweet girl. With all my heart."

Chapter Thirty

Isabeau
Now

There's a piano in the hotel suite on our wedding night.

"A room with a piano, and you," Laszlo says, kissing me. "What else do I need to make me happy?"

I get out of my white lace dress and take out cello, and sitting in a white corset and suspenders, my hair hanging in long curls over my shoulders, we play together. We play *Vocalise*, and for the very first time in my life it sounds different to my ears. The two instruments, once so alone, have found each other.

Laszlo looks thoughtful. "When we played this together in the airport in Singapore a woman came up to you after and spoke to you."

"She said, '*It's not in his face, but it's in the notes he plays. He loves you.*' And I shook my head because I never knew you loved me. I couldn't hear it."

He gets up from the piano and comes over to me, cupping my cheek. I turn my face into the warmth of his palm as he asks, "Do you hear it now, how much I love you, sweet girl?"

I do hear it, all the beautiful notes of his love, my *maestro*. I have been his ward, his protégé, his lover and now his wife. "I hear it, daddy. All of it. Every note."

He smiles, as he always does when I call him that. Laszlo picks me up and takes me over to the bed, his hands tight around my corseted waist. "And you'll come to Bangkok, my love, my world-class soloist, as often as you can?"

Laszlo has accepted the role of musical director of the new Bangkok symphony orchestra, and I've accepted Ms. Sanchez as my agent. I've already booked several performances in London and Italy with premier orchestras. It will be hard, being away from him so much, but Bangkok is always only a flight away, and when I'm with him there will be a place for me to play in his orchestra, filled while I'm not there by a temp. So I get the best of both worlds, a career as a soloist and the pleasure of playing with Laszlo, which will always be one of my keenest pleasures in the world.

I take his finger in my mouth and suck it lovingly, saying between licks, "I'll always come back to you, no matter how many times I leave. Wherever you are in the world is my home."

Laszlo's eye narrow with heat as he watches me, his words a purr that cascades through my body. "Good girl. Are you going to keep being my talented, beautiful Isabeau, my wife, my sweet protégé?"

I take another of his fingers into his mouth and continue to suck, showing him how happy he makes me. All those things. "Yes, daddy. Yes, sir. Yes, *maestro*."

I can't wait to perform with the new orchestra. Meanwhile I've been playing with the RSLO until we leave for Bangkok, just because it makes me happy. The violist who made me feel so small and ashamed at the airport and was rude to me in Bangkok looked disconcerted to see me there. A little guilty, too.

Domenica, my section leader, was able to explain. "She took a picture of you and Mr. Valmary kissing in the street in Bangkok and put it on Facebook. That's how we all found out about you."

I tell the violist that I think we got off on the wrong foot and it was awkward at first but I think we've cleared the air, though I doubt we'll ever be best friends.

In the days that followed Laszlo's proposal he told me more about his relationship with my father. How he enjoyed writing about me as much as my father loved reading the letters. How proud both of them were of me. How they both just wanted to protect me. I don't need to take just Laszlo's word for that, because my father wrote letters, too. Not as many as Laszlo and not as long, but he kept them all for me, in case he would be allowed to show them to me one day.

"I think it's time you saw these, sweetheart," he said, handing me the box the night of our engagement. I read them sitting on the couch in Laszlo's home. In our home.

It was so good to be home.

One letter in particular stays strong in my memory, that Dad wrote after Laszlo's furious letter when I was sixteen. The one where Laszlo begged Dad to tell me he was trying to get better.

Valmary,

The pain isn't too bad today and I'm not too stoned to write. I know you're angry but it's my decision to keep this from her, not yours.

I don't get her smiles, or the sight of her over the breakfast table, or hear her questions or see her doing her homework or the million other things that make up a life. But thanks to you I get her music. And I get to know she's happy. It's better this way. I've got nothing for her but sadness and disappointment. You're standing between her and all that pain, protecting her from it.

I suppose this is me saying thank you. For being someone that Isabeau deserves. And for loving her, like I know you do.

Laurent

Epilogue

MARRIED TO A MAESTRO: INSIDE THE CONTENTIOUS UNION BETWEEN LASZLO AND ISABEAU VALMARY

On the eve of their relocation to Bangkok, biographer EVANGELINE BELL talks with performance power-couple Isabeau and Laszlo Valmary about music, marriage and making waves in the classical music world.

When I arrive at the Valmarys' London home I'm greeted by a barefoot Isabeau in a cream dress, her long auburn curls tumbling over one shoulder. "Come up and see the music room," she says to me with a welcoming smile. "It's the best place in the house."

Just twenty-one, the soloist exudes the confidence of a young woman used to the spotlight. Sitting down at her cello she treats me to an unaccompanied performance of her signature piece, Saint-Saëns' *The Swan*. Her playing is filled with the honesty and pathos which has earned her critical acclaim and the hearts of audiences during a recent three-night performance of the Brahms *Double Concerto* with violinist Hayley Chiswell in Birmingham.

While she plays her husband appears, as if drawn by the sound of her cello. Laszlo Valmary stands in the doorway watching her. It's a sight he must have witnessed a thousand times over the years since Isabeau came to live with him when she was just eight years old, but to look at him one would think he was hearing her for the first time.

Valmary, thirty-eight, is polite though reserved, and shakes my hand with a firm grip, his hazel eyes guarded and assessing. I've heard rumors that husband and wife play together often, him accompanying her on the grand piano that stands on one side of the room. When I ask if he'll perform something too he tells me there's coffee downstairs in the living room and turns away.

"We're not sure what to do with the house," Isabeau explains when we're settled on the sofas. "It's Laszlo's family home and he doesn't want to sell it. I'll be flying back and forth between London and Bangkok a lot for performances so I'll stay here. Hopefully other touring friends will be able to use it as well. There should always be music in this house."

Valmary was recently appointed as musical director of the new Bangkok Symphony Orchestra and will begin auditions for orchestra members as soon as he's back in Asia. "I'm very keen to gather new talent around me and shape the orchestra's sound," he tells me. "There's a huge appetite for classical music in Asia and the audiences are open to experimentation."

Image, above: Laszlo and Isabeau embrace on the sofa in the Hampstead home they've shared for most of the last thirteen years. Isabeau twists her fingers through his hair. "It's always too long," she says, referring to what she calls his conductor's mane. "Should I cut it all off?" he teases.

On the mantelpiece are photographs, mostly of Isabeau over the years, and she takes me through them. Isabeau as a child of eight playing a three-quarter size cello in the room upstairs. "Laszlo bought it for me not long after I came to live with him because my instrument—my mother's instrument—was too big." Isabeau onstage with the RLSO at age fourteen as she plays *The Swan* in a pink dress while Mr. Valmary conducts. A candid shot of a teenage Isabeau looking exhausted but happy sitting cross-legged amid a sea of instrument cases. "Laszlo took that while we were on tour in Edinburgh." A photograph of their wedding day two weeks earlier, which is the only picture Valmary appears in. It shows Isabeau in a long white lace bridal gown and tiara and Valmary in a grey suit and black tie. The couple are embracing, their profiles to the viewer, Isabeau leaning close as if to whisper secrets to her new husband, pink roses clutched in one hand.

"It was all done in such a rush," she explains with a breathless smile. "But it was the most perfect day." When she resumes her seat her hand slips comfortably into his, and his thumb rubs absently-mindedly over the diamond ring on her left hand.

On a nearby coffee table I notice a few more pictures that include the conductor: Isabeau and Valmary backstage at an event that I recognize as Isabeau's last performance with the Royal London Youth Orchestra on the night of her eighteenth birthday. Isabeau notices me looking and regards the pictures, chewing her lip. "We're not sure where to put these photographs. It was a very happy night but…it's complicated, too."

Valmary, who's been doing very little talking, speaks up. "I want them where I can see them. As a reminder of what we've been through to get where we are today."

Isabeau turns to look at him, and nods. She gets up and places one of the photographs next to their wedding portrait. In the picture, Valmary appears to be talking to someone just out of shot, mirror-ball sunglasses atop his head and unbuttoned shirt gaping. One of his arms is around Isabeau who has both of hers wrapped around his waist, and is smiling up at him. It's a bright, easy smile showing no sign of the impending complications the pair have hinted at.

They're reticent to talk about exactly when they became lovers. "I always loved Laszlo, and he didn't know. When I was old enough I sprang myself on him and it went very badly. I think I shocked him. In fact I know I did."

Valmary declines to answer.

"Later, we were able to figure things out," Isabeau adds. When asked if the figuring out happened on the recent tour with the RLSO during which Isabeau was second cello, she merely smiles, refusing to answer the question. Isabeau Valmary seems to have as much tenacity as her husband beneath her charm and beauty. While researching the pair I found no evidence that Isabeau and Valmary performed together after the night of her eighteenth birthday, until the most recent tour.

In February of this year Isabeau joined the RLSO on a limited contract and there are several professional photographs of the couple on stage during a tour of Southeast Asia. Neither have posted any informal photographs of themselves separately or as a couple from this time on social media.

There was a photograph taken by an orchestra member that appears to show the pair embracing, Isabeau possibly unwell, on Khaosan Road in Bangkok but it's since been removed from Facebook and neither admit to knowing of its existence.

The first candid photograph of them together and the first public indication that they were a couple is from four weeks ago: a slightly blurry untagged photograph of Isabeau and Valmary on Hayley Chiswell's Instagram. Miss Chiswell was concertmaster in Valmary's youth orchestra and is now an accomplished soloist and one of Isabeau's closest friends and co-performers. The photograph shows the couple laughing together over dinner, Valmary's arm around his bride-to-be with Isabeau's engagement ring clearly visible. It is simply captioned, *Gorgeous fucking idiots*. At time of publication the post has over twenty-one thousand likes.

Isabeau speaks of her mother, a cellist who passed away when Isabeau was seven. "She taught me to love music. After she died my father struggled with pain and addiction. We weren't close, but Laszlo sent my father regular letters and recordings as I grew up. I saw him briefly before he died."

Is she angry with him for not being there for her?

"He tried to get better, but sometimes people aren't able to. It's a great comfort knowing he tried, for my sake."

When I ask if there was any formal or legal arrangement between Valmary and Isabeau's father both decline to answer. Adopted children are not legally able to marry their adoptive parent so it's doubtful an adoption took place. There are no records of any other sort of formal guardian and ward arrangement, though several of Valmary's friends and colleagues have stated that he referred to Isabeau as his ward during the ten years up until her eighteenth birthday.

Finally, I ask the question that's been at the back of my mind since arriving in their home. What would they say to people who find their relationship objectionable, even abhorrent? Isabeau seems to be have been expecting this and answers easily. "I was so happy for ten years living with Laszlo, and then what followed was a very sad and lonely time. We both worked hard to get where we are now. I think we've earned our happiness."

I turn to her husband and see that Valmary's jaw is set and his face his closed. Those who have worked with him or tracked his career over the years are familiar with this Laszlo Valmary: formidable; severe; someone who was able to hold his own against the classical music elite at the age of twenty-five. He has weathered his fair share of censure and disapproval. "I have nothing to say to anyone about our relationship."

I thought this defiant statement was all I would get out of Valmary but his eyes land on his bride and his face softens. As his hand caresses her cheek I see a glimpse of Valmary's private, affectionate side. The sort of man a girl of eight could cherish. The sort of man a woman could fall for.

"Isabeau is happy, and I have her love. Keeping it, being deserving of it, that is all that matters to me. That is everything."

TO THE LIMITS, Evangeline Bell's biography of composer and former musical theater star Frederic d'Estang, is now available.

Acknowledgments

Mr. Hale, I couldn't ask for a more supportive, kind, loving partner. I'm just so lucky to have you in my life. I love you. Thank you for finding all my typos. I love you even more for that.

Thank you so much to my gorgeous beta readers who helped me spank this book into shape, namely:

Bear (I have to call you Bear, you're Bear on my PS4 headset so you're Bear here) who is a truly wonderful and supportive friend through the best times, good times and awful times. Thank you for letting me ask you a hundred questions about classical music. Eyes up, Guardian.

L.R. Black, who would like everyone to know that she's called dibs on Laszlo, she did it first, he's hers, sorry I don't make the rules!

Abby Gale, who is a breath of fresh air and inspires me with her strength and kindness.

Andi Jaxon, your incisive ideas made so much difference and I'm so happy to know you.

Lylah James, the other day I found an email I sent you with an ARC of PRINCESS BRAT and I remember thinking OH SHIT LYLAH JAMES WANTS TO READ MY BOOK. It's still pretty much my reaction when you read anything of mine.

Liz Meldon, you are a ray of sunshine and loveliness in the world. Never change, beautiful.

Writing taboo and dark books can be a nerve-wracking experience when it comes time to set the pages free into the world. So thank you, dear reader. I couldn't do this without you.

Finally, curious about that epilogue and want to know who Evangeline Bell and Frederic d'Estang are? Keep reading…

Brianna Hale

Read on for an excerpt of SOFT LIMITS by Brianna Hale

"If you test my limits I'm going to test yours back, twice as hard. If you push me you'll find you run out of ground long before I do."

Frederic d'Estang: performer, professional villain and my youthful crush. He calls me *chérie, ma princesse, minette*.
And I call him daddy.

Adult, sexy and daring. Brianna Hale gets better and better - **The Book Bellas**

sigh All the stars in the world for SOFT LIMITS - **AnObsessionWithBooks**

Brianna Hale knows how to write a damn good love story ... her books keep getting better and better - **The Romance Rebels**

As soon as I reached the end, I could have read it all over again - **Wicked Reads**

Beautiful and dark in all the best ways - **Honeyed Pages**

This book is the perfect combination of vulnerability and dark fantasy - **Book Talk By Sarah**

Brianna Hale just keeps getting better and better! SOFT LIMITS is so dirty and sexy that I couldn't put it down - **Reading Cafe**

Chapter One

Evie

I'm not paying attention when it happens. The laneway is deep with silence and noonday shadows, and there's a fresh breeze blowing. My eyes are following tiny birds as they hop among the cow parsley and tangled wildflowers, but my mind is far away, in a dark and bitter East Berlin winter of razor wire and searchlights and snarling German shepherds. I picture Mrs. Müller, not as I left her just now, a sturdy, gray-haired woman in a cream blouse, but as a young woman of twenty with a pale, determined face and clear blue eyes. She laid photos out before me of friends long dead. *Shot going over the Wall. Arrested by the Stasi. Arrested. Disappeared. This one betrayed us—she was an informant and we didn't know it.*

There's a break in the hedgerow and I cut across the laneway, heading for the stile. The path beyond leads a mile across the fields to my parents' country house, where I'm staying over the summer with my mother, father and my sisters. All three of them.

Suddenly a car races around the bend. I freeze, turning toward this black, rushing thing, as silent as it is sleek — Why is it so quiet? — but then the driver slams on the brakes and the air is filled with the screech of tires and smoking rubber. The car stops six inches from my legs and I'm finally released from terror-induced paralysis. I scurry to get out of the way but my feet tangle and I go down with a yelp. Papers and books cascade from my shoulder bag. I stare at my burning hands pressed against the gravel, my chest heaving.

A car door opens and rapid footsteps approach. Someone hovers over me, saying something about the driver and not seeing me and asking me if I am hurt.

"No, really, I'm fine, the car didn't touch me, I just fell," I say, brushing gravel from my bare legs and scraped palms while simultaneously trying to grab at loose pages that are fluttering into the hedge.

His hand catches mine. "Miss," he says, in a voice that cuts through my babble. He's got an accent of some sort. "I will collect your papers. Are you sure you're all right?"

I look up, and recognition and dismay stun me into silence. The man bending over me has dark, curly hair with a few silver flecks and slanted green eyes above pronounced cheekbones. His mouth is full and slightly parted. It's a mouth I've seen thinned with anger, twisted into sneers and plumped with self-satisfaction. It's the mouth of a villain.

"Monsieur d'Estang," I say automatically.

His eyebrows shoot up, and then his concerned expression becomes a sleek smile. "*Oui, mademoiselle.*"

Oh, god. He thinks I'm a fan. *Well, you are a fan.* No—not really, not anymore. "I'm not—" And I take a deep breath, because even I can only bear making a fool of myself so many times in one day. "I think you are on your way to see my father."

Dad didn't mention that Frederic d'Estang, the French Canadian musical theater performer, would be coming to the house, but then he's not much in the habit of warning us about these things. As he's a theater agent, and a gregarious one, it's not unusual for a star to pull into the drive while you're eating your toast or plump down next to you at dinner.

Monsieur d'Estang studies me for a moment. "You are Anton Bell's daughter?"

"Yes. Well, one of them."

He puts a hand over his heart. "Miss Bell, I deeply apologize." And he continues to apologize in the most eloquent way for several minutes while he helps me up and collects all my notebooks and papers. I try to get them off him but it's hard to get a word in while he talks on, and then he's taking my elbow and steering me toward the car.

"No, please, I'm fine to walk, it's not far across the fields."

"But Miss Bell, we are going the same way, I believe." His eyes are so much greener in person and I feel like a mouse pinned by the jeweled gaze of the cobra. He's had more than twenty years' professional experience convincing people of things with those eyes and I've only had minutes to try and discover how to refuse them.

I fail, and get into the car.

The driver adds his own apologies to Monsieur d'Estang's while I'm buckling on my seat belt. It's an electric car, he explains, which is why I didn't hear it. I mutter something about not getting many of these in the countryside around Oxford.

"What were you thinking about so deeply when we nearly knocked you down?" Monsieur d'Estang's accent is unusual, a slight North American inflection with a clipped Frenchiness about the vowels. It's a very nice voice, and surprisingly gentle for such a tall, sultry man. I think about all the actresses and singers he's been romantically linked with over the years. He probably knows it's very nice.

"Communists," I say.

He looks amused. "Oh?"

"I mean, it's just something I'm working on," I say quickly. "East Germany, Cold War." Why can't you say, "It's a book I'm writing for a client"? Is that so hard?

"Ah, so you're a writer. That explains the daydreaming." He glances out the window and I glare at the back of his head. I'll put up with being pigeonholed as awkward and boring by my sisters, but it's irritating from strangers.

But it seems he was just checking where we were, as he turns back to me. "What are you doing out here in the middle of nowhere?"

"What, walking?"

"No, I mean here in the countryside. Why aren't you in London, or Paris? Somewhere with a little more excitement."

"University," I say, waving my hand in the general direction of Oxford. I'm working on a PhD in Victorian literature but he probably thinks I'm a gormless undergrad. I'm dressed like a gormless undergrad, in scuffed shoes and denim shorts.

"During summer? Do they not allow you any holidays in England these days?"

I'm about to reply when we turn into the driveway of my parents' house. It's something of a spread, all white columns and twining ivy and gray stone. There's a fountain in the center of a circular gravel driveway. Lisbet, just fourteen, is lying in the grass reading a book. My elder sister, Mona, appears at the sitting-room window, and I see her peer at the car and then turn and call over her shoulder, probably to our other sister, Therese.

I realize that if I stay where I am I'm going to get mobbed by the whole family. *Why are you in the car with Monsieur d'Estang? What happened to you? You fell? Oh, Evie, how funny you are! Everyone, come and look.*

"Well, thanks for the lift!" I cry, grabbing my shoulder bag and jumping out of the car.

Lisbet looks up from her book as I scurry past. "Who's that?"

But I just push into the house and run upstairs. It's not until I'm standing in my bedroom with my back against the door that I remember I've left all my books and notes in Monsieur d'Estang's car.

"Drinks!"

THE PROTÉGÉ

My father's voice is a roar up the stairs. I glance at my phone: six thirty. He'll have been banging around in the kitchen for the last hour and will want everyone to come and have a gin and tonic before we eat. I pull off my T-shirt and shorts and yank the first sundress I lay my hand on over my head.

Lisbet, Mona and Therese are occupying all the good spots in the sitting room when I go in, and they're arguing about whether this year's Dancing with the Stars contestants were as good as last year's. Monsieur d'Estang is standing in the door to the kitchen, his back to us, talking to my father.

"He was rubbish, Lisbet," Mona is saying. "The producers wanted to keep him on because he's weird, and weird means ratings. Don't look at me like that, Evie said it."

Lisbet turns her red-cheeked glare on me as I sink into the scratchy embroidered chair by the fireplace. "Sorry, Betty-bun." I did say that, but mainly because I was miserable about Adam and it felt good to be nasty about a stranger.

I wait for my sisters to screech at me about falling down in front of Monsieur d'Estang's car, but they don't so perhaps he didn't tell them.

Mum comes in through the French doors, pulling gardening gloves off her hands. "Frederic, I didn't know you were here." Monsieur d'Estang turns around at the sound of his name and breaks into a smile. My mother is attractive and blonde, and her eyes are very blue. She kisses him on both cheeks. "How simply wonderful. Are you staying the week?"

"Just a day or two, if I may. I have to be back in Paris on Monday."

Lisbet's voice rises in outrage in defense of her favorite dancer, and Mona and Therese laugh.

"Keep it down to a dull roar, you lot," Dad says, coming in. Then cheerfully to Monsieur d'Estang, "I'm sorry for the dreadful gaggle of women in this house. Everyone's come home to roost for the summer holidays."

"Not at all," Monsieur d'Estang replies, smiling round at us.

Mona and Therese give him coquettish glances. It's so easy for some people, flirting. I finger the scrape on my knee, trying not to think about Adam. The scrape hurts. I press it harder.

"Have you all got drinks?" Dad asks. "Mona, Therese, Evie?"

They ask for gins. I ask for sparkling water.

"Go on, have a proper drink," Therese urges me.

"I have to write later," I say, accepting the water from my father. Out of the corner of my eye I see Mona roll hers.

Therese looks up at Monsieur d'Estang. "Dad says you've been cast in a new production. What is it?"

He turns to her with a smile. "I'm playing Rochester in a new musical production of *Jane Eyre*."

I look at him from beneath my lashes. Well, he'll be perfect. Stormy, dark features, penetrating eyes and high cheekbones. He's in a crisp white shirt now, but I can just imagine his broad figure in a frock coat and his legs in leather riding boots. Musically he'll be good too. His singing voice can rattle windows with fury or caress with love.

Mona frowns at me. "You've read that book, haven't you, Evie?"

About a thousand times. "Oh, that book. Yes, I should think everybody's read that book."

"Evie loves that—" Lisbet begins.

"A musical adaptation, that's different," I say. "What made you interested in the part?"

Monsieur d'Estang accepts a gin and tonic from my father. "It's just such a different sort of role for me. When I was a young man I was called elfin and allowed to grow my hair out and play romantic leads. But then someone noticed what an excellent scowl I have, and my face began to harden with age, so they sheared off my curls, et voilà." He sweeps his hand in a little flourish. "I am a villain. And, I thought, typecast for life. So it was a surprise, and a pleasant one, to be invited to play a romantic hero once more."

I've seen photographs of Monsieur d'Estang as a very young man, and he was elfin, but very striking all the same. I think about the role and whether you could call Mr. Rochester, so driven by his passions, so contemptuous of the laws of society and the Church, a hero. "Some would say Mr. Rochester is a villain," I muse out loud.

He tilts his head to one side. "Oh, that's interesting. Would you say so?"

I'm not used to being asked to speak my opinion out loud in this house, and certainly not about something as achingly dull, as Mona would say, as nineteenth-century literature. "I don't know," I say, plucking at a loose thread on the side of the chair. "Maybe."

We all finish our drinks and are herded into dinner. The talk is dominated by my father and sisters, particularly Mona and Therese. Mum and I eat and listen, and Lisbet, who hates being left out of anything, tries desperately to edge herself into the conversation.

"And what do you all do when you're not summering here?" Monsieur d'Estang asks us.

Lisbet tells him about her dressage ribbons and Therese her law degree. Then Mona brings up her upcoming audition with an opera production company in London, and the talk inevitably becomes music-focused.

Finally Monsieur d'Estang turns to me. "You're a writer, Evie. What are you working on?"

Therese cuts across me. "She ghostwrites autobiographies for old ladies and things."

Thanks, Therese. You make it sound so interesting. She catches my baleful look and opens her eyes wide in a *well, you do* expression.

"Now, there's a thought," Dad says to Monsieur d'Estang. "Your Canadian agent emailed me yesterday and said he's been trying to convince you to write your memoirs. Get Evie to do it for you," he says, laughing. "She can cast a good sentence."

Monsieur d'Estang gives him a tight smile. "Martin told you that, did he?"

Oh, Dad, shut up, please… I'm counting the number of weeks until the university opens again when Mona's phone buzzes. An email has just come in. She's got the audition she was hoping for. "God, it was like, the most perfect thing. I saw the director in a café so I went in and I just started singing. No hello or anything, I just burst into the aria and then left her my email address."

Dad purses his lips, but his eyes are glimmering with amusement. "My daughter. I have to work with these people, you know."

Tapping a reply into her phone, Mona mutters, "What? It worked, didn't it? You understand, don't you, Monsieur d'Estang?"

I'm fairly certain Monsieur d'Estang always had too much class to make a twit out of himself like that, but he just smiles and says, "Anything for a part."

After dinner Lisbet goes straight to the living room and hunts through the DVD collection for one of Monsieur d'Estang's recorded performances, which she's never been interested in before. She chooses *The Phantom of the Opera*. I know it well. The man who plays Raoul is romantic in a bland sort of way. The Phantom, played by Frederic d'Estang, is manic, bold and powerful.

Lisbet's mouth is open as she watches him on the screen. I'm familiar with the sensation she's feeling: She's in the early throes of her first proper crush, an innocent, naïve infatuation that will cycle from daisy-plucking to wistful diary entries and back again.

Little idiot, I think, and stalk upstairs.

Chapter Two

Frederic

"Now, Frederic. About that memoir."

I accept the tumbler of whisky from Anton, but my heart sinks. That again. Martin promised he wouldn't talk about the book deal he's negotiating with the Canadian publisher with anyone. I know what he'll say if I complain. Anton isn't just anyone, he's your British agent. I suspect he told Anton about the book so there'd be someone else to nag me to do it.

"What about it?" The casement windows are open and the scent of daphne is wafting in on the night air. I was just starting to relax but now I feel on edge again.

Anton sinks into the armchair next to mine. His youngest daughter—Lisbet, I think her name is—is watching Phantom on the television on the other side of the room. She's cross-legged on the carpet, and I would find her rapt attention sweet if I couldn't hear myself singing.

Anton gives me an arch look. "I sense you're not keen on the idea."

"I'm not," I say heavily.

"It would sell."

"That doesn't make it a good idea."

Anton grins. "Tell that to Martin. No, but seriously, why don't you like the thought of a book?"

If I tell Anton the truth, he'll ask a hundred more questions that I can't answer. What can I say instead? "I don't know. Who wants to read me banging on about my stage career for four hundred pages? I did this, I did that." In a way that's the truth, or at least a secondary truth. And I'm too young to publish an autobiography. I'm forty-one. I haven't done everything that I want to do yet. "And it's not like I can even write."

"Then hire someone to write it for you."

I grimace. "That would be worse. I'd have to read someone putting words in my mouth."

Mona comes in and plops herself on the sofa behind her sister. Bored and hot, she seems to cast about for something to do. After a moment she scoops up a handful of Lisbet's long hair and starts working it into a complicated braid.

Anton sips his whisky, thinking. "Do a biography then. Third-person. Someone interviews you and the people who know you best and writes it up. All the dirt along with all the bragging. I'm sure any biographer worth their salt could dig up a few dozen people who hate the very sight of you. It's what's called a balanced view, I hear."

"People in the theater world who hate the sight of me? Oh, easily. The problem with a biography, though, is how do you end it? I'm not dead."

Anton waves this away. "Oh, that's the writer's problem. They'll figure something out, and it doesn't need to be flashy. Marianne Faithfull's book ends with a recipe for chicken."

It's not the writer's problem. It's mine. I have no idea what happens next.

Mona's been half listening to our conversation, it seems, because suddenly she turns to us. "Honestly, get Evie to do it. She knows your career back to front and she's read every character you've ever played. She could probably write half of the book off the top of her head."

Anton gives me an appraising look.

More to put an end to the conversation than anything else, I say, "Have you got anything she's written?"

Mona thinks for a moment. "Good question. All her ghostwritten books must be at college because I haven't seen them here. She's so private about that stuff. There's probably something on her hard drive…" She makes an exasperated face, as if asking her sister about this is more trouble than it's worth. Then she brightens. "I know! Give me your email address and I'll send you a link."

Anton digs his phone out of his pocket. "I've got his address, Mona. I'll send it to you now." Once he's done this and laid his phone aside he looks back at me, thoughtful. "Why is Martin so keen for this to happen? Why now?"

I consider whether to tell him. I should tell him, as he's going to find out sooner or later. But an irrational fear grips me. *You have to get on the stage in this country in a few months' time. Do you really want to speak it aloud?* I thought I was immune from silly theater superstitions, but it seems I'm not.

"Wants his cut, doesn't he?" I say, forcing a smile. "Been talking about getting a holiday house for the last year. Then he comes up with this book idea."

Anton grins. "That sounds like Martin."

Once I've finished my whisky I head upstairs. It's very still outside, not even the slightest breeze stirring the net curtains on this hot, sticky night. I check my email on my laptop and see that Mona has sent me a link. I click through and frown at the screen. I'm not sure what I'm looking at. There's a list of pieces and their characters and word counts. A name catches my eye. That's curious… I click through and start to read.

Two hours later I sit back, bewildered and amused. Evangeline Bell. Who would have thought?

Closing the laptop, I ponder things for a moment. The book's a pain in the ass but it's not going to go away.

Maybe, with Evie, I've found a way to make it a worthwhile project after all.

SOFT LIMITS is available now in Ebook and Audiobook

Also by Brianna Hale

LITTLE DANCER

PRINCESS BRAT

MIDNIGHT HUNTER

THE NECROMANCER'S BRIDE

COME TO DADDY

VOW OF OBEDIENCE

About the author

There's nothing Brianna Hale likes more than a large, stern alpha male with a super-protective and caring streak, and when she's not writing about them she can usually be found with a book, a cocktail, planning her next trip to a beautiful location or attending the theatre. She believes that pink and empowerment aren't mutually exclusive, and everyday adventures are possible. Brianna lives in London.

Printed in Great Britain
by Amazon